To Kevin

LANCELOT'S LADY

Warning: May cause hot flashes 😊

Cheryl Kaye Tardif
writing as

Cherish D'Angelo

*Cherish D'Angelo
aka
Cheryl Tardif*

Lancelot's Lady is the winner of an Editor's Choice award from Textnovel.com. It was also the #3 Most Popular Semi-Finalist in the Dorchester 'Next Best Celler' contest hosted on Textnovel.com

LANCELOT'S LADY

First Edition

Cover designed by Imajin Creations
Cover art: photo licensed from www.romancenovelcovers.com
Cover model: Jimmy Thomas

ISBN: 978-1-926997-04-9

Praise for Lancelot's Lady

"Romance, mystery, danger, black-mail, and twists and surprises, this tale contains them all... Despicable intentions threaten every character in this finely crafted tale of sweet tension...Lancelot's Lady is a non-stop adventure combined with the agonizing struggle to not give in to the magnetism between them. Enticing. Fun." —*Midwest Book Review*

"From the cold rocky shores of Maine to the extravagant mansions of Miami to a lush tropical island in the Bahamas, Cherish D'Angelo takes her heroine through a series of breathtaking romantic adventures that mirror the settings, often in surprisingly ironic ways. A page turner in the best possible sense." —Gail Bowen, author of the award-winning Joanne Kilbourn series

"Cherish D'Angelo has got that mythical "voice" down to a fine art." —Jennifer L. Hart, author of *River Rats*

"*Lancelot's Lady* is riveting. It holds on and won't let you go! Cherish D'Angelo's descriptive powers are amazing. She summons up scenes like genies from bottles!" —Susan J. McLeod, author of *Soul and Shadow*

Lancelot's Lady **is dedicated to my Textnovel fans.**

You have supported me, encouraged me, embraced my writing, loved my characters, and followed Rhianna and Jonathan's journey. Without you, my words are just words.

Chapter 1

Pacing in the expansive marble foyer of Lance Manor, Rhianna McLeod tried to calm her nerves as she waited for her life to change. One man's decision would determine her fate. Would she have a new job and a place to call home? Or would she be sent packing?

A tall, thin man in a dark gray suit approached her.

"Are you Mr. Lance?" she asked, holding her breath.

The man smiled and fine lines crinkled the corners of his warm brown eyes. "I'm Higginson, Mr. Lance's butler. He's resting at the moment. Perhaps you can leave your name."

Rhianna blinked back tears. She couldn't be turned away. The trip to Florida had taken most of her savings and she didn't have enough money to fly back to Maine. Besides, if it weren't for Mr. Lance's letter, she wouldn't even be in this predicament.

"But Mr. Lance is expecting me. I'm Rhianna McLeod, the palliative nurse he contacted. In his letter he said I'd have the job if I came here."

"I'm dreadfully sorry. Mr. Lance already has a nurse."

"But I don't have anywhere else—"

Somewhere in the stately mansion something crashed to the floor. Before Rhianna could comment, a crystal-shattering shriek pierced the air. This was followed by a terrible wailing sound.

The butler groaned. "Oh, no. Not again." He rushed off in the direction of the commotion.

Unsure of what to do, Rhianna took a determined breath and followed him. When they passed beneath a pillared arch and into a long hallway, she saw a reed-thin elderly man dressed only in a threadbare blue plaid bathrobe. It gaped open in the front, threatening to reveal more than just a hairy chest. Beside him, a plump woman in white scrubs was trying her best to calm him down, even though she was dripping wet and very upset.

As they approached the dueling pair, Rhianna tried to remember everything she could about her potential employer. In the past year, the tabloids had been filled with stories of multi-millionaire JT Lance and his fight against an aggressive disease, a cancerous brain tumor that made him an unruly and difficult patient. From what she could see, the rumors were true. Once exuding strength, confidence and perhaps a touch of arrogance, JT now looked frail and helpless.

"JT?" the butler called out.

"Higginson, get this woman a towel. She spilled my water."

"I did not spill it," the nurse snapped. "Mr. Lance refuses to take his meds or draw a blood sample. Now he's having a temper tantrum. He threw that water pitcher at me."

JT's eyes flared. "That's because you keep trying to poison me, you old bat!"

"I am *not* trying to poison you," the nurse sputtered. "The medication will help—"

"How the hell do you know what will help me? Half the time, you keep me so drugged that *I* don't even know who I am when I look in the mirror. The other half, you're busy taking my blood for your *test*s."

JT turned his back on the nurse and staggered toward Higginson, oblivious of the broken glass and water on the floor.

"Sir!" the butler warned.

With a resigned sigh, JT leaned against the wall for support. Then he caught sight of Rhianna. His mouth gaped and electric blue eyes lit up like twin lanterns.

"Anna," he whispered. "You came back."

He moved toward her and she suddenly found herself wrapped in his scrawny arms. Her first reaction was panic. It gripped her around the throat, strangling her. She wanted to fight him off, but then something strange happened. Calmness washed over her and she felt connected, a sense of belonging. For once in her life, she knew what it felt like to be welcomed home.

But this isn't my home.

She pulled back, embarrassed. "Mr. Lance, my name is Rhianna McLeod. I'm the nurse from Maine. Remember?"

"Nurse?" He studied her face and something akin to recognition flickered in his eyes. "Ah, yes…"

"What's going on, sir?" Higginson asked.

"I'll explain later. First, I need a drink."

Higginson gave Nurse Simpson an apologetic look. "Get Mr. Lance a fresh jug of water, please. I'm sure he won't let his temper get out of control now that he has company. Will you, sir?"

All eyes watched as the portly nurse waddled down the hall. Her disappearing act seemed to make the old man extremely happy.

JT nudged Rhianna. "That woman's a *vampire*."

"As you can see," Higginson said, "Mr. Lance and the nurse don't exactly get along." He turned to JT. "Let's get you back into bed before you end up on the floor—again."

"Come along, Anna." JT took her hand. "You can visit while Higgie tucks me in."

Rhianna stifled a laugh. *Higgie?*

When she caught his eye, Higginson shrugged.

She followed the two men up a spiral staircase, her shoes clicking on the Italian marble steps and echoing around her. When she entered a handsomely decorated suite accented with polished mahogany and brass, she sucked in a stunned breath.

The suite was larger than four bedrooms put together. A plush sitting room with two suede sofas and a wall of bookshelves greeted her first. Double French doors with glass inserts opened into the bedroom area. On one side of the bedroom, an open door led to a massive walk-in closet that held rows of suits, dress shirts and ties in every shade, and a shoe collection that would be the envy of any man on Wall Street. Another door opened into a bathroom ensuite featuring a Jacuzzi, a glass and tile shower and a sauna room. A sliding door on the other side of the spacious bedroom led out onto a small balcony overlooking a delicately scented rose garden. Between two tall windows stood a huge carved bed, a work of art in itself. A tan-colored suede armchair was positioned next to it—probably for the nurse—and a kaleidoscope of pill bottles lay scattered across the nightstand.

"What do you think, Anna?" JT asked once he was settled in the bed.

"I think it's definitely a man's domain."

Nurse Simpson returned, carrying a plastic jug of ice water. Shoving the pill bottles aside, the woman set the jug on the nightstand and crossed her arms, every muscle in her face pinched in disapproval.

JT dismissed her with an impatient flick of his hand.

In the doorway, the nurse hesitated. "Mr. Lance needs his rest. Even if *he* doesn't think so." Sensing competition, her eyes narrowed in Rhianna's direction. "Or anyone else, for that matter."

"Maybe we should talk later," Rhianna mumbled.

"Nonsense," JT said. "Stay with me a while."

The butler glanced toward the door. "Nurse Simpson, why don't you take a break for an hour or two?"

JT nodded. "Anna will take good care of me."

As the door slammed shut behind the nurse, Rhianna took a step closer. "Mr. Lance, my name is Rhianna McLeod."

"Rhianna?" JT sighed. "Well, yes. I guess you are."

Confused, she turned to Higginson. "I don't think he remembers writing me about the nursing position. He even contacted the hospital I used to work in and—"

"I hate it when people talk as if I'm not in the room," JT fumed. "Of course I remember you, uh...Rhianna. And I do want you to be my nurse. Higginson! Make up the Rose-Mist Room for Ms. McLeod. She'll be staying with us indefinitely."

"Are you sure?" Rhianna asked, surprised. "You may want someone more experienced. I've only worked in one hospital and one nursing home before coming here."

Higginson cleared his throat. "Have you checked her references, sir?"

"References are for untrusting fools. It's my blasted memory that's disintegrating, not my eyes." JT eyed the door. "And references sure didn't make a difference with Nurse Dracula. Which reminds me...see that the old bat gets a nice severance package."

As the butler's footsteps faded, Rhianna was at a loss for words. "I...uh...thank you."

"You can thank me by getting my pills over there." JT pointed to the nightstand. "The ones in the red bottle."

She fetched his medication and quickly scanned the bottle. The prescription was for Vicodin, a narcotic pain reliever. She shook out two pills and poured a glass of water before approaching his bedside.

"Thank you, Ann—Rhianna." His breathing was strained.

"Are you feeling all right, Mr. Lance?"

"JT, my dear. When you call me Mr. Lance, I feel so damned ancient, like some old geezer waiting to croak." He chuckled at his own joke.

After he was resting comfortably, she sat down in the chair and studied him. His thinning gray hair and handsome face suggested the rather dashing young man he must once have been. A once-strong jaw line, now softened by age and illness, still held traces of stubbornness. But it was his eyes, bright and kind, that held her attention. They seemed sad. Tired and sad.

"Now, Rhianna, tell me a bit about yourself."

"Well, I grew up in Bangor, Maine, and graduated—"

"Not the technical interview stuff, dear. I want to know about *you*. What are your goals, your dreams?"

Nobody had ever asked her about her dreams. For nearly two years, she had hidden herself in the nursing home in Portland, afraid to let anyone too close. Afraid to dream.

In that bedroom, sitting beside a dying man, she found more than an employer—she found a friend. Tentatively, she told him bits and pieces about her life. It started slowly, like a gurgle of water bubbling up from the center of the earth.

Within an hour, Rhianna had told him all about her childhood, about the terror she had endured, and the fear and abuse that had drained her soul of all self-worth.

Chapter 2

Settling into her new job had been easy for Rhianna. JT had made it easy. Although occasionally prickly, her patient was also compassionate and kind. He gave Rhianna full run of the mansion while he napped, which was often.

As she wandered through the various rooms, admiring antique furniture, expensive ornaments and a collection of massive oil paintings in ornate frames, she caught sight of a painting in the foyer. It had mesmerized her since her first day at Lance Manor over six weeks ago. A rectangular brass plate on the bottom of the frame displayed no date or artist name, only the name of the work.

Lady in the Mist.

On the canvas, a woman's naked body, wrapped only in a thin veil of mist and caressed by soft blue moonlight. She stood in the shimmering stillness of a murky lake, her long, slender legs half-submerged in the water. Rich auburn hair cascaded down her shoulders and swirled over the peaks of firm breasts, and brilliant jade-green eyes gleamed with such yearning and expectancy. The mist rose from the lake in spiraling tendrils, like fairy hands grasping at the woman's body. The wind whispered in hot, humid breaths. Water trickled from the falls above, showering the plants with glistening moisture, while the Lady in the Mist appeared to be waiting for something.

Or someone, Rhianna thought.

There was something primal about the painting.

It was alive.

"It's a lovely painting, isn't it, Miss McLeod?"

She spun around at the sound of Higginson's voice.

"The resemblance is uncanny," he observed. "She looks like you."

"You say that every time—as if she predicted my arrival."

"Well, look at you." Higginson smiled. "You're here. And part of the family."

"You and JT have shown me the meaning of family—I'll always remember that."

"Don't talk as if you're leaving us," he chided.

"I will be. One day."

Rhianna's heart ached at the thought. Her job could end in a heartbeat. Or the lack of one. They both knew that. Though they'd given him six months at most, not even the doctors knew how much time JT really had left.

It had been difficult at first, watching a grown man waver between being fully cognizant one moment and barely lucid the next. Some days he had a hard time remembering the simple things, like how to tie his shoes or the cream went in his coffee not over his eggs. But she loved the old man. JT was like the father she'd never had.

Orphaned at birth, she'd been sent to live with her mother's sister, until Aunt Madeline and Uncle Bernard died in a ferry accident. After the funeral, Rhianna went into foster care and remained there until she was sixteen. The last place she was sent to was the home of Gwen and Peter Waverley. She spent three long years there—three years of hell.

She shook her head. *The past is the past.*

Flicking a look at Higginson, she noticed a single tear had escaped down his cheek. The man was a loyal employee, more like a companion and dear friend than a well paid butler. He'd been with JT for over twenty years. They often argued over business matters, yet JT always respected him, and that had won the butler's eternal devotion.

"There's something magnetic about her," Higginson said, before leaving her alone.

Rhianna's gaze was drawn back to the mysterious canvas. She often felt the woman in the painting was watching her. The artist had captured the sensual yearning in the young woman's expression, a sense of desperation, torment and passion that haunted her beautiful eyes. However, there was one thing that stood out—a flaw of sorts. The artist's signature was illegible.

"Good evening, dear."

Turning, Rhianna smiled as JT approached. "You're wearing your new robe."

He frowned. "New? Oh, yes. I can't seem to find my other one."

She'd given him a new bathrobe when he turned sixty-seven a week ago, but every now and then he'd forget about it and go in search of the ratty, threadbare one that she and Higginson had secretly thrown out.

"Why didn't you answer me when I called your name?" he asked.

"Sorry, I was daydreaming." She glanced at the painting. "It's so beautiful I get lost in it."

"I know, dear. It's your favorite."

"Who's the artist?"

JT's eyes went cloudy. "What artist?"

She indicated the painting.

"I don't have a clue." He frowned. "I think I knew once, but..." His voice trailed away.

"It's okay, JT."

"What is?" he asked, bright-eyed again.

She let out a sigh. JT's memory lapses were becoming more frequent.

Higginson approached them. "Everything is ready, sir."

"Then let's get this show on the road."

JT winked and Higginson disappeared down the hall.

"What's going on?" she asked JT. "You should be upstairs resting."

"I'll have plenty of time for that when I'm dead."

Her eyes watered. "Don't say that."

"I'm sorry, dear. You know I wouldn't hurt you for all the world, but if I'm going to die soon I might as well enjoy life now." He gave her a secretive smile. "Anyway, I can't very well miss tonight's celebration, can I?"

"What celebration?"

He frowned. "Your birthday party, dear girl."

Oh no. This was the last thing Rhianna wanted.

"It's no big deal," she mumbled.

"No big deal?" JT's arm swept across her shoulders. "My dear Rhianna, you're twenty-five now. When you're as old as I am, you'll be thankful for every single birthday you ever had. It means you lived one more year, saw one more year of sights and loved one year longer."

She smiled. "I suppose you're right."

"Of course I'm right. Besides, I have to dance with the birthday girl at least one time." He kissed her forehead. "You know, my birthday is coming up soon. I'll be sixty-seven." He frowned and scratched his chin. "Or is it seventy-six?"

She didn't have the heart to tell him he'd had it already.

His sudden burst of energy the past few weeks worried her. So did his insistence upon having a glass of brandy every night before bed, even though it was against doctor's orders. He'd been given six months. That was three weeks ago.

JT took her arm for support. "Take me to the dining room. And no arguing."

The first thing she saw when they entered the room was the bouquet of pink and mauve roses in a crystal vase. Instead of being positioned as a centerpiece, it sat on her plate. Beside the rose bouquet was a large box wrapped in pastel paper and tied with a lop-sided pink bow.

"I couldn't quite get that blasted bow right," JT muttered.

"Oh, JT," she said, not sure if she wanted to laugh or cry. "You didn't have to buy me anything. I'm your employee."

"No, Anna, you're like a daughter to me." JT's eyes widened. "Well, go on. Open it."

Some days he's just like a child, Rhianna thought, bending her head so he wouldn't see how much his thoughtfulness meant to her.

Blushing, she pulled out a mint green bikini with tiny lavender rosebuds on it. "I, uh…thank you."

"There's more," JT prodded.

Under a layer of tissue lay two sheer skirt-wraps and a pair of white leather sandals.

"This is very generous of you, JT, but I'm not sure where or when I'd ever wear these. They're not very practical for a nurse."

JT's eyes twinkled. "That's the point, Rhianna. Look how I had to argue with you just to get you to wear normal clothes instead of those ghastly nurse uniforms that only remind me that I'm dying." He smiled. "Besides, a pretty gal like you should be spoiled on her birthday. Someone needs to remind you that life is for living, not for holing up in an empty house with a cranky old geezer like me."

"Well, you do know how to spoil a girl." She grinned. "And I suppose if I have to put up with a 'cranky old geezer' like you, I'll survive. If nothing else, you keep things interesting."

"Now for the real gift," JT announced.

Higginson handed him a white business envelope before vanishing from the room.

Rhianna frowned. "Where's he going, JT?"

"Oh, don't worry. He'll be back."

She opened the envelope and gasped. "What's this?"

"It's your vacation. A plane ticket to Angelina's Isle, a resort island just northeast of Nassau in the Bahamas. I want you to take the next three weeks off."

"But I can't take a holiday."

"Yes, you can. And you will. You need a bit of fun."

"Fun? How can you say that when you…"

"I'm not going anywhere," he assured her. "I'll still be here when you get back."

Her voice trembled. "How do you know that?"

"I just do."

"But what if something happens while I'm gone?"

"Higginson will make sure I have expert care."

"But why are you sending me away? I don't understand." A tear trickled down her cheek.

"Rhianna, don't cry. I'm doing what's best for you. Trust me." He looked her straight in the eye. "I want you to have an adventure you'll never forget. You can't get that here. Besides, you could use a break. You're too devoted to your job."

I'm devoted to you, she wanted to say.

"When you come back," he said, "you'll be rested and ready to face the inevitable."

They both knew he was talking about his looming death.

"You're paying me to look after you," Rhianna argued. "Not to go gallivanting off to some resort in the Bahamas."

Even as she said this, a thrill of excitement raced through her. She'd never been anywhere except Maine and Florida. There was so much of the world she yearned to see, so many things she'd never experienced. Like freedom, adventure…love.

"You've done a terrific job caring for me," JT said. "But there's more to life than looking after an old man. Higginson will drive you to the airport tomorrow morning. When you come back, I want to see you tanned, healthy and happy."

She opened her mouth to protest, but he held up a hand. "If you won't do this for yourself, do it for me."

She let out a heavy sigh. "Fine then. For you."

Rhianna could tell JT was elated by her decision. The way he'd ordered her around one might think he was her father.

As if reading her mind, the old man reached across the table for her hand. "You know I love you as if you were my own flesh and blood. You've certainly shown me more affection than my son."

"You never mentioned you had a son."

"He left home years ago. Shortly after he got married, we had a terrible argument and I haven't heard from him since."

"You mean he just disappeared? Hasn't he at least written you?"

"He wanted to make me pay for my sins," JT said, the light in his eyes dimming. A minute later he looked at her, confused. "What were we talking about?"

Before she could reply, Higginson returned with a small item wrapped in a piece of soft cotton. It was rectangular in shape and the size of a large book.

"And now I have two more gifts for you," JT said, giving her a conspiratorial wink.

Still fuming about JT's errant son, she watched him unveil a miniature print of the Lady in the Mist. Matted in deep blue and framed with a silver-edged frame, it was almost as exquisite as the original.

"I love it," she said, swiping at a rogue tear. "Thank you."

"Take it on your holiday," he suggested. "So you have a piece of home with you."

She couldn't hold back. "What's the second gift?"

JT grinned so widely that if he were dressed in a Santa suit he'd have passed for good old Claus. Well, Santa on Weight Watchers, maybe.

"The original Lady in the Mist is hanging in your room." At her stunned expression, he added, "It's all yours."

Rhianna was more than stunned. She was speechless. The very painting that she had gazed at for almost two months was actually hers. There were other paintings in Lance Manor, some even painted by the same artist, but none affected her quite like the one of the woman with the long red hair and deep green eyes.

"JT...I don't know what to say. You're too generous."

"That's what friends do," he said in mock sternness. "Now, just make an old man happy and say thank you."

She grinned at him. "Thank you."

Without hesitation, she wrapped her arms around the dying man and hugged him fiercely. "You are an honorable friend, JT, and I am so glad you're in my life."

"I haven't always been honorable. I've done some things in my life that I'm not proud of. And I've hurt people too." He lowered his voice. "There are no guarantees in life. But any risk is worth taking when you love someone. Remember that, Rhianna."

Alarmed by the tremor in his voice, she pulled back and saw tears in his eyes. "What's wrong?"

He blinked twice.

"JT?"

He gave her a blank look. "Anna..."

She sighed. "It's past your bedtime."

"When did you get here, Anna? Did you bring the baby?"

Rhianna had asked Higginson about this Anna person JT always mistook her for. The butler didn't have a clue. And now it seemed this mystery woman had a baby.

It must be someone from his past.

Maybe his son's mother.

Escorting JT to his room, she tried not to think of what would happen once he was gone. In some ways he was already gone. It was emotionally draining to watch him flip-flop between bouts of memory loss and total comprehension. Witnessing this grand man's decline was devastatingly heartbreaking. Today, one would never know by looking at him that he had less than six months to live.

She blinked back tears, then pasted a smile on her face for the man who meant so much to her. He gave her more than a paycheck, more than a place to call home. He restored her sense of safety and belonging.

Yes, JT was one of a kind.

She scowled. *Too bad his son hasn't realized that.*

If she ever met the guy, she'd have a few things to say to him. And none of them would be polite.

Chapter 3

The airplane droned over cottony clouds and Rhianna was lulled into sleep. She dreamed of coming home to find JT lying in his bed, still and lifeless. Waking suddenly, she shook off an uneasy feeling.

It's just a nightmare.

She smiled, recalling JT's words before she left.

"I'll wait for your return before I go anywhere," he promised, "including Heaven's pearly gates—or that other place—whichever will take me."

God, please don't take him before I return. I'd never forgive myself.

She yawned and rested her head against the window.

Then restless dreams once again claimed her...

After being dumped off on Mrs. Emerson, a foster mother with very little money and too many mouths to feed, Rhianna had given up hope of finding a real family. She was a lost soul for a couple of years, until the "system" found her new foster parents when she was almost sixteen.

At first, Peter and Gwen Waverley seemed kind, but the honeymoon stage didn't last long. By the second week, Rhianna was making dinner, doing the dishes, vacuuming the house, and on weekends she did laundry. Sometimes her foster mother would ask her to dust too. Plus she had to keep her own bedroom spotless. Between school, chores and homework there wasn't much time left for a social life.

It didn't take her long to realize that the Waverleys were more interested in having a live-in housekeeper than a daughter. Later, she found out that her foster father saw her as anything but daughter material. In fact, he saw her more as a possession. A possession he had to have.

Peter's lecherous advances behind his wife's back made Rhianna so nervous that she remained in her room unless she had chores to do. At night, she'd lock her bedroom door, holding her breath as his footsteps slithered past her door.

Most of the time she was able to avoid being alone with him—until one evening when Gwen decided to go see Phantom of the Opera.

Rhianna saw the evil twinkle in Peter's eyes.

"Please don't go, Mrs. Waverley," she cried. "I don't want you to leave."

"Quit your whining," Peter snapped.

Sweat trickled down his brow as he waddled over to his wife and handed her a twenty dollar bill. "Have fun."

Gwen eyed Rhianna with disdain. "See to it that all your chores are done before you retire. I don't want to come home to a pile of dirty dishes and wrinkled laundry. And quit that sniffling."

"But Mrs. Waverley, I'd just feel much better if you were home. And I don't think the agency would like—"

Peter whipped around. "You don't think I can take care of you?"

"Now, Peter," Gwen said with a sigh. "The girl is just missing me, that's all. I'm sure you'll do a fine job looking after our...*daughter*." Her eyes narrowed. "And don't worry, she won't say anything to the agency. She knows there isn't another family for miles that would take her in."

Peter glared at Rhianna. In a cold voice he said, "It's a good thing your parents are dead. I don't think they'd be too proud of your behavior."

"Yes, you behave yourself," Gwen commanded. "And get those chores done while I'm gone. I'll be back around ten o'clock."

The door slammed shut behind her.

Rhianna watched as Peter flicked the lock.

When he turned around, his eyes were gleaming and his mouth was stretched into a sadistic smile. "Come to Daddy."

Her heart stopped beating.

"Miss?" a voice called from the blackness. "Wake up."

Rhianna opened her eyes and a face swam into view.

"Why, hello there," a flight attendant said, her accent placing her from Ireland. "Boy, that was one doozy of a nightmare, if I do say so. You better have a drink, and I don't mean water. Can I fetch you something?"

"No, thank you." Rhianna shook off the remnants of her dream. "When will we be landing?"

"In about twenty minutes, give or take. Course we have to make it through the Bahama Triangle first."

Rhianna's pulse raced. "The Bahama Triangle?"

The flight attendant grinned. "Just kidding. No such thing."

In the aisle seat across from Rhianna, a man in a business suit nodded. "I've taken this trip dozens of times, and they still use the old

Bahama Triangle joke." He smiled. "Where you headed?"

"To a resort on Angelina's Isle. Have you been there before?"

The man frowned. "No, can't say I have."

Over the speaker, the captain asked everyone to fasten their seatbelts for their descent. The plane softly touched down and coasted down the runway.

Rhianna's heart raced with anticipation, mimicking the rumble of the plane's engine. Fifteen minutes later, she disembarked from the plane and followed the ant trail of tourists and residents down the narrow hall.

Once she passed through the airport, she hurried outside. A wall of heat and humidity hit her, and she sucked in a breath, grinned and hailed a cab.

"I need to get to Bayshore Marina," she said, checking the directions JT had written down.

A kaleidoscope of island colors and scenery rushed past the open taxi window. The seductive aroma of exotic flowers mingled with the fresh but humid scent of an earlier rain that had left evaporating puddles on the road. Between lush palm trees, she saw houses painted in tropical shades of orange, pink, yellow and green.

It was breathtaking, unspoiled. Like another world.

Almost too soon the taxi pulled up to Bayshore Marina. A small dock jutted out over the water and boats of various sizes and styles were moored there, while others dotted the water. In the distance, small islands appeared to float on the ocean's surface.

She wondered which one was Angelina's Isle.

Walking along the dock, she noticed two men arguing about the boxes they were loading into a brightly painted powerboat. Moving closer, she discovered that the paint job was meant to detract from the rickety shape the craft was in.

"There isn't enough room for all of them!" yelled the dark-skinned man.

"You'll have to make room, Roland," his older companion replied. "Tyler wants these supplies *this* month, not two months from now."

"I'm telling you, Denny, I can't transport them all. The boat'll sink."

The older man cursed. "Tyler pays you to make sure he's well stocked. You don't wanna get on his bad side. Remember what happened to Daniel O'Brien? Tyler just about took his head off when the poor kid forgot his brushes."

"Excuse me," Rhianna said.

Neither man noticed her.

"Hello there!" she hollered.

The two men looked up, their eyes widening in shock. Roland nearly dropped the box he carried. And Denny missed going for a swim by about six inches.

"I'm looking for a boat called Siren's Call," she said. "Can either of you tell me when it's supposed to arrive?"

"What do you want with the Siren?" Roland asked, white teeth gleaming as he smiled in her direction.

"The captain is supposed to take me to Angelina's Isle," she explained, backing up as the men jumped onto the dock. At their doubting looks, she said, "If you could just tell me when he'll arrive, I—"

"The captain won't be taking you anywhere," Denny said. "The Siren isn't taking passengers today."

"But I don't understand. I was told the captain would take me across." She shaded her eyes with one hand and surveyed the boats nearby. "Maybe I can take another boat."

"There aren't any others that dock there," Roland answered. "Lancelot's Landing is private property."

"Well, I'll just wait until the Siren's Call gets here," she said in a tight voice. "I'm sure once I've explained why I'm here, the captain will take me across."

Roland laughed. "Ma'am, this *is* the Siren's Call. At least it used to be, until the boss changed her name."

Denny let out a scornful snort. "Long overdue, if you ask me."

"Now she's Misty's Dream," Roland said with pride.

"So you're the captain?" she asked.

The young man nodded. "But like Denny told you, I can't take passengers today. I have enough on board already. Besides, the boss didn't say he was expecting anyone."

"Then the *boss* is in for a big surprise." Rhianna reached into her handbag and dug out the envelope addressed to 'Captain'. "This is for you. From my employer."

Roland suspiciously peered at the envelope. Ripping it open, he quickly read the note.

"Your employer paid me five hundred dollars," he said. "Looks like you're heading to Lancelot's Landing."

"Roland," Denny warned.

"I need the money. Leave the last two boxes on the dock. I'll run them out to Tyler in a couple of weeks."

Helping Rhianna aboard, Roland tucked her suitcase by her feet.

"You won't get in trouble for leaving supplies behind, will you?" she asked.

"Not enough to turn down the money you gave me."

With a wave to Denny, Roland pushed the throttle forward and the powerboat took off, leaving a frothy wake in its trail.

"I guess your boss forgot he had a new guest," she said, smiling as the wind caught at her hair.

"Tyler never forgets."

He did this time, she almost said.

She found herself wondering about the resort's boss. How could he not pay attention to his guests' arrival? And how would he feel when Roland explained that they had to leave two boxes behind in order for her to come on board?

Rhianna leaned back and closed her eyes while the boat raced across the water, the outboard purring like a kitten. The coolness of the breeze was a welcome change from the scorching heat she'd felt when she deplaned. Loosening her hair from the restraints of an elastic band, she ran her fingers through the wavy strands.

"You're definitely not in Maine anymore," she said beneath her breath.

Roland pointed at a small island. "That's Angelina's Isle."

"It's very isolated."

"You have no idea."

The way he said it made Rhianna's heart sink.

Minutes later, Roland slowed the engine and aimed the boat for a worn dock that jutted out into the water.

A weathered sign nailed to a post at the end of the dock read, *Welcome to Lancelot's Landing, Angelina's Isle.* Underneath, a second sign warned, *PRIVATE PROPERTY. TRESPASSERS WILL BE PROSECUTED.*

It was an odd warning for a resort.

Rhianna squinted, searching the bushes for signs of life. There wasn't a building, road or person in sight.

Roland hefted the suitcase over the side and set it on the dock with the boxes he'd already unloaded. Then he opened a small mailbox under the warning sign.

"Tyler's next order," he explained. "He should be here any minute." Roland jumped into Misty's Dream and prepared to cast off.

"Wait! Where are you going? There's no one here yet."

"Don't worry. Tyler'll be here. He hardly ever misses his supply drop." He waved once, then steered the boat toward open water.

"What do you mean *hardly ever*?" she hollered.

There was no reply.

She moaned. "Where do I go if Tyler doesn't show?"

As she watched the powerboat speed away, anxiety crawled over her like fire ants at a picnic. There wasn't a soul in sight. Not even a proper path through the overgrown brush to show her the way.

"Wait until I get a hold of this Tyler," she muttered. "I've got a thing or two to tell him about customer service. Some kind of resort this is."

She grabbed the Gucci suitcase—a birthday present from Higginson—and dragged it in the direction she hoped would lead to the resort. Using her handbag to ward off errant tree branches, she gradually made her way through the dense foliage, although the grass was slippery and she came close to falling more than once.

"Where the heck is this place?"

After ten minutes of fighting an unforgiving jungle, she turned around and headed back to the beach.

When the boss comes for his supplies, I'll be waiting.

She would register a complaint with the front desk. Guests shouldn't be dumped off in the middle of God knows where and left to fend for themselves for God's knows how long.

She checked her watch. It was almost three o'clock.

Damn. How long is Tyler going to keep me waiting?

Mindful of slivers, Rhianna sat at the end of the dock and dangled her bare feet in the warm water. It had been a long trip, and worrying about JT definitely didn't help. She smiled, thinking of the old man's stubborn pride. He didn't like to be babied, especially by her.

Staring out at the glittering ocean, a sudden pain flared deep within. Her only taste of what family was like would end in less than six months.

She couldn't go back to Maine, not now.

Not ever.

Tears trailed down her cheeks, and for the first time in months, she broke down. If only she could have picked a father. She would have picked JT.

The shrill cry of an unseen bird reached out to her as loneliness enveloped her, wrapping her in exhaustion. She couldn't resist lying on her back, her toes skimming the ocean. Before drifting into a deep sleep, she had one last thought.

I'm like the Lady in the Mist. Waiting...

A misty dream pool beckoned, calling her name.

Rhianna...

She waited expectantly, observing the still surface. Warm water closed around her toes as she stood at the shore, her white nightgown fitting the curves of her body like a second skin.

A ripple disturbed the water, as if someone had dropped a stone from above. From its center a form arose, sleek and graceful.

It was him! She had found him at last.

This man of her dreams, all bronzed and muscular, brushed the water from his jet-black hair and waded to the shore. His muscles gleamed in the moonlight as he stepped, naked, from the pool. He moved toward her, his eyes smoldering with passion. Arms outstretched, he reached for her and pulled her close.

She reached up, her fingertips gently tracing a path up his smooth chest. Winding her hands around his neck, she clung to him, barely daring to breathe.

He bent his head, those sapphire eyes mesmerizing her, drowning her. Not a word was said. He leaned forward, caressing her lips with his, lighting a fire that swept through her very soul.

His kiss deepened, growing more urgent.

Then he whispered her name…

Chapter 4

"Hey, lady! What the hell are you doing on my island?"

Rhianna held her breath and clamped her eyes shut. She didn't want to face the man whose voice simmered with fury. She was sure that he would look as ugly as he sounded.

Finally, she raised her head and forced herself to focus on the imposing man before her. She took in paint-splattered jeans that hugged well-formed thighs, a purple t-shirt covered in various spatter colors, muscular arms folded in front of an impressive chest, and thick black hair that curled at the nape of his neck.

The contours of his handsome face were chiseled as only an ethereal sculptor could, with strong lines enhanced by a dimple on his left side, the only side unmarked by streaks of paint. His nose was straight and proud, just bordering on arrogant. But it was his eyes that fascinated her. Framed by thick black lashes, they were the deepest sea-blue she had ever seen, and right at this moment, those eyes were trained on her with sniper precision.

She felt her throat constricting. Whether it was from fear or attraction, she didn't know. But she did know one thing. He was the most gorgeous man she had ever met.

"I asked you a question!" the man demanded. "Who are you and what are you doing here?"

She glared back at him. "My name is Rhianna McLeod. Who are you?"

"I'm no one important."

Rhianna couldn't agree more. From the looks of him, he was probably the handyman.

"And you, Ms. McLeod, are on private property," the man continued. "I'd appreciate it if you would go back to wherever the hell you came from." He kicked her suitcase for good measure.

"Hey!"

He stabbed a finger at the sign. "Can't you read?"

"Look here, whatever-your-name-is, I'm a guest here. Now if you'd just take me to your boss, I'm sure he'll explain this to you."

She rose abruptly and tried not to blush as she unrolled her pant cuffs until they covered her feet. Then, with sandals and handbag in one hand, she grabbed the handle of her suitcase and lugged it to the shore end of the dock.

On the sandy beach, she flicked a look over her shoulder. "Are you coming?" With hands on hips, she gaped at him, fighting the impulse to wipe that smug look off his face. "What?"

"Just get back on your boat and—"

"Boat?" she shrieked. "Do you see a boat anywhere?" Infuriated, she waved her hands in the air. "The captain just dumped me here in the middle of God knows where and took off in his blasted boat."

And if she ever saw young Roland she'd have a few things to say to him.

"There's obviously been a mistake," he said.

"I'll say there's been a mistake," she snapped. "When your boss hears about this, I'm sure he won't be too happy. Is this the way you treat all your guests?" She reached into her handbag for a pen and paper.

"What the hell are you doing?"

Rhianna didn't answer him. She was livid. Her vacation wasn't going the way she had planned. She should be lying on a beach in her new bikini, drinking strawberry margaritas like JT had promised. Instead, she was arguing with an insulting, paint-splattered, black-haired Adonis, while she looked like a homeless street-person.

"What's your name?" she demanded.

"Jonathan."

"Last name?"

"Just Jonathan. Everyone here knows who I am."

She scribbled his name on the paper.

"What do you intend to do with that?" he asked.

"I'm going to report you to your employer. Now take me to the resort—or lodge, or whatever you call it."

Jonathan laughed again, catching her off guard, his deep voice sending a shiver down her body. His eyes gleamed and she watched in disbelief as he vanished into the bushes.

"Jonathan?"

No answer.

She was about to go after him when he returned with a large wheelbarrow. In one swift movement he stripped the t-shirt from his body and tucked it around one of the wheelbarrow handles.

She eyed him nervously. "What are you doing?"

"I'm getting my supplies." He cocked his head to one side. "You know, the boxes that were dropped off...with *you*."

The way he said it made her feel like she was some kind of bug. One that needed to be squashed.

She watched while he loaded the wheelbarrow. It was difficult not to stare at his rippling muscles, especially when he exuded strength, confidence and arrogance in every breath. She'd never met a man as infuriating as this one.

Something about him seemed...familiar.

Suddenly recalling her dream, she gasped. *It's him!*

The man from her dream.

Jonathan almost laughed at the woman. How dare she look at him as if he were some uneducated, impoverished bum. If she could only see herself. Most of the women he'd known would never allow themselves to be seen in such disarray, with hair tousled by the wind, no makeup on whatsoever—not that she needed any—and tired, angry eyes.

Approaching, he surreptitiously studied her. The woman's creased cotton pants were slightly damp at the hem. The blouse she wore, while feminine, was primly buttoned to the top. And her unmarked suitcase screamed *brand new*, suggesting this woman either wasn't well-traveled or worldly, or she was and she bought a new suitcase for every trip.

Rhianna, he recalled.

She had eyes the color of jade, and right now they were flinging daggers at him.

He chuckled. *She's feisty, I'll give her that.*

Now that she was standing, he could see that her head only came as high as his chest, but she was curved in all the right places. She had long, slender legs—the kind he'd like to wrap around him.

Now where the hell did that thought come from?

"Where are you from?" he demanded.

"Miami."

He let out a huff. "City girl."

Staring into her thick-lashed eyes, he felt a shock of something akin to recognition. Yet he knew they'd never met before. Shaking his head, he reminded himself that women were nothing but trouble. He'd had enough of that to last him a lifetime.

Liars and cheats. All of them!

"How far is the resort?" she asked.

His laughter echoed through the trees.

Without looking at her, he pushed the wheelbarrow along the dock, then carefully inched it onto the sand below. It was a bit of a struggle pushing the wheels through sand, but he finally made it to the grass.

Wiping his brow with the t-shirt, he said, "What boat did you say brought you here?"

"Misty's Dream." Her voice was soft, like a summer breeze.

"Roland," he muttered. He'd have to have a talk with the guy. Roland should know better than to bring anyone to the island.

"Sorry about the other boxes," Rhianna said behind him.

He froze. "What other boxes?"

"The ones we had to leave behind on the dock."

He gaped at her. "You left my supplies behind?"

"It was the only way I could fit..." Her voice drifted away when he cursed loudly.

"You've got a lot of nerve, lady."

"I'll explain to your boss why the boxes are missing," she offered.

"You'll explain?" He clenched his fists. "I'm sure that'll make things all better."

She scowled at him. "You don't have to be so angry."

Jonathan was angry all right. Angry with Roland for leaving his supplies on a dock where anyone could steal them. Angry that this woman had invaded his privacy. Angry that she accused him of being angry.

"I'm not angry," he said, clenching his jaw. "I'm furious."

"I said I was sorry."

"Let's just go back to the house." He heaved up the handles of the wheelbarrow, aimed for the trees and stomped off.

"Wait!" Rhianna said. "Who's going to carry my suitcase?"

He glared over one shoulder. "Who do you think?"

Jonathan felt some satisfaction knowing that his uninvited guest would be fighting with that blasted suitcase all the way to the house.

Behind him, he heard a few words that no lady should ever say. A smile tugged at the corner of his mouth.

"It's not too far," he lied.

Realizing that he wasn't going to wait for her, Rhianna stumbled after him, half carrying, half dragging the suitcase. It seemed to have magically increased in weight and she groaned inwardly. That'll teach her for not packing lighter.

She scowled at Jonathan's back, hoping he was just as hot, tired and sweaty as she was and wishing he'd fall flat on his face so she could have a good laugh. She certainly needed one. The man didn't even have the decency to look over his shoulder and check on her.

What a lot of nerve!

Trudging through the tall grass, she stole a few furtive glances at the man ahead of her. His arms bulged in rebellion to the weight of the boxes in the wheelbarrow, yet he didn't seem to notice. The jeans he wore hugged his hips, and fit him in all the right places.

Without warning, he spun around and caught her staring. He raised one mocking eyebrow, then let out an aggravated huff. He stalked over to her, wrenching the suitcase from her hands. He threw it on top of his boxes and without a backward glance continued trekking through the woods.

Rhianna had a terrible feeling that her holiday had just gone down the toilet.

Chapter 5

Rhianna gasped. "It's beautiful."

Flowers bloomed everywhere—roses of every color, morning glories and hibiscus. The air was delicately scented with a potpourri of luscious fragrances, each mingling with the summer breeze. In the middle stood a pastel peach-colored house.

"But it's not the resort you were expecting," he said dryly.

She shrugged. "No, but it has its own...charm."

The two-storey house had a whitewashed roof and a wide wraparound veranda, complete with a swinging chair and a screened porch.

It wasn't at all what she had expected.

"I thought the resort was bigger," she blurted.

"For the last time, it's not a resort," Jonathan said through his teeth. "I thought you'd figured that out."

"If it's not a resort, then what is this place?"

"Lancelot's Landing. I call it home."

Stunned by his revelation, she realized that Jonathan was probably much closer to Tyler, the big boss, than she'd hoped, which would make it far more difficult to complain about Jonathan's rudeness.

"Are you all right?" he asked, touching her hand.

She couldn't help the quickening of her pulse. She told herself that her reaction was because she was dead tired and stressed. It had nothing to do with the man eyeing her, touching her hand. And it had nothing to do with the yearning she felt when she looked into his fathomless eyes.

No, she thought. *It has nothing to do with Jonathan.*

Jonathan saw the faint blush that brushed the woman's cheeks. "Ms. McLeod?"

"You aren't joking, are you? I mean, I was told this was a resort. My employer said—"

"Your employer was mistaken." Her hand trembled in his and he sighed. "Look, we'll have to make the best of a bad situation. This may not be a resort, but I think you'll survive just fine."

Suddenly self-conscious, Jonathan let go of her hand.

"This way," he said, pushing the wheelbarrow toward the house.

Leaning against the frame, he held the front door open for her. As Rhianna ducked under his arm, he caught a whiff of fresh citrus and vanilla.

She smells good.

"Are you coming inside?" Rhianna asked.

"I, uh...of course."

He led her through the house, all the while thinking that it had been ages since they'd had a real guest.

He caught himself. *No one invited her here.*

"It's beautiful," she said, "but I really should go back to the mainland. Can you arrange for a boat to take me?"

"There is no boat."

The woman looked like she was going to cry.

"Roland keeps my boat on the mainland," he explained. "He's not coming back for another six weeks, when the next supply is due." He ran his fingers through his hair. "Mind you, he could return earlier, seeing as he still has to deliver the rest of the supplies."

He felt tired and dirty. He had worked longer than usual today, which was why he was late picking up the supplies. All he wanted was a bath and a good night's sleep. The last thing he needed was some spoiled city girl invading his privacy.

"Can't you just call him and ask him to come back?" she begged. "I can pay him for his trouble."

"No phone service out here." The disbelief in her eyes made him add, "No cell phone service either. No tower. Closest one is too far away. And I haven't repaired the long-range radio yet, but now that I have the parts..." He shrugged. "It looks like you're stuck here until I fix it."

Whether we like it or not.

He watched Rhianna as she examined the spacious living room and settled into a plush chair by the window. Her skin was slightly pink from the sun, and she shifted uncomfortably. For a Miami city girl, she seemed unusually flustered by the heat.

"Want a drink?" he asked, heading for the bar.

"Water, please."

He grabbed a bottle of water from the small fridge.

"Glass?"

Wordlessly, she shook her head.

As he handed the bottle to her, their fingers brushed. He jerked his hand away, confused by the sudden energy that fused through his body.

"Let me show you around, Ms McLeod."

"Rhianna," she said in a weary voice. "Since I'm stuck here, we may as well be on friendly terms...Jonathan."

He frowned.

The last thing he wanted was to get friendly with this castaway. But God only knew how long she'd be stranded here.

He swallowed hard. "Do you want a tour?"

Rhianna was surprised by Jonathan's question. He hadn't seemed too happy about her intrusion. Why was he being so nice all of a sudden?

Then she remembered.

He doesn't want me complaining to his boss.

She followed him into the kitchen. There was a large island in the center with a grill for indoor barbecuing. A skylight had been installed above the island, filtering in beams of warm sunlight. The dining nook area harbored a small oak table and two chairs, an oak china cabinet, and a number of potted plants. A sliding door near the table led onto a two-tiered cedar deck.

"It's not much, but it's home," he said.

"I think it's lovely. How many people live here?"

"Besides the help? Two."

Tyler must be married, she thought.

"Are you hungry?" he asked. "We already ate supper, but I think there are some leftovers."

She stifled a yawn. "I ate on the plane. All I want now is to crawl into bed."

"Well, lucky for you, I've got an empty bed you can crawl into."

A fiery heat rose from her neck to the top of her head. She turned away, praying to God that he hadn't noticed.

"Can you show me my room?"

Jonathan led her into the den. It housed an enormous library, one she'd give anything to explore. From the look of Tyler's collection, she surmised he must be a wealthy man. There were books of many genres, including children's books.

"A collector?" she asked Jonathan.

"Yeah. It's a hobby."

She waited for him to say something more about his enigmatic boss, but he beckoned her upstairs. On the second floor, they walked down an open hallway that looked down into the living room. They reached the door at the end of the hall.

"This is the only unoccupied room," he said, pausing.

When he opened the door, Rhianna blinked twice. The bedroom was stunning. Someone had decorated it with pale lilac wallpaper, delicate watercolor paintings and leafy potted plants. An antique cedar dresser and vanity stood in one corner of the room. French doors led to a small balcony that overlooked part of the back yard. On the far side of the room, under an arched window with aqua and mauve sheers, was a large four-poster bed draped in lilac sheets and a satin rose comforter.

Her eyes lingered for a moment on the tempting sight. She was so tired and confused by the day's events that all she wanted to do was curl up on the bed and sleep. For a week. But reality set in. She was staying on a private island, uninvited and unwanted. Her holiday had turned into a nightmare.

How could this have happened? she fumed. *How could JT have made such a mistake? He's always so organized, and Higginson confirmed all the details.*

She had heard JT tell him to make sure everything was arranged. Now here she was trapped on this island with a man who obviously didn't want her around, and a boss she dreaded meeting.

"Do you like this room?" he asked.

She turned to him. "It's beautiful. Thank you."

"No problem," he said with apparent relief. "If you need anything…"

Her skin burned at the suggestiveness of his words.

Had he meant it that way?

Convinced that she had just imagined it, she said, "When can I meet your boss?"

Jonathan's mouth thinned. "Trust me, all your questions will be answered in the morning. Have a good night."

After he was gone, Rhianna stared at the closed door and wondered what she'd done to make him so angry. With a frustrated sigh, she wandered around the room, fingers trailing over polished wood and soft fabrics. Someone kept the place spotless.

There must be another woman on the grounds.

She hooked a finger on one of the sheers and pulled it aside. Her room overlooked a backyard deck. Not a soul was around, but off in the distance she noticed two smaller buildings. She was sure one was a barn and she wondered what kind of animals it housed. A thin trail of smoke rose from the chimney of the other, a small cottage that looked like something out of a Thomas Kinkade painting.

I wonder—

A knock on the door interrupted her thoughts. When she opened it, the only thing in sight was her suitcase. Jonathan must have brought it up.

The man was a mystery. One minute he was cold and unwelcoming, the next minute thoughtful.

"Tonight you need to de-stress," she said aloud.

In the adjoining bathroom, her eyes widened at the sunken Jacuzzi in the corner and the jar of rose oil on a shelf above it. "Yes, that'll do just fine."

While waiting for the tub to fill, she twisted her hair and fastened it with a clamp. Then stripping off her clothes, she lit the candles that surrounded the tub, turned off the overhead light and stepped into the scented water.

"Ah," she moaned. "That's what I'm talking about."

Soothing, warm water enveloped her and she leaned back, closing her eyes. The day's tension slowly seeped away, leaving her tired but relaxed. While soaking, she let her mind drift, thought after thought released to the universe.

Until Jonathan's powerful physique came to mind.

She couldn't shake the image of him pushing the wheelbarrow. The strength of his arms, the glint in his eye. Even when angry, he was an incredibly attractive man.

She sighed. What was it about him that disturbed her?

She stared at the flickering candlelight patterns on the walls and wondered what Jonathan would tell Tyler. If he wasn't happy about her presence, how would his boss feel? And was there really no way off the island for six weeks?

She chewed on her bottom lip.

Perhaps if I help in the kitchen and stay out of Jonathan's way, Tyler won't be too upset and the time will fly by.

An hour later, she pulled the plug and watched the water swirl down the drain. After toweling off, she strode into the bedroom and eyed her suitcase. She'd packed a nightgown on the very bottom.

"No unpacking tonight," she muttered.

She pulled back the comforter and slid, naked, between the petal soft sheets, the fragrant fabric whispering against her skin. It was a piece of heaven, and more than a little sensual.

"This isn't so bad," she said before shutting her eyes.

There were far worse places to be stranded than on a private, tropical island. She had a beautiful home to stay in, even if she had to share it with the most irritating—and devastatingly attractive—man she'd ever met.

Drifting into sleep, she was greeted silently by her dream lover. He stepped from the depths of a natural hot spring, draped only in moonlight, wisps of steam and a warm breeze.

She stared into blue eyes and whispered his name.

Jonathan.

Chapter 6

Morning arrived too quickly and Rhianna groaned at the merry chirping of birds outside. She stretched, yawned, then opened her eyes.

The yawn caught in the back of her throat.

It hadn't been a nightmare. She really was stranded on an island in the Bahamas.

"With a guy who hates me."

She yanked the comforter over her head. As she lay there, she heard the tinkling of laughter coming from somewhere outside.

It's time to get up and face the head honcho.

Climbing out of bed, she wondered if Jonathan had already told Tyler about her. She hoped not. She'd rather that the boss make up his own mind about her, rather than be influenced by a rude handyman.

After a quick shower, Rhianna put on a teal sun dress. Then she dried her hair and pulled the long waves into a high ponytail, securing it with a decorative elastic band. To her dismay, a few stubborn curls fought their way free near her face.

I'm ready, she thought as she brushed on some blush and applied a light shade of lipstick. She wasn't sure exactly who she was preparing to meet—Tyler or Jonathan.

Feeling confident, she headed for the stairs but froze on the top step.

"Lord, have mercy!"

A plump woman of Caribbean descent was rooted in one spot at the bottom of the stairs. She stared at Rhianna as if she'd seen a ghost.

"Sorry, I didn't mean to scare you."

The woman fanned herself with one hand. "I couldn't believe my ears when I heard we had a guest."

"I'm sorry to be such an imposition—"

"Stop your apologizing, dear. It's been far too long since we've had a beautiful young lady in the house."

Rhianna blushed.

"You must be Ms. McLeod," the woman said, beaming a wide smile and brushing the flour off her hands. "I'm Mrs. Atkinson, the housekeeper. Come in and have a seat, dear. You must be hungry."

"I'm famished."

"Did you sleep well?"

A platter of pancakes and sausages, along with a bowl of sliced fruit materialized in front of Rhianna the minute she sat down.

"Like a baby," she said, filling her plate.

She glanced at the dirty dishes Mrs. Atkinson was removing from the table. Jonathan and Tyler must have eaten already.

"Sorry," she apologized. "I should have gotten up earlier and eaten with everyone else. I assume Tyler is up?"

"Oh, he's been up for hours," Mrs. Atkinson replied.

"Do you know where he is? I need to talk to him."

"Mr. Tyler always works long hours during the summer. And he doesn't like interruptions."

"What time will he be back?"

"Oh, Mr. Tyler will be busy all day, dear. We won't see him until supper time. If we're lucky." Handing Rhianna a napkin, the housekeeper added, "You might as well make yourself at home."

After breakfast, Rhianna returned to her room and unpacked her suitcase. With everything in its place, she rummaged through her handbag for her plane ticket and passport. Under the ticket folder was her cell phone.

Taking it out on the balcony, she flipped it open and turned it on. "Crap. No service."

Jonathan hadn't been pulling her leg.

"Six weeks?" She let out a groan. "You can do it. Anyway, what could possibly go wrong in that time?"

She leaned against the rail and gazed across the yard. A corner of the cottage she'd seen last night was in view and something moved there. Shading her eyes, she squinted into the sun. A man was standing stock still near the cottage. She couldn't make out his features, but she was sure of one thing.

He's looking straight at me.

Jonathan—or the illusive Tyler?

For a moment she was tempted to go after the man, but she recalled what Mrs. Atkinson had said. Tyler didn't like to be disrupted. And if it was Jonathan, that would be even worse.

She stepped inside her bedroom and tucked her passport, ticket and cell phone under the t-shirts in the dresser. Then with a fortifying breath, she headed downstairs.

"Mrs. Atkinson?"

No answer.

Unable to resist temptation, Rhianna stepped into the den. It had a pleasant lingering scent, musky and masculine. Tyler's room. She thought of Mrs. Atkinson's use of his name. Mr. Tyler. Very formal. It made her wonder how imposing the man really was.

The various titles on the shelves surprised her, and she was ecstatic to find some of her favorite authors—Dean Koontz, Stephen King, Andrew Gross, M.J. Rose, Rick Mofina, Lisa Unger and Daniel Kalla, to name a few.

"Quite the book collection, Tyler," she said, her hand pausing above a shelf. "What's this?"

It was a book on hearing loss. Next to it was an ASL manual. Someone at Lancelot's Landing was learning American Sign Language.

Frowning, she wondered who. And why?

She pulled both books from the shelf and took them outside. "Might as well brush up on my skills, since I'll be looking for a new job soon."

"Are you talking to me?"

The books landed on the deck with a thud.

"Jonathan," she murmured, heart pounding.

"Sorry I startled you." He rudely pushed past her. "I have to get something from inside the house. I'll see you later."

She blinked once and he was gone. *Like a mirage.*

She picked up the books and settled into a lounge chair under the sizzling tropical sun. The only thing missing from her 'holiday' was a meandering swimming pool. Of course she could always venture back to the beach for a swim, but she'd probably get lost. The brush was too dense and the pathways nonexistent to someone who didn't know the lay of the land.

She opened the book on ASL. It was the same one she'd studied when she had gone to work for Mrs. Fletcher. Sign language had come easily to Rhianna, and it had definitely made her job easier with the cranky old gal.

When Jonathan emerged from the house and strode past her, a book tucked under his arm, she didn't say a word. Neither did he. Without even a flicker of response, he made a beeline for the far end of the yard, for the cottage-like building with the chimney.

"No pool?" she yelled, miffed.

"We're surrounded by one," he called back.

She let out a huff. *He wants me to get lost.*

Just before lunch, she examined the paintings in the hallways and living room. Some of them she was sure she'd seen in an art gallery, although it had been months since she'd gone to one, and she never would have if JT hadn't encouraged her to take a day off.

She wondered how he was doing. Was he worried because she hadn't called him? Somehow she had to figure out a way to get a message back to the mainland.

"Hello there," Mrs. Atkinson said from the doorway. "Have you eaten lunch yet?"

Rhianna shook her head. "I didn't want to go snooping around in your kitchen."

"Well, you snoop all you want, dear. I should've warned you I serve breakfast, lunch and dinner at eight, one and six o'clock. If you want anything earlier, just help yourself."

"I can do that. As long as Mr. Tyler doesn't mind."

"Wouldn't matter if he did." Mrs. Atkinson grinned. "It's more *my* kitchen than his. Since I'm here now and you haven't eaten, what would you like for lunch?"

"Something I can take outside?"

Working side by side, she couldn't help smile at Mrs. Atkinson's jovial spirit. She answered the housekeeper's questions and tried to ignore the occasional piercing stare.

"So you thought you were coming to a resort?" Mrs. Atkinson laughed. "I bet you were shocked when you found out otherwise."

Rhianna nodded, though she didn't tell the woman how shocked she was by Jonathan's rude treatment.

"I can't eat all this," she said.

Together they'd made a platter of cheese, crackers, vegetables and dip. Enough for a small family.

"I usually bring Mr. Tyler his supper," Mrs. Atkinson said. "I'll leave you a plate if you don't mind. You can heat it in the microwave." She glanced at the kitchen clock. "And Misty might return soon. She eats like a horse."

"Misty?" *Must be Tyler's wife.*

The woman smiled. "You'll like her, Ms. McLeod."

"Please…call me Rhianna."

"Misty spends most of her days now with Mr. Tyler," Mrs. Atkinson said, bustling around the kitchen in an effort to tidy up. "So I expect you'll have a lot of alone time here."

"That's fine. I don't mind being on my own."

Rhianna was dazed by the realization that there was another woman on the island. It would explain the feminine touch in the décor of the house, and all the flowers inside and out. It would be a relief to share some female conversation, especially if Mrs. Atkinson only made an appearance before the meals. Maybe Misty would provide her with the necessary diversion, so Rhianna could keep her mind from straying to a lean, muscled man with wavy black hair and features so finely chiseled that he resembled an ancient Roman god.

She gave her head a sharp shake.

Where did that come from?

With platter in hand, Rhianna determinedly brushed away all thoughts of Jonathan and his muscles and stepped out onto the deck. She returned to the lounger and picked at the cheese and vegetables. Her stomach was tied in knots, but as the day progressed, she relaxed and forgot all about the mysterious Tyler and his wife.

And the exasperating handyman Jonathan.

Just after seven that evening Rhianna heard the front door slam.

Misty? Or Jonathan?

She waited, but no one joined her.

"If the mountain won't come to Mohammed..."

She strolled through the house, expecting to be greeted by a beautiful, fashionable woman. It was the least she'd expect from the wife of Tyler, the mystery man who obviously had money. How else could he afford his own island in the middle of paradise?

She paused at the bottom of the stairs.

A door closed overhead.

Taking a deep breath, Rhianna climbed the stairs, hoping to God that curiosity wouldn't kill the cat. She had a lot more living to do.

Upstairs, something thumped on the floor.

She hurried up the last six steps. A quick glance down the hallway showed only one closed door. It was at the opposite end of the house from Rhianna's room. She paused in front of the door. Knocking on it, she waited nervously. But there was no answer.

She knocked again. "Hello in there."

A chill swept over her and she shivered. She didn't believe in haunted houses, but the unearthly silence paired with her conviction that someone lurked within the room behind the door unnerved her.

She pressed her ear against the wood. Someone *was* moving about—or some*thing*.

"I know you're in there," she snapped.

She tested the doorknob. It was unlocked.

This is ridiculous, she thought. *Why are they ignoring me?*

"I'm coming in."

She pushed the door, then sucked in a startled breath.

The room was inhabited by shadows. Someone had pulled the heavy blinds down low, so that no light entered the room. In the far corner a table lamp bestowed warm golden light in a small radius, illuminating an elaborately carved rocking chair with its back to the door. The chair creaked and rocked, slowly but with purpose, and although Rhianna couldn't make out the person sitting in the chair, there was no doubt it was occupied.

By human or ghost, she wasn't quite sure.

She stepped into the room, expecting the person to acknowledge her presence by jumping from the chair or whirling around.

Nothing happened.

Light from the hall glowed amidst the shadows, and the eerie silence—save the creaking—awarded the rocking chair ethereal, ghostlike properties.

Rhianna felt a surge of fear. Her palms grew sweaty and she wiped them on her pants.

Holding her breath, she approached the chair.

"Hello?"

Creak, creak, creak...

"Sorry I'm interrupting but I—"

She froze as the chair's occupant came into view.

A young girl of six or seven stared back at her, her small fingers clamped on the armrests. The contrast of jet-black hair and pale ivory skin made the child's eyes seem unnaturally large and luminescent.

Rhianna smiled. "Well, hi there."

The girl watched her, but said nothing.

Rhianna reached out to touch the girl's curly mop of hair and was startled when the child twisted her head away.

She's afraid of me.

"What's your name?" Rhianna asked.

No response.

"My name is Rhianna. I'm visiting. From Florida."

Suddenly, the child leaped from the chair and ran toward the door, while Rhianna watched in dismay.

"I'm sorry. I didn't mean to scare you."

Rhianna followed the girl into the hallway and was surprised to see her enter the room next to hers. The girl had left the door slightly ajar, so she peeked inside.

It was a room right out of a fairy tale. Unicorns danced on the walls, a castle dollhouse stood in one corner and a brass canopy bed was situated between two window seats. A waist-high bookshelf held assorted children's books and a leafy glass terrarium with two live chameleons.

Everything was in its place.

Except the child. She was gone.

A quick survey of the room told Rhianna there were few hiding spots. She knocked on the closet door and opened it slowly. No girl.

That left one other hiding place.

She walked slowly toward the canopy bed.

"You have a beautiful room."

The toe of a black shoe peeked out from beneath the frilly bed skirt. In a flash it was gone.

"I'm sorry." Rhianna knelt on the rug by the bed. "I didn't mean to scare you."

She peered under the bed. "There you are. Why don't you come out of there?"

The girl shook her head.

"Please. My name is Rhianna."

The girl made rasping noises in the back of her throat.

"What's wrong?" Was she ill?

Strange sounds erupted from the girl, sounds that were familiar to Rhianna. Thinking back to the books she'd discovered in the den, she realized it all made sense now.

The child was deaf.

Chapter 7

"My name is Rhianna," she signed. "What's your name?"

"Misty," the child replied, her hand carefully forming each letter. "I don't want to talk to you."

"I'm not here to hurt you. I just—"

"Go away!"

Misty turned away, but Rhianna tapped her shoulder and signed, "Is Tyler your father?"

"Yes, now go away. I don't want you here. I hate school, and I hate teachers."

"I'm not a teacher. I'm a guest."

Misty wandered over to the shelf, reached into the terrarium and gently stroked one of the chameleons.

Rhianna flinched. If there was one thing she didn't like it was lizards. And bugs. And snakes.

Misty spun around, a glimmer of a smile on her face. She held out her hand and the tiny lizard scampered up her arm. She beckoned for Rhianna to take the chameleon.

Rhianna shivered. "No, thank you."

The lizard reached the girl's amber t-shirt and began changing color.

Misty watched Rhianna for a minute, then the girl's eyes narrowed and she moved closer.

"It's okay," Rhianna signed. "I'm not big on lizards."

But Misty ignored her, rushing forward and placing the chameleon on the front of Rhianna's dress, just above the waist.

"Please get it off me, Misty."

Rhianna held out her arms and held back a shriek as the lizard scurried up her dress toward her face, its tail slowly turning teal.

"Misty, please!" she signed.

The girl just stood there grinning, especially when Rhianna started dancing a nervous jig, pinching the front of her dress and holding it away from her skin.

"Help me! Get this thing off me!"

Misty's gaze drifted past Rhianna, her grin widening.

In all the commotion and panic, Rhianna was unaware that someone else had entered the room.

"What's going on here?" a deep voice thundered.

Oh crap. Jonathan.

As Rhianna turned to face him, the chameleon moved to the neckline of the dress. She nearly fainted when the creature cocked its head to one side and stared at her. She glanced up, pleading for help, but Jonathan met her gaze with a scowl.

"I see I can't leave you alone unsupervised without you getting into trouble."

"Are you talking to me?" she asked in a heated voice.

"Who else?"

With all the dignity she could muster, she looked him in the eye and raised her chin. "Can you please get this creature off me?"

Jonathan eyed the chameleon. Then his gaze moved from the lizard to the soft swells of her breasts and up to the curve of her neck. Her skin burned as if he'd lit a match along the way.

"Please," she whispered.

He frowned. "It's just a chameleon. They don't bite."

He plucked the lizard from the neckline of her dress, his knuckles grazing her skin, sending a tingle through her body.

Relief, she told herself. That's all I'm feeling.

Jonathan returned the unfortunate creature to its habitat, then looked at Misty. "I see you've met the real boss, Ms. McLeod."

"I know she's Tyler's daughter."

"*My* daughter."

"Your daughter? But I thought..."

"Yeah, I know."

There was more to the sudden twinkle in Jonathan's eye. The cad was actually laughing at her, and he wasn't even trying to hide it.

"But if she's your daughter, then that means you're..."

"Jonathan Tyler." He bowed mockingly. "At your service, ma'am. But everyone around here calls me Tyler."

Rhianna glared at him. "And all this time you let me go on about your boss, about how I was going to report you." Her face grew flushed. "Of all the—"

"Yes?" His brow arched, daring her to continue.

Thankfully, Misty interrupted them by throwing a book at Rhianna, who ducked just in time. The girl ran around her bedroom, shrieking in a raspy voice and knocking toys and books on the floor.

"Misty!" Jonathan yelled and signed at the same time.

Teary-eyed, Misty tugged on his sleeve, and her hands moved slowly. "Daddy, is she my new teacher?"

"No," he signed.

Rhianna noticed the cruel twist to his lips. He was taking great pleasure, savoring that single word.

"Jonath—Tyler, whoever the heck you are, you don't have to be so—"

"Misty's worried that I've hired you to replace Mrs. Vermont." He reached out, stroking his daughter's unruly curls. "I'm simply reassuring her that that's not the case."

"What happened to the teacher?"

"Which one?" He gave her a wry smile. "Misty's been through three teachers in the past seven months. She can be a bit of a handful, and it's hard to find someone with experience in teaching ASL and in dealing with…well, let's say her streak of stubbornness." His voice grew gentle as he watched his daughter. "I don't know what to do with her anymore."

"What about your wife? Can't she home-school Misty?"

He looked at her, his jaw clenched and eyes burning with contempt. "Her mother is no longer in the picture. And even if she was, she'd be absolutely useless."

Rhianna swallowed hard. "That's kind of harsh, don't you think? I mean, she is Misty's mother."

He grabbed her arm and pulled her into the hallway.

"My wife abandoned us seven years ago, Ms. McLeod. She left us the day the doctor confirmed that Misty was deaf—the day she found out she didn't have a *perfect* child."

Rhianna's mouth gaped in shock.

How could a mother voluntarily leave her own child—especially a deaf, yet beautiful little girl who needed her?

She thought of her own mother, of the tragic car accident that had ripped Rhianna from her parents and forced her to grow up afraid, abused and so alone.

"I didn't know," she whispered.

"Of course you didn't," he snapped. "You're a stranger here. You know nothing."

"You're right."

He was silent.

"I-I'm really sorry."

Her apology seemed to diffuse his anger. His shoulders relaxed, his hands unclenched and his mouth softened. She couldn't take her eyes off his lips.

He looked at her for a long moment, then glanced away. "It's a touchy subject. My apologies, Ms. McLeod."

When they entered Misty's bedroom, Rhianna studied the small child with the wild hair and untamed temperament.

"There must be a suitable teacher on the mainland," she suggested. "One that's qualified."

Jonathan shook his head. "I think we've gone through them all. I'll have to put an ad in some of the other island newspapers."

Misty sat on her bed and played silently with two Barbie dolls. She was mimicking an argument, one that resulted in one of the dolls slapping the hands of the other. After a moment, the girl raised her head and locked eyes with her.

"I'll do it."

The words were out of Rhianna's mouth before she could even contemplate the consequences.

Taken aback, Jonathan gawked at her. With auburn hair framing a heart-shaped face, Rhianna McLeod sure didn't look like any teacher he'd ever met.

I could probably teach her a thing or two.

Unable to resist, he glanced at her full lips covered only with a touch of pink gloss. He wondered what it would be like to kiss those lips. What would she taste like? Cotton candy came to mind.

"You'll teach my daughter?"

"Yes."

"The last teacher said Misty is uncooperative and undisciplined. Why do you think you'll have any better luck?"

There was a spark of challenge in her eyes.

"It's not a matter of luck. It's a matter of trust."

He smiled. "You think you can get Misty to trust you?"

She shrugged.

"And why should *I* trust you, Ms. McLeod?"

"Because you've got no one else."

He leaned one hip against the wall and crossed his arms. "There's a private school for deaf children in Miami. They have a great success record. I've been thinking of maybe sending her there."

"You'd send your own daughter away?" she asked, shocked. "To live with strangers?"

"It's not the best scenario, but it might be better for her."

"How can you be so insensitive?"

"Maybe it's what she needs."

"Misty needs her father," she hissed. "Not some cold institution surrounded by strangers."

"It's just an option. I'm not ready to make that kind of decision yet, but it might be good for her. She'll have other children to play with, proper education, and—"

"And it'll be the worst mistake you ever made."

Her words cut him deeply. "Why do you say that?"

"Trust me. I know what it's like to be separated from your parents. *And* to be foisted off on strangers. You don't want that for Misty. Or for yourself."

Rhianna was right. He couldn't jeopardize his relationship with Misty. He loved his daughter far too much.

"So what do you suggest I do, Ms. McLeod?"

"Well, for starters, you can call me Rhianna."

His lips lifted on one side. "I can do that...*Rhianna*."

She moved toward the door. "If I'm going to be here for six weeks, then I want to help out. I have certain skills that might be useful."

"Are you experienced?" he asked.

She spun around. "P-pardon me?"

"Are you experienced? As a teacher?"

She let out a soft hiss of air. "No, I've never taught before. But I'm a nurse, Mr. Tyler, and one of my clients was deaf. I'm quite fluent in ASL."

"I see. Then that's what you can do. To be useful."

"Thank you, Mr. Tyler."

He frowned. "There is one rule though."

"What's that?"

"If I'm to call you by your first name, then I'd appreciate it if you did the same."

"Jonathan it is," she said. "Or would you prefer I call you Tyler like everyone else here?"

"Jonathan is fine." He grinned and extended a hand. "Let's seal the deal then, Rhianna."

She tentatively placed her hand in his. The sudden warmth caught him off guard. Seconds later she withdrew her hand and he clenched his fist, missing the softness of her touch. An unexpected need surged through him, a yearning so intense that the only thing he could do was watch her walk away.

He released a pent-up sigh.

Rhianna McLeod had a strange effect on him.

And he didn't like it one little bit.

"I'll read you a story when you're in bed," Rhianna offered.

Misty gave her a suspicious look. "Why?"

The question stumped Rhianna.

"Because I'd like to," she signed. "Don't you like books?"

With an eager nod, Misty smiled. "Yes."

Rhianna grinned back. *Score one for the new teacher.*

She glanced at Jonathan. He watched them from the corner of his eye, yet tried to appear disinterested.

"You want to read to her?" she signed.

Jonathan's face reddened. "I'm afraid my signing skills are worse than hers."

Her eyes widened in surprise. "I'm sorry. I assumed from the books in the den that you were fluent."

"I'm trying to learn." He glanced at his daughter. "For Misty's sake."

"Believe me, I understand. Signing comes more naturally to children than adults."

"Misty's sign language is limited," he said. "Her teachers said her communication skills were lacking because she wouldn't study. They blamed it on Misty's disruptive behavior."

Rhianna frowned. "I think it's the other way around."

"What do you mean?"

"Because she can't communicate well, she's frustrated, and that leads to her behavior problems."

"According to the last teacher, Misty is the most rebellious, impatient and stubborn six-year old she'd ever met."

She shot him a smug look. "I wonder where she gets it from."

Jonathan actually grinned. "Yeah, I guess the apple doesn't fall far from the tree."

Caught up in his smile, she barely heard him.

He's very handsome when he smiles.

She cleared her throat. "I don't mean to pry, but what have the doctors said? Can they do anything for Misty?"

Jonathan sighed. "She has a hearing aid, but she refuses to wear it. I've tried bribing, threatening and pleading. Nothing works."

Misty appeared in the doorway. "Read," she signed, handing Rhianna a book of fairy tales.

Jonathan took his daughter's hand and led her inside the room. "First we have to get your PJs on," he said, signing the letters *PJ*.

"No!" Misty tossed the two-piece pajama set on the floor and tried signing something to him. She let out a huff and made the same awkward signs.

Jonathan's mouth hardened. "I don't know what you want," he said, his hands resting at his side.

"She'd like the purple nightgown instead," Rhianna said softly. "The one that's hanging inside her…" She paused, looked at Misty and signed, "Closet?"

The girl nodded.

Minutes later, Misty was in her bed, snuggled up with a stuffed penguin. "Story?" she signed.

She surprised Rhianna by patting the bed.

"You want me to sit?" Rhianna asked.

"Yes."

"You seem to have made an impression," Jonathan said behind her.

She glanced at him. "Have I?"

There was a moment of silence.

"With Misty," he said softly.

She slowly blew out the breath she was holding. Lowering her head, she fumbled with the book, opening it to the first page. "I knew that's what you meant."

There was no reply.

Jonathan was gone.

Chapter 8

As Rhianna closed the door to Misty's room, she thought of how the young girl had tried to copy her as she signed the story. Misty was smart. No doubt about it. With a little encouragement, she could learn to sign more proficiently.

She thought of Jonathan. Where was his ex-wife? Had she remarried? Did she ever come to visit?

Does he still love her?

Shaking her head, she backed away from the door.

"Is she asleep?"

"Jesus!" she hissed, grabbing her throat. "Don't sneak up on me like that."

Jonathan emerged from a shadowed doorway and stepped into the dimly lit hall. "Sorry. I didn't mean to scare you."

"You don't scare me."

"I don't?" His mouth curled into a lazy smile.

Rhianna frowned.

Why did everything the man say sound so evocative?

"I'll go say goodnight to Misty," Jonathan said.

"She fell asleep before I finished the fourth book."

"You should've gotten me."

"You could've stayed while I read to her."

"And have you work your magic spell on me too?"

She laughed. "What are you talking about?"

"I've never seen my daughter take to someone so fast. She wouldn't let the other teachers get one foot inside her room." He started down the stairs.

"I'm not a teacher," she said, right behind him. "She thinks I'm your…"

At the bottom of the stairs, he turned. "My what?"

"Friend," she said, swallowing hard. "I don't know. I'm just some stranger who showed up here."

"Yet there you were, a complete stranger, sitting beside her when usually she throws a temper tantrum." He shook his head. "Magic."

If she reached out she could touch his shoulders. But she kept her hands glued to her sides.

Look but don't touch.

Jonathan was doing his own observing. It was making her self-conscious. His eyes trailed over her, from the top of her head down to her bare feet. She held her breath as his gaze swept back up, pausing on her mouth.

She licked her lips.

Suddenly, Jonathan jerked his head toward the living room. "I think we both deserve a nightcap."

The spell broken, she moved down the last two steps and followed him to the bar. He poured two glasses of wine and handed her one.

"Thank you," she said, sitting on the sofa.

"No, thank *you*." He took a sip of wine before adding, "Misty's teachers said she was so far behind in signing that they couldn't waste time reading to her."

"I don't consider reading a waste of time."

"Those were their words, not mine." He studied her hands. "You sign beautifully."

"I'm a bit rusty," she admitted, "but it's kind of like riding a bike. Once you learn ASL, you never really forget."

"Unless you're me," he said sheepishly.

"Don't worry about whether your signing is perfect. It's all about communicating with someone you love." She blushed. "And I know you love your daughter."

"That I do. So teach me."

The wine was making her lightheaded. "Teach you?"

"To sign. I could use some lessons."

"I don't know if you'll make a very good student," she blurted.

His eyes narrowed. "I don't know if you'll make a good teacher."

She couldn't resist a challenge.

"My name is Rhianna," she signed.

He signed his name.

"Nice to meet you, Jonathan."

He reached to take her empty wineglass and his hand brushed hers. As before, a spark of energy made her pull back, her smile fading ever so slightly.

Does he feel it too?

Rhianna was alone with Jonathan for the first time all day. She felt like an awkward school girl, shy and unable to think of anything intelligent to say. So she stared at him instead. He paced the room, moving with feline grace, a jungle cat on the prowl. His eyes darted toward her and she looked away. Finally he sat on the edge of an armchair, poised to pounce.

The silence was excruciating.

She thought of JT. Was the old man okay? Was he worried because she hadn't called him? She hoped not. JT didn't need the stress.

Jonathan cleared his throat, bringing her back to the present. "Rhianna, I-uh...I'd like to take you up on your offer. Misty could really use some signing lessons, and since you're here I thought, perhaps..."

"You want me to teach her." It was a statement, not a question.

"If you wouldn't mind." He exhaled. "I know you're supposed to be on holiday—"

She gave him a wry smile. "Some holiday this has turned out to be."

"I'll pay you, of course. The same as the other teachers."

She set the wineglass on the coffee table. "You don't have to pay me, Jonathan. You didn't know I'd end up stranded on your island. Six weeks is too long to sit around and do nothing. To be honest, I'd be happy to help Misty. She's a lovely child."

A sad look crept into his eyes. "She is."

Jonathan stared into his wineglass, swirling the fragrant liquid. *Misty is a beautiful child, even though she looks like her mother.*

He tried not to think of Sirena. Every time he did, he felt a surge of fresh rage for his ex-wife. She'd left them when they needed her most. He remembered that day like it was yesterday. She wanted to continue with her acting career and felt that Misty's special needs would hold her back. She resented their daughter, but she resented him even more.

"You have no time for me," she said.

He'd never understand how she could just walk away. When the divorce papers had arrived, he signed them with relief. Now Sirena was somewhere in Europe, from what the newspapers reported, sleeping with anyone who would benefit her.

Forcing his ex-wife from his mind, he poured another glass of wine and watched Rhianna. What was it about this woman that made him so edgy and grateful at the same time?

The answer came quick.

Rhianna was very attractive—and she'd read to Misty when none of the teachers could be bothered.

"That was pretty generous of your employer to send you to the Bahamas," he said, struggling to end the silence. "You must have worked for him for a long time."

"Less than a year, actually."

"Really?"

She gave a nod.

His eyes narrowed. What kind of favor had she offered her employer to get him to splurge on an expensive holiday?

Rhianna noticed Jonathan's scowl.

He looks like he's swallowed a fly.

"My employer is the most wonderful person I've ever met," she stated. "He thought I needed a break, so he made all the arrangements and gave me this trip as a birthday present." She snorted. "If he'd known I'd be stranded on your island, I'm sure he'd be mortified."

Jonathan stared at her, his eyes aglow like flames.

Was she the moth?

Watching him, a strange tingle coursed through Rhianna's veins. The intensity of his gaze seemed very personal, as if he'd skimmed the surface of her skin with his fingertips instead of his eyes.

She shivered. Why did her body feel so inflamed?

Jonathan took a sip of wine and licked his lips. Then he smiled, a satisfied gleam in his sapphire eyes.

Her breath caught in her throat.

He knows I'm attracted to him.

The heat rose in her cheeks and she prayed that the soft lighting of the room would hide her reaction. She mentally cursed her sudden weakness. What the hell had gotten into her? She never reacted this way to men. Ever. All the men she'd met were uninteresting and forgettable. She could shrug them off because she never allowed them to impact her emotions. Or her life.

But how many men like Jonathan had she met? She'd spent years holed up with old people—dying people. She'd cut herself off from the world of dating and romance. She didn't want or need a man to complete her, and she certainly could live without physical intimacy.

Yet, here she was wishing Jonathan would kiss her.

She had to think of something else. *Anything* else.

Higginson's face came to mind. How would he react if saw her stretched out on a sofa, sipping wine with an extremely attractive man? A man who oozed sensuality and made her want to—

Don't think of that, Rhianna!

If Higginson could see her now, he'd probably faint.

She giggled at the thought.

"What's so funny?" Jonathan asked softly.

"I, um, was just thinking about someone back in Florida. He'd have a fit if he knew I was stranded here."

Another warning flashed in Jonathan's eyes.

Oh for crying out loud, she thought. *What's he ticked off about this time?*

"You were given a holiday," he said in a tight voice. "If I were you I'd take advantage of it." He finished his wine in one quick gulp and stood up. "I don't expect you to teach Misty, then hide in your room for the rest of the day. There are lots of things you can do to entertain yourself, and if you get really bored, just remind yourself it's only for six weeks. Maybe less if I get the parts for the radio before then."

"I thought you said the parts you needed were in the boxes Roland brought you."

He gave her a dry smile. "You mean the boxes that were left behind?"

She winced. "Oh…crap."

Jonathan raised a brow. "Crap? That's it?"

"I'm sorry, but it wasn't my fault."

"Then whose fault was it?"

From the stormy expression in Jonathan's eyes, Rhianna knew a tempest was brewing. One that was out of her control.

"Your presence has uprooted my quiet life here," he said. "Not only was I not expecting company, you managed to leave behind the one box we needed the most. Without a radio, we're at the mercy of fate."

She chewed her lip. "Let's just make the best of it."

"The best of it." His mouth turned down. "I guess that's what I should expect from a spoiled city girl."

"Hey!" She jumped to her feet, swaying slightly from the wine. "I am *not* a city girl. I was raised in a small town in Maine, I'll have you know." She let out an unladylike snort. "And I'm far from spoiled. You have no idea how hard I've had to work."

"I'm sure you do work…hard."

She glared at him, unable to wrap her tongue around a simple retort that would put him in his place. That ticked her off even more.

"Maybe your employer was planning on joining you on your holiday," he added. "I bet he's married too. Rich and married."

Rhianna was in complete shock. The fact that Jonathan saw her as nothing more than some rich guy's play toy was beyond comprehension.

A surge of ancient guilt brought bile to the back of her throat. Peter Waverley's face flashed before her. He'd thought she was a play toy too, an innocent child who would never argue…or fight back.

Don't think about that!

Looking into Jonathan's eyes, a knifelike pang pierced her heart.

"You don't know me, Mr. Tyler," she said coldly. "And you have no right to judge me."

"If you're teaching my daughter, I damned well do."

"I volunteered," she snapped. "You seem to have forgotten that."

She watched the muscles contract in Jonathan's neck as he clenched his teeth. Without a word, he strode to the bar and poured another glass of wine before speaking.

"Maybe I need to reconsider your offer."

"What?" Rhianna was enraged. "Of all the—"

"I'd watch it if I were you."

The warning in Jonathan's voice scared her.

Without a second thought, Rhianna spun on one heel and darted to the front door. Shoving her feet into her sandals, she stepped out into the humid night and slammed the door behind her. She pushed through the foliage and prayed she was going in the right direction—toward the beach and the dock. She'd sleep there if she had to. She certainly wasn't spending another night in that house with such an insufferable man.

"How dare he insinuate I slept with my employer to get a vacation!" she fumed. "What the hell kind of—"

Her words were cut short by a sudden drop in the ground. Her shoes skidded over the grass as she went hurtling through the bushes, the cacophony of snapping branches and crackling underbrush following behind her.

Finally, a tree blocked her path. She smacked into it and sucked in a startled breath. Relieved that her plunge down the hill had ended, she straightened her dress and took in the sight that the foliage had hidden.

She let out a soft gasp.

Chapter 9

Before her, the ground dipped then rose steeply, giving way to a massive slab of limestone carved out in the center by Mother Nature's gracious hand. Between sheer rock walls, the wandering trench of a narrow waterfall meandered downward about four yards and ended in an oblong pool of dark, mysterious water.

Rhianna had never seen any place so breathtaking.

She smiled. "Now this is what I call heaven."

Closing her eyes, she inhaled slowly, deeply. The warm night air carried the sweet scent of allamanda and frangipani. The drumming of the falls slowed her pulse, and for a single moment she was lost in the heartbeat of the island.

Until a raspy, croaking sound interrupted the stillness.

Her eyes flared open. She searched for a sign that she wasn't alone, but she could see nothing, and the only sound she heard was that of the waterfall.

Overhead, a soft breeze disturbed the jungle-like canopy. The leaves parted, revealing a polished pearl of a moon, then hiding it again.

It was a beautiful night—a perfect evening for romance under the stars.

But there was no chance of romance on *this* holiday.

Of that, she was sure.

Thinking of Jonathan, she wondered what had set him off. One minute he seemed quite friendly; the next he was snapping at her. It shouldn't bother her, but it did.

She sighed.

This could be the longest six weeks of my life.

"But once you leave Lancelot's Landing," she murmured, "you never have to speak to that arrogant Jonathan Tyler again."

It was an unsettling notion.

She stood in the shadows of the tree line, which consisted mainly of coconut and casuarina trees. The latter had scattered thin, needle-like leaves on the ground.

Rhianna suddenly felt a deep yearning for JT to live long enough to see a sight as beautiful as the one she was experiencing.

"JT told me to relax," she said, kicking off her shoes.

With a self-conscious look over her shoulder, she peeled off her sundress and hung it over a tree branch. Wearing only panties and bra, she made her way over the casuarina leaves and around a patch of mud.

She stepped into the water. There was no gradual deepening, like wading into the ocean. Instead, cool water came up to her knee and she nearly lost her balance before she placed her other foot in the pool. The floor sloped toward the center and she waded out until the water reached her stomach.

Giggling, she bounced on her toes. *One, two, three!*

Rhianna plunged beneath the surface and swam underwater until she reached the bubbles caused by the waterfall. When she surfaced, she licked her lips. The water had a faint chalky taste. She swam to the far edge of the pool and stretched out, her body resting on the sandy floor while her head rested against a smooth rock.

"Ah," she said. "This is just what the doctor ordered."

She didn't want to leave. Ever. She realized something. Her discovery tonight might just save her sanity. If she could escape here every night—

Crrrack!

Before she could move, a bulky shadow appeared above her.

So Rhianna did what any woman would do.

She screamed.

A warm hand curled around Rhianna's mouth, cutting off her scream. Then a voice growled in her ear. "Be quiet, you silly fool! It's just me."

"You!" she stammered when the hand released her.

Jonathan stood slowly. "Last thing I expected was for you to be skinny-dipping on my island."

Realizing her state of undress, she self-consciously moved into the depths of the pool where she watched Jonathan restlessly prowl the edge. He didn't look at all happy.

"I'm not skinny-dipping."

"Really?"

The single word sounded threatening.

"You nearly gave me a heart attack," she said in an angry voice. "I thought you were a bear—"

"A bear?" He chuckled. "On an island in the Bahamas?"

"How the hell do I know what kinds of wild animals live here?" Wild like you, she almost said. "What are you doing following me anyway?"

"I wanted to make sure you didn't get lost. But I had no idea you'd be here." He sounded bitter. "How did you know about this place?"

"I didn't. I just…stumbled across it tonight."

It was literally the truth.

"Aren't you afraid of snakes?" he asked. "Or bugs?"

Panicking, she eyed the surface of the water. "Are there snakes in here?"

"No."

"Then why would you say that?" she demanded.

He shrugged. "You're a city girl."

Rhianna clenched teeth. "Stop saying that!"

He moved toward the trees.

"What are you doing?" she called out, nervous.

When he returned, he had her sundress in his hands.

"Put that down!" she fumed.

"It was on the ground," he said dryly.

For a long, awkward moment neither of them said a word. Jonathan stood motionless, staring at her, waiting. She watched him too, unable to take her eyes away or draw in an even breath.

He held out a hand. "Come out of the water."

"No."

"Rhianna…"

She shivered at the sound of her name on his lips.

"Go back to the house," she said tightly.

"I'm not leaving here without you."

Jonathan flung her dress over the nearest tree branch, then began unbuttoning his shirt.

"W-what are you doing?" she squeaked.

"What does it look I'm doing?" He slid his shirt off and added it to the branch. Then he eyed her. "If you won't come out, I'll come in and get you."

Moonlight gleamed off Jonathan's tanned, smooth skin and the muscles that rippled as he moved. When his hands hovered near the zipper of his jeans, she gasped.

"What's it gonna be?" he asked softly.

Rhianna swallowed hard. If she went to him, he'd see her near nakedness. A wet bra and panties left nothing to the imagination, even in the moonlight.

But if he comes in after me…

She didn't want to think about what could happen. In fact, she'd give anything to wake up and find that it was all a rotten nightmare.

"Hold my dress out and turn around," she demanded.

He laughed and the sound carried into the night.

In a low voice he said, "You come out. Or I come in."

Rhianna's cheeks burned with humiliation.

"Since you leave me no choice, you insufferable—" She bit off the list of names she yearned to call him. The man was, after all, someone she had to deal with every day.

At least until the radio is fixed or Roland comes back.

Crossing her arms, she waded toward the edge of the pool, the water line dipping lower with each step, until it was at her belly button.

Jonathan watched her every move. His gaze was so intense that it rattled her.

"C-can you please look away?" Embarrassed, she choked on the words and tears well in her eyes.

Something in Rhianna's voice told Jonathan he'd gone far enough. He'd intended to embarrass her a bit, not bring the woman to tears. One part of him felt guilty for goading her, the other felt tremendous pleasure in watching the city girl squirm.

"Please," she whispered. She looked as though she might faint.

Heaving an irritated sigh, he grabbed the dress from the branch, held it out and averted his face. "There. Satisfied?"

The soft splash of water was the only reply.

He felt a cool, damp hand brush his as she took the dress. He glanced sideways, unable to resist a peek.

His breath stopped.

Damn. It's been far too long.

The natural curves of Rhianna's body and the movements she made as she struggled to pull the dress over her head, drew a physical response from him, one he hadn't felt in months. He wanted her. Of that, there was no question. The dress clung to her, absorbing the wetness of her skin, and she fought to smooth the fabric

"Let me help you," he offered.

"No!" She caught his gaze and spun around. "Stop watching me!"

"But you need some—"

"Don't touch me!" she shrieked. "You know, you didn't have to follow me out here. Or sneak up on me. And I certainly don't need you...to..." She let out a strangled huff.

"I made enough noise on that path for three people," he snapped, standing with his back to her. "And if you hadn't stormed outside, I wouldn't have felt obligated to go after you."

Hell, he wasn't going to defend his intentions to some woman. It was his damned island, after all. He could go wherever the hell he pleased.

He made the mistake of glancing over his shoulders at the same time Rhianna leaned forward to shimmy the dress over her hips.

Jonathan swallowed the lump in his throat. "Just make sure you don't—"

He didn't have time to complete his warning.

A shriek echoed through the night.

One minute Rhianna was standing an arm's length away from Jonathan; the next she was sitting on the ground, covered in mud. She wiped her mouth on her arm, wanting nothing else but to have a good cry. She deserved one after tonight.

She glared up at Jonathan. The corners of his mouth jerked in small spasms. The bastard was laughing at her.

"Don't even think about it," she warned. "It's not funny!"

A grin spread across his face. "Actually, it kinda is."

"You bastard."

"Possibly." He shrugged. "I'm sorry."

"Yeah, right. Sure you are."

Rhianna couldn't take her eyes off him. Moonlight filtered through the trees, emphasizing the hardness of his body and the tension in his face. As his eyes drifted from hers down to the mud smeared on her thighs, an unfamiliar ache snaked through her body, weaving its way downward. It was as if he'd stripped away her last remnants of clothing with his thoughts, leaving her naked and trembling.

She shivered.

"Come on, city girl," he muttered, breaking the spell. "Only animals roll around in the mud. You look—well, how can I put it politely? You look like hell. And you need a bath."

She couldn't believe his audacity.

A wicked idea formed in her mind.

"You're right," she said, holding out her hand.

Jonathan leaned down, and before he could guess what she had in mind, Rhianna clasped his hand and gave it a quick, hard tug. He landed on his stomach, sliding past her in the mud.

Rhianna snorted. "Didn't you say that only animals roll in the mud? Who needs a bath now?"

Jonathan raised his head slowly and she saw the warning in his narrowed eyes. It told her she was down to one choice.

Run!

With a startled yelp, she leapt to her feet and took off into the dense brush. Branches caught at her already-ruined dress, ripping a long tear in the shoulder. Behind her, she heard Jonathan crashing through the bushes.

"For Christ's sake, stop running!" he bellowed.

There was no way in hell she was going to do that.

As she raced toward the faint golden light that she prayed was the house, two thoughts occupied Rhianna's jumbled mind. Was Jonathan as angry as he looked?

And what will he do when he catches me?

Chapter 10

Rhianna tried to use the moon as a guide, but eventually she had to admit she was lost. The path didn't lead back to the house as she had expected. Instead, it led to the small cottage she'd seen from her bedroom window. As she approached, she took in the well tended vegetable garden and pruned bushes. Candlelight flickered through a window. Soft music flowed from inside, an unspoken invitation.

Mrs. Atkinson's home, she realized.

Rhianna raised a hand to knock, but the door opened.

A startled Mrs. Atkinson gasped in shock. "Ms. McLeod! You gave me quite a start. I thought my husband was imagining things when he said someone was outside." She smiled. "Come inside, dear."

Rhianna hesitated on the porch. That's when Mrs. Atkinson noticed the torn, mud-splattered dress.

"What happened to you, dear? Are you hurt?"

"I'm fine, Mrs. Atkinson. I went for a walk and lost my balance at the falls."

"And I tried to rescue her," a familiar voice growled behind her.

"Is that what you call it?" Rhianna muttered, refusing to turn around.

Mrs. Atkinson gaped at Jonathan. "You're covered in mud too, Mr. Tyler. What happened to the two of...?" Her voice faded as a glimmer crossed her eyes. "Ah..."

"It's not what you're thinking," Rhianna said quickly.

"Of course not, dear."

Rhianna whipped around. "Tell her."

Jonathan's eyes narrowed and he cocked his head to one side. "Tell her what?"

"That we didn't—that we weren't—you know."

"Do I?"

Rhianna let out an aggravated sigh. "Nothing happened, Mrs. Atkinson. I slipped in some mud and when Jonathan tried to help me up, he slipped. End of story."

Mrs. Atkinson shook her head slowly and made 'tsk-ing' sounds with her tongue. "Jonathan Tyler, take your guest on home. She needs a warm bath. And you could use one yourself." She herded them off the porch. "Run along now. It would be a shame if either of you caught a chill."

"Yeah," Jonathan mumbled. "A damned shame."

Rhianna clenched her jaw.

Jonathan stomped off in the direction of the house, while Rhianna tripped and cursed behind him. There was no way he was slowing down for her. His stranded houseguest was turning out to be a real pain in the ass. Already, she'd made him look like a fool in front of his housekeeper.

Whose side is Mrs. Atkinson on, anyway?

Last thing he needed was a troublemaking *guest.*

A vision of Rhianna's smooth skin to mind. He recalled gently rounded breasts encased in a wet bra, the droplet of water that had trickled down her throat and disappeared between her breasts, and long, limber legs made for wrapping around—

You don't want her!

But he knew that was a lie.

Rhianna trailed after Jonathan, although he wasn't making it easy. It was more like a marathon than a moonlit stroll. Was he taking a longer route just to pay her back for dragging him into the mud? It sure felt that way.

She cursed the day she'd set foot on Angelina's Isle. Higginson and JT would have a lot of explaining to do when she got back home.

Home. It seemed so far away.

She thought of Mrs. Atkinson's last remark. *'I'm not blind.'* What exactly was she seeing that no one else could? Or could it be that the housekeeper was simply being protective, motherly?

He doesn't know how lucky he is, Rhianna thought.

She would have given anything for a strong motherly role model in her life. But that wasn't what fate had in store for her.

A few yards ahead, Jonathan whirled around, his open shirt flapping in the breeze. "Let's not be out here all night."

"I'm walking as fast as I can."

Looking away, she noticed a small, barn-like shed situated within a copse of trees. "What's that?"

"That," Jonathan stated, "is off limits to you."

"Why? What is it?"

When he didn't answer, Rhianna couldn't resist having a little fun. At Jonathan's expense.

"I bet it's a secret still. You're brewing moonshine back there." She let out a false gasp. "Or maybe you're a drug smuggler."

He stopped in front of her and turned slowly.

"Maybe I'm storing the body of the last woman stranded on my island," he said in a soft, dangerous tone.

Rhianna swallowed. "That's not funny."

With a sigh, he said, "It's none of your business what's in there. And if I tell you to stay away, I expect you to listen."

He grabbed her arm and steered her past the shed.

"Hey, let go!" she demanded.

Jonathan didn't release her until the foliage parted and they stepped into the backyard. Without a word, he kicked off his muddy shoes and began to undress right in front of her. He reached down, pulling his shirt over his head, his muscles flexing with every movement. His pants dropped next, revealing black boxers.

The man exuded primal maleness and Rhianna couldn't take her eyes off of him. As she removed her own shoes, she found it difficult to breathe. Her body tingled all over and her nipples hardened.

From the cool air and wet dress, she told herself.

"I, uh, should take a bath and go to bed," she mumbled, pushing past him and opening the door.

"Rhianna?" Jonathan called softly.

She turned expectantly.

"For a spoiled city girl, you sure have a way of looking like something that's been washed up on a beach."

His laughter followed her all the way to her bedroom.

Humiliation reddened her cheeks and Rhianna slammed the bedroom door. Jonathan Tyler was the most exasperating man she'd ever had the misfortune to meet.

"Washed up on the beach," she muttered. "I don't look like..." The words drifted as she caught sight of her reflection in the mirror over the dresser. "Crap."

Peeling off her clothes, she tossed them into the sink. A bath wouldn't do. Not when she was caked in mud. She stepped into the shower and watched the dirt swirl down the drain.

She closed her eyes. As the water caressed her face, she pictured Jonathan. Lean, sculpted, handsome Jonathan. A man of mystery. A secretive man who was incredibly, irresistibly...rude.

And sexy.

She hitched in a breath at the image of flexing muscles and gleaming skin, of fine dark hair that trailed from his belly button and disappeared below the waistband of his boxers.

Oh God. Why can't I have normal thoughts?

In the living room, Jonathan poured a second glass of brandy. He hadn't really meant to goad Rhianna with that last remark, but he couldn't help himself. Something about her demanded that he insult her at all cost. It was the only way to keep her at arm's length, and something told him it was vital she stay there.

"I didn't mean it as an insult," he grumbled.

Rhianna McLeod *did* look like something washed up on a beach. A mermaid princess. Like the one in the story his mother used to read to him when he was a child.

Putting his glass down sharply, he berated himself for juvenile fantasy. Rhianna was no mermaid. She was a stranger who had so far managed to bewitch Mrs. Atkinson, earn Misty's trust and irritate the hell out of him.

He climbed the stairs, suddenly feeling he'd aged fifty years. At Rhianna's door, he paused. No sounds came from the room. He pressed a hand against the door, yearning for something he refused to name. Then with a soft groan, he clenched his fist and turned away.

In his bedroom, Jonathan took a quick shower. Crawling between the sheets, he stared up at the ceiling. Why had this woman been dumped on his island? It didn't make sense. As he closed his eyes, he made a mental note to ask her about her employer in the morning.

Before he fell into a restless sleep, he recalled Rhianna's long legs sprawled in the mud, the wet dress clinging to her hips. She was beautiful. Even covered in mud.

His dream started off innocently enough. He was walking through the woods at night, alone. The pool appeared before him, the surface of the water eerie and still. He could hear the night sounds—the frogs, crickets, night birds…tribal drumming. Then a musical laugh.

What's that?

An illusive vision shimmered in the falls. Something moved behind the veil of water.

He squinted, trying to make sense of what he saw.

A woman stepped through the waterfall and dove into the pool. That's when he saw the iridescent tail.

A mermaid?

Drawn by an undeniable magnetic attraction, Jonathan strode into the water. He tried to catch her, but his pants weighed him down and she was too fast. Finally, he gave up and waded back to shore.

He glanced over his shoulder. And gasped. "Rhianna?"

The mermaid with Rhianna's face smiled and blew him a kiss. Her auburn hair streamed behind her in the water and her jade eyes sparkled with mischief. Then she dove beneath the water.

As Jonathan held his breath and waited for the mermaid's return, the drumming intensified. His pulse quickened. His senses quivered. Apprehension clung to him. He couldn't shake this feeling of impending doom. With every drum beat, he felt certain that something was coming. Something very dangerous.

The pool's undisturbed surface shone like glass.

"Come back," he whispered in his sleep.

Chapter 11

Blazing sunlight tore Rhianna from another taunting dream, one that starred Jonathan Tyler, baring far more flesh than she ever wanted to imagine.

"Just a dream," she said, waiting for her pulse to slow.

Anticipating a day of teaching, Rhianna dressed in what she thought was close to schoolteacher attire. She even contemplated twisting her hair into a tight bun. In the end, she twisted it loosely and fastened it with a plastic clamp.

When she stepped out into the hall, Misty was waiting for her.

"I'm ready for school," the little girl signed.

Rhianna smiled. "I need a cup of coffee first. Is your father downstairs?"

Misty shook her head. "He's working."

With a shrug, Rhianna took the girl's outstretched hand and followed her downstairs.

"Good morning," Rhianna said when she spotted Mrs. Atkinson in the kitchen.

"Coffee, dear?" The housekeeper hurried over with a carafe in hand. "I made some fresh muffins. Blueberry and bran. Or if you prefer, I could make you some eggs."

"Coffee and a muffin sound perfect."

When Rhianna sat down, Misty sat beside her.

"What would you like for breakfast?" Rhianna asked.

The girl began to sign, then changed her mind.

"We play this game every morning," Mrs. Atkinson explained. "I can't make out what she wants."

"Toast!" Misty signed. "With…" She growled and dropped her hands.

"Toast with jam?" Rhianna signed.

Misty shook her head. "Toast with..." Her hands fell away.

Stumped, Rhianna held up her hands. "I'm sorry. I don't know what you want."

With a loud bellow, Misty jumped up and swept an arm across the table, knocking over a glass of orange juice.

"I want brown toast!"

Rhianna eyed Mrs. Atkinson. "Do you know what she means by brown toast?"

"No, dear. We have whole wheat bread all the time, but when I make her toast, she gets angry and throws it on the floor." The woman smiled softly at Misty. "She's frustrated, the poor little one. I suppose I would be too if no one understood what I was saying."

Misty sulked in the corner of the kitchen, arms folded across her middle, eyes burning a hole into the ceramic tile.

Rhianna frowned. "Then we need to make sure everyone starts understanding her." She raised her eyes to Mrs. Atkinson's. "That goes for you too."

The housekeeper smiled warily. "The last teacher said I was too old to learn. You know, you can't teach an old dog new tricks."

"One of my patients was eighty-seven years old when she learned ASL," Rhianna said. "You're a spring chicken compared to her."

"Well, I don't know about that," Mrs. Atkinson said with a giggle. "But I'll try to learn if you're willing to teach me. I did pick up a few signs." She demonstrated a dozen or so signs with only a bit of hesitation.

"Sit down," Rhianna signed to Misty. Surprisingly, the girl obeyed.

"How about we spend one hour every afternoon teaching Mrs. Atkinson some sign language too?"

The scowl on Misty's face lifted. "My Daddy too?"

Rhianna swallowed hard. "I, uh..."

"Of course I'll learn too," a masculine voice said.

Rhianna studied Jonathan, who was dressed in ripped shorts and a faded t-shirt. At least he looked cleaner than the last time she'd seen him.

But he wore less in your dream.

A nightmare had kept Jonathan from a restful sleep. He'd spent the long night chasing an illusive Rhianna deep into the jungle, where predators lay in wait. He had to catch her, because behind him something ancient and evil stalked them. When he'd awoken, he was covered in a thin sheen of perspiration and his heart pounded in his chest. He'd bolted from the bed and paced the room.

Something was coming. And it wasn't good.

He muffled a derisive snort. *You idiot. Nothing bad is gonna happen.*

He glanced at his daughter. The little traitor was sitting beside her teacher, all grins and giggles.

"Does two o'clock work for everyone?" Rhianna asked, without looking at him.

"Works for me," he replied.

"Me too," Mrs. Atkinson said. "This will be quality family time."

Jonathan frowned at her. What was the woman up to?

"Sit down, Mr. Tyler," Mrs. Atkinson ordered.

He slumped into the chair across from Misty. "I'll take my coffee black today, Mrs. Atkinson."

The housekeeper raised her brows in surprise. "No cream?"

"No. Just keep my mug filled."

"You're supposed to be working, Daddy," Misty signed.

"I wanted to make sure you and Ms. McLeod were settled into school first," he signed self-consciously. "How are you this morning, Angel?"

Misty giggled. "I'm not an angel."

"Then you must be a…" He flicked a look at Rhianna. "How do I sign fairy or princess?"

Rhianna showed him and he mimicked the moves, much to Misty's delight.

"I'm a fairy princess," Misty signed to Mrs. Atkinson.

"That you are, dear love. That you are."

Jonathan settled back in his chair and took in the strange scene. They rarely ever ate together like this. He was usually locked in his studio by now. Misty would visit after lunch and he'd often miss supper.

It was kind of…nice.

He watched Rhianna. She was good with his daughter. Patient, kind, caring. He saw her wipe a smudge of orange juice from the corner of Misty's mouth. It was such a natural act, yet it annoyed him. Sirena should be sitting there, looking after their daughter. Not some stranger.

Jonathan pointed to a small stack of books he'd set on the counter when he'd arrived. "Those are the books that the last teacher used, Ms. McLeod. You can use this table once Mrs. Atkinson has cleaned up, and if you feel you need anything else, let me know the night before."

"That's fine."

That she barely looked at him irked him to no end.

For a long moment, Rhianna couldn't look at Jonathan. She still felt mortified from being caught nearly naked in the pool, although she'd gotten him back for sneaking up on her and nearly scaring her out of her skin. There was a sense of justification in her actions. So she'd yanked him down into the mud. So what?

She studied him now from beneath her lashes. A willful wave of hair fell across his ruggedly handsome face, and his tanned skin set off the brilliant blue eyes. She could see his pulse beating steady and strong at the base of his throat.

His hands cradled the mug and she noticed that his fingers were long, tanned and very tense. She remembered how they felt across her mouth, soft yet firm. Her body tingled at the thought of his hands caressing her skin. What would it be like to have those hands touch her in other places?

"Rhianna?"

She realized he'd asked her something. Her cheeks burned and she lowered her head. "Sorry. What were you saying?"

"I said you look well this morning. No chills, I take it?"

He was laughing at her. She could hear it in his voice.

As Jonathan left the room, she stared after him.

Thank God he isn't the type to take revenge.

Jonathan *was* thinking of revenge, but his was of a much sweeter kind. He'd waited this morning, specifically putting off going to work just so he could see Rhianna. He couldn't help but notice how the sheer peach blouse glowed against her skin, or how the navy pants outlined her long legs. She looked radiant and fresh.

And completely unsuspecting.

The kind of revenge he had in mind was personal in nature. He didn't even stop to consider why he felt it necessary. Sure, she'd frustrated him enough that he'd chased her into the night. He could have shrugged that off. But when he saw her lying in the pool, his breath had nearly stopped. Later, she'd embarrassed him, caught him off guard. Now his pride egged him on.

The plan had brewed all morning. He'd find a secluded corner where he could be alone with the troublesome Ms. McLeod. Then he'd make her pay for giving him that mud bath.

Her hair would look much better down, he decided.

He imagined how silky it would feel and how beautiful she would look with soft waves tumbling about her shoulders. She'd be at his mercy and he'd take what he wanted. It would be enough to put Rhianna in her place and show her she couldn't mess with him and escape unscathed.

And what did he want from her exactly?

One simple kiss.

Then he'd be done with her.

As he strode across the backyard, he grinned. Yes, his revenge would be very sweet indeed. Best of all, Miss City Girl wouldn't even see it coming.

The morning passed quickly for Rhianna. She went through sign language basics with Misty to get a feel for where the girl stood academically. Jonathan's daughter was very bright, especially when it came to learning signs for objects in her environment, a method Rhianna had used with Mrs. Fletcher.

"It's important to learn the signs for things around you," Rhianna told Misty at lunch. "Later, you can teach these to your dad and Mrs. Atkinson."

It was nearing one o'clock when Misty yawned and signed, "I'm tired. I want a nap."

"Of course," Rhianna said. "I'll wake you up at two."

Misty headed for the stairs. On the first step, she paused and looked over her shoulder. "Will you tuck me in?"

"Sure."

Ten minutes later, Rhianna skipped down the stairs, feeling very pleased with Misty's progress. But her happiness diminished the second she saw Jonathan waiting in the dining room.

"It's not two yet," she said.

"I know. I can tell time."

"Of course you can."

"Is Misty having a nap?"

"I just put her down." She smiled. "She did great at ASL today. She knows more than anyone realized and she catches on fast. I think she'll be caught up in a week or two."

She was rambling, but his unwavering stare made her uneasy.

"Why are you back so early?" she asked.

"I forgot something."

"Oh."

Jonathan moved toward her. "I was trying to think of something appropriate."

"For what?" she asked, backing up against a wall.

His lips curved into an innocent smile. "It's payback time."

"Payback?" she squeaked.

In answer, he leaned forward and pulled the clamp from her hair. "Your hair looks better down."

Rhianna was stunned into silence. She couldn't have spoken even if she'd wanted to. She was too wrapped up in conflicting emotions—excitement and fear.

Jonathan mussed up her hair. "Now you look like you did the first time I saw you."

With her cheeks aflame and her nerve endings firing on all circuits, even his breath against her hair made Rhianna quiver. She reached up to stop him from playing havoc with her hair. And her mind.

When their hands met, a sudden shock jolted through her body. Then their eyes locked. She saw turmoil in his.

Without warning, Jonathan grabbed her hands and pinned them above her head. He eyed her, his mouth curved in a lazy smile.

"Let...me...go," she said between clenched teeth.

"Not yet."

"Let me go, Jonathan."

"Not until I get what I want. Last night you called me an animal." Lips brushed her ear. "You haven't seen the animal in me until now."

She couldn't breathe.

His burning gaze traveled the length of her body. His eyes heatedly took in her tousled appearance—her flushed face and trembling lips. He held her captive hands above her head, causing her breasts to strain against the sheer fabric of her blouse.

Jonathan lowered her arms and moved closer. His hard chest rubbed against her blouse and the friction made her gasp.

What is he doing to me?

Jonathan leaned forward, exchanging his breath for hers. She should resist him, push him away or at least tell him to stop. But she couldn't move.

"Just remember, city-girl, it's dangerous to tease a wild animal."

When his mouth made contact with hers, she pulled back. "Don't."

He ignored her. His lips touched hers, moving more urgently, coaxing her submission. Heat raced through her blood and her pulse quickened as his tongue sought refuge, sweeping and drawing something primal from her.

Lust, she told herself.

Her eyes drifted shut, her treacherous body responding against her will. An intense hunger for something more—something she couldn't name—overwhelmed her. Even though her head told her to fight, her heart told her to give in to this new pleasure.

Jonathan's breaths were coming quick, his mouth growing more demanding. Her body was aflame with desires she'd never felt before. She couldn't fight the feelings he drew from her.

So she closed her eyes and gave in.

His hot mouth skimmed her neck and moved lower.

"Rhianna..."

She shivered. "What?"

"I never thought revenge would taste so good," he murmured.

She froze. *Of course! He warned me.*

"Stop it!" She ducked under his arm. "Just because this is your island doesn't mean you can manhandle me."

"I wouldn't call that manhandling," he said dryly.

Flustered, she crossed her arms over her chest. "This is your idea of revenge?"

"Don't tell me you weren't enjoying it." He shrugged. "Anyway, it was only a kiss."

Rhianna gaped at him. *Only a kiss?*

She couldn't get to her bedroom fast enough. Once inside, she locked the door and leaned against it. She touched her lips, recalling his kiss.

He was right. She had liked it.

What the hell am I doing?

Rhianna hid in her bedroom. With her senses on high alert, she listened for footsteps or sounds that Misty was awake.

She tried to ignore the truth. Jonathan had kissed her and she'd liked it. It was so different from the kisses in her past, the dirty ones.

A wave of ugly memories assaulted her. Peter Waverley's angry face, his hands touching where he shouldn't, the pressure, the invasion…the blood. He had abused her in every way, and even after she'd left them, she was haunted by what he'd done to her, what he'd taken from her.

This unwanted initiation had caused her to spurn advances from handsome, young interns while she attended nursing college. And the few times she'd gone on dates, their groping hands and sloppy kisses had made her push them away.

Disgust. That's all she'd felt back then.

She sighed. *What's changed?*

"I wanted him to kiss me."

She still did.

This realization was beyond comprehension, as was the fact that her body yearned for much more than a kiss.

Downstairs, a door closed.

Rhianna strode to the window just in time to see Jonathan crossing the lawn, his hands tucked in the pockets of his shorts. As he approached the ridge of bushes, he paused and turned toward the house.

Mortified, she froze. Could he see her?

Jonathan raised a hand.

"Of all the—" She ducked from view and groaned. "Great, Rhianna. Now he's going to think you're interested."

She flopped on her stomach across the bed.

"I am *not* interested in Jonathan Tyler." *I'm not!*

The lie made her shiver.

Her eyes wandered to the photo on the nightstand. Higginson had taken the picture on one of JT's good days, shortly after Rhianna's birthday party. Full of life and healthy color, JT grinned in the photo. He had one arm thrown over Rhianna's shoulder, while she beamed back at him.

Life was far less complicated back in Miami.

Rhianna picked up the photo. "You're the only man who's ever loved me, JT."

A surge of homesickness hit her. All of a sudden she wanted nothing more than to go home. Back to JT's mansion. Back to her familiar life, the one that held no demands or expectations other than her nursing skills.

Where I know the rules.

She missed everything, even JT's grouchy moods.

"You must be worried sick," she said to the photo.

That concern would only increase as each day passed without a phone call from Rhianna.

Her eyes watered. "No crying."

The old man's kindness and fatherly love had done more for Rhianna than two years of counseling. There was no doubt in her mind that he only wanted the best for her.

What would he think of this situation?

She kissed the photo. "I miss you, JT."

Please be okay.

Chapter 12

When the phone rang, JT was tempted to ignore it. But he couldn't. What if it was Rhianna?

It wasn't.

"Mr. Lance," a man said cheerfully.

JT scrunched his face. He knew that voice. Didn't he?

It took a long moment before things slipped into place.

"What do you want, Chambers?"

"We have some business to discuss."

JT swirled the brandy in the glass and stared at the amber liquid. "We've already concluded our business. And you've been paid quite handsomely, may I add."

He'd paid Winston Chambers fifty thousand dollars.

"Well, there's the problem," Chambers said. "We have differing opinions as to what constitutes a *handsome* payment."

JT heard the flick of a lighter.

"I have no more work for you," he said.

Chambers chuckled. "I don't want more work. I just figure that since you went to all the trouble to find the girl that you'll be open to…a bonus."

JT heard Chambers inhale deeply. The man was probably puffing on one of his obnoxious smelling cigars.

"What kind of bonus are you thinking, Chambers?"

"Two hundred and fifty thousand should suffice."

"How much?"

"You heard me."

"This is blackmail!"

"I know what it is, Mr. Lance. You're a rich man. What I'm asking for will barely make a dent in your bank account."

JT downed the brandy and slammed the empty glass on the table. "No!"

There was silence on the other end.

"Did you hear me?" JT yelled. "I won't cave in to blackmail."

"Then you'll be very, very sorry."

"What can you do?" He tried to laugh.

"I can tell her."

JT's breath stopped for a moment. "What do you mean?"

"You know what I mean. I'll tell her everything. How you made me search for her all these years. How you followed her every move."

"So tell her," JT said with a shrug. "It's not that big a deal."

Laughter sounded on the other end. JT wanted to slam down the phone.

"She'll want to know how you got her name," Chambers said.

That's where JT had him. He hadn't given the private investigator all the details. *Just her name, thank God.*

His head began to throb.

"I came across her name when I was researching homecare," he said, hoping he sounded convincing.

"Liar."

JT rubbed his eyes. Everything was blurry.

"Listen, you bastard," he snapped. "I'm not paying you a cent more than I already have."

"That's where you're wrong, Mr. Lance. In fact, the price just doubled."

"What? Are you out of your mind?"

"Five hundred thousand dollars. In my account by midnight tomorrow."

JT's heart pounded out an unsteady beat. "Or what?"

"Or I tell your precious Rhianna everything."

As Chambers revealed what he knew, JT massaged his aching head. The pain was excruciating. But if Rhianna ever found out about the secret he'd kept all these years, his pain would be far worse.

"The money will be there," he said, broken. "But you have to promise me you'll take it and disappear."

"You have my word," Chambers said.

JT hung up the phone. He stared at it, afraid it would ring again and bring him more trouble. Finally, he tried to stand. His legs wobbled. Then an explosion of bright light assaulted him and everything went black.

Before he passed out, he had one last thought.

If Rhianna discovers the truth, she'll never forgive me.

When JT awoke, he was back in bed. He surveyed the room through hazy eyes. Curtains drawn, water jug beside the bed, door closed leaving the room in shadows.

Something moved in the corner.

JT blinked twice and his vision cleared.

Aw, crap.

A worried Higginson sat in the chair, his arms folded tightly across his chest and his expression dark and moody.

"You look like the grim reaper," JT said dryly.

"He'll be by any minute if you keep this up."

"Then he'd better bring reinforcements. I'm not ready to go yet."

"You've got one foot in the grave. And it's sinking."

JT scowled. "Stop treating me like I'm dying."

"You *are* dying," Higginson said sharply. "When are you going to get that? You need to conserve your energy."

JT closed his eyes, wishing he could drown out his friend's voice. He knew he was dying, but that didn't mean he had to lie back, play the feeble invalid and wait for it to happen.

"You're pushing yourself too hard."

JT flashed Higginson a smile. "I have things to do, places to visit, people to—"

"Piss off?"

"People to see, and—"

"Floors to pass out on," Higginson finished for him.

JT sighed. "That wasn't my plan." He struggled to sit up, then gazed out the window. "I miss her, Higgie."

"I know, my friend."

"The house just isn't the same without her."

Higginson pulled the chair closer. "JT, you remember why you're doing this. To make amends. To fix what's broken."

"To find some peace," JT whispered.

"You have to take better care of yourself. If not for yourself or me, then do it for Rhianna. When she comes home—"

"She *is* coming home," JT interrupted. "Isn't she?"

Higginson nodded. "I'm sure she'll be back. You're like a father to her."

"I'm old enough to be her grandfather and you know it."

"You're all she's got," Higginson said, standing. "So you'd better be here when she returns."

JT gazed into his old friend's eyes. "She's going to be pissed."

"I expect so, sir."

"She won't like that I tricked her."

"You're probably right, sir."

"Did I do the right thing?"

Higginson rested a hand on JT's shoulder. "My friend, I have known you for many years, and in all this time I've come to recognize that you always do the right thing. In the end."

"Fine." JT pushed the covers aside. "Now help me out of this blasted bed. We've got to plan Rhianna's welcome home party."

"Your wish is my command, sir."

Higginson held out a hand, but JT slapped it away.

"Knock it off with the *sir* crap, Higgie."

"Yes…sir."

Sitting in the shadows of his compact office lit only by the golden glow of a table lamp, Winston Chambers tamped out the cigar and stared at the dead butt in the ashtray. *Cohiba Behike.* One of the most expensive cigars ever made. He'd paid twenty-five thousand for the cigars. Only one hundred desktop humidors had been manufactured, each with forty handmade, numbered cigars. The ring of paper around the top also boasted his name—*Winston Archibald Chambers.*

He licked his lips, savoring the rustic blend of coffee and cedar flavors on his tongue. Like an orgasm, the cigar had been good while it lasted.

He glanced at the manila folder on his desk. He'd scribbled his client's name across the tab.

JT Lance's guilt had more than paid for the Cohiba Behike cigars. Now what? A new car? A casino weekend in Vegas?

Scratching his chin, the fleeting thought that he should have shaved crossed his mind. Then again, it worked for Winston. Being a private investigator meant he had to blend in, not get made. It meant he could go places where law enforcement types couldn't. It meant he got results, whether with a bribe, a threat or his fists.

Which reminds me, I haven't been to see Miss Shirl's girls for a while.

Miss Shirl was the owner of Bare Essentials, a downtown Miami gentlemen's club. At least that's how Winston preferred to think of it. The girls there had been brought in from exotic countries—Jamaica, Mexico, Japan, China, Malaysia. Even Canada.

Winston preferred Japanese girls. Small and meek, they knew their place—on their knees or their backs. He could easily lay down ten grand at Bare Essentials for a night of debauchery and fun. Sometimes more if he had to pay for damages. Like the fat lip he gave the last bitch, a smart-mouthed little Malaysian whore who'd fought him when he wrapped his hands around her scrawny neck.

Should've strangled the bitch.

He leaned back in his chair. It groaned rebelliously under his weight, a hundred pounds of it superfluous.

By tomorrow he'd be a wealthy man.

And I'll have JT Lance to thank.

He laughed. "If he really thinks he's seen the last of me, he's got another thing comin'"

He recalled the day he'd met the multi-millionaire. It was at an art auction. Lance was bidding on artwork for his mansion, while Winston was screwing the auctioneer's pretty, young girlfriend in the coatroom. Unbeknownst to him, Winston had dropped his business card on the floor when he'd dropped his pants. Lance found it later that evening.

"I have a job for you," he'd said to Winston the following day when he'd called. "I'll pay you double your rates."

The offer had intrigued Winston.

"What's the job?" he'd asked.

"I need you to locate someone for me. A girl."

At first, Winston thought the old man had wanted the girl to satisfy his sexual urges. But this wasn't the case. Lance said something about wanting to make things right—whatever the hell that meant.

Then Lance had sent him the photo.

The first time Winston had seen it, he'd freed Willie and pumped him until he was spent. He'd had to wipe his shoes off.

He slid the top drawer open and pulled out the worn photograph of Rhianna McLeod. It was her graduation picture, from nursing school. She was barely twenty-one, but she looked about sixteen. There was a haunted innocence in her fathomless green eyes.

He stroked her face. "You can play nurse with me any time."

Finding the girl wasn't that difficult. He'd had her parent's names. Bribes had paid for her birth records, school records and a complete file from Social Services.

At first, Winston didn't understand what the old man wanted with her. Lance wasn't related to the girl.

Or was he?

That thought had cropped up in Winston's mind a few times. What if the girl was actually Lance's daughter? Was he perhaps looking for his missing heir?

This led Winston to delve more deeply into JT Lance's background. His past seemed to be an open book. Self-made millionaire by thirty. Married once. Divorced. One kid, a son. Still, what if Lance had a daughter by someone other than his wife?

It had taken some digging. He'd scanned newspapers, school records, anything he could find.

Then he found it. The connection.

He held the photo up to the light. "I know who you are now. But you have no idea who JT Lance is, do you?" Wet lips smacked against the photo.

He wiped away the trace of saliva he'd left behind, then picked up the phone and dialed a number.

"It's Win," he said to the woman on the other end. "I'll be in tomorrow night and I want your best room, a vial of E and your best champagne."

Minutes later, he hung up. He was thrilled by the prospect of an entertaining adventure. This time he'd asked Shirl for a young redhead with green eyes and luscious curves.

Oh, the things I'll do to her.

Clasping pudgy hands across his ever-expanding girth. "I think I should take a holiday soon. Where to go?"

He glanced at the map on the wall. A smile slowly creased his grizzled face, yet never fully reached his hardened gaze. "I've never been to the Bahamas."

But first, he'd have to plan his retirement.

Chapter 13

At the beach near the dock, Rhianna relaxed on an oversized towel and listened to soft waves lapping against the powdery shore. The air was misted with the scent of the ocean and tropical flowers, an aroma she now identified with Angelina's Isle.

They should bottle that scent.

Flipping onto her back, she adjusted the top of the green bikini, applied some sunscreen to her face and slipped a fashionable pair of sunglasses over her eyes. Higginson had called them her *"movie star shades"*.

Sorry to disappoint, Higginson, but I don't feel like a star out here.

She inched up onto her elbows and took in the view.

Palm and coconut trees lined the beach with its pale sands and the ocean glistened as if a painter had taken a brush and swirled turquoise, violet and sapphire pigments together.

It was peaceful here. *Maybe too peaceful.*

There wasn't a soul in sight. Mrs. Atkinson had taken Misty to her cottage to do some gardening, giving Rhianna the rest of the afternoon off. And Jonathan…well, he was off working.

Since that day when he'd kissed her, he'd been avoiding her. That suited her fine. She wasn't sure what to say to him anyway. Dinners had been quiet and most often he wasn't there when Mrs. Atkinson laid out the plates.

Rhianna had spent the past six nights in her room after dinner, her nerves a jumbled mess as she waited to hear the front door slam. Jonathan always tiptoed upstairs and disappeared into Misty's room before locking himself away in his bedroom.

Her days were spent teaching sign language to Misty, a welcome reprieve from worrying about a stupid kiss that meant nothing.

Jonathan's daughter was a fast study. Every sign was followed by its use in a sentence, a technique that Misty enjoyed. It was while they were in the kitchen, signing about the use of ingredients in the pantry, that Rhianna solved the mystery of Misty's *brown toast*. The girl loved buttered toast with cinnamon and sugar sprinkled on top. It was something one of her past teachers had made for her once, but the woman hadn't bothered to teach her the sign for cinnamon.

She smiled, thinking of Misty. Such a sweet child. And very sensitive. Just this morning she'd asked why Rhianna didn't talk to her Daddy.

"Your Daddy's very busy," Rhianna had explained, though she still didn't have a clue what the man did.

I never asked.

In her attempt to distance herself from Jonathan, it had completely escaped her to ask her host what he did for a living. Banking? Some kind of Internet mogul? Whatever it was, Jonathan wasn't hurting for money.

She flipped over onto her stomach and clenched her teeth. "Don't think of him."

"Don't think of who?"

Gasping, she scrambled to her feet, nearly tripping over her handbag. "Jesus!"

Jonathan flashed perfect pearly whites. "Not quite."

"Stop doing that!"

"Doing what?"

She grabbed her towel and hid behind it. "Sneaking up on me."

A dark brow arched mockingly. "I don't sneak."

"That's exactly what you do."

He took a step forward. She froze.

When he reached out a hand, she jerked away. "What are you doing?"

"Relax," he hissed. "You've got a blob of sunscreen on your chin." His finger lightly grazed her face. "There. It's gone."

Rhianna tried to still her trembling hands. Wrapping the towel around her chest, she clasped it close, then leaned down to retrieve her handbag.

"You didn't answer my question," he said, not moving.

"What question?"

"Who were you so determined not to think of?"

Rhianna swallowed hard. Then she said the first thing that came to mind. "My employer. I miss him."

A shadow crossed Jonathan's face. His lips curled downward. "I see."

As quickly as he had appeared, Jonathan vanished into the woods, and Rhianna was left feeling that something was terribly wrong.

Muttering a few choice curses, Jonathan fled through the overgrown brush and headed for the one place he always found sanctuary. As the roof of the small cabin came into view, he let out a frustrated growl and wiped the sweat from his brow.

"What the hell is the matter with me?"

There was something about Rhianna McLeod that made his blood boil, something that made him want to grab her and shake her—when he wasn't thinking of other things he'd like to do to her.

"She'll be gone soon enough," he said, shoving open the wooden door.

He took a deep breath. The air inside smelled of vanilla and cinnamon. There were bowls of scented oils scattered throughout the room. There were also other underlying aromas. The tang of paint and turpentine. Combined, the scent was welcoming and familiar.

Jonathan studied the room.

His sanctuary was small but inviting, with wood plank walls, rustic log furniture, a tiny kitchen in the corner, a small bathroom with a shower, and two bedrooms at the back that held only a bed each and a side table. The main room featured a sofa and one chair, pushed up against the back wall.

He'd built the place with his own two hands. And a bit of help from some of the local islanders. He'd been so proud of the house. It was the starter home he'd promised Sirena, a way for them to get out of the cramped one-bedroom apartment they'd shared in New York. Sirena hadn't been happy when he purchased the island.

"I don't want to live way out here in the middle of nowhere," she'd told him.

He had to promise they'd leave the island often. And they had. Every week he took her to the mainland. They often flew to New York and sometimes to L.A. so Sirena could pursue her acting career.

That was before he'd sold the boat to Roland. Before Misty was born.

After the divorce, he'd retreated to the island with his tail between his legs. Not very manly, he supposed, but that's the way it was. Thankfully, Sirena hadn't fought for custody of Misty.

"I want Misty to live with me," he'd told her as she prepared to leave the hotel on the mainland for California.

"Take her," she'd replied. "I never wanted her anyway."

He'd fought to stay calm. But all he wanted to do was tell Sirena what a coldhearted bitch she was.

"I'll have my lawyer draw up an agreement for sole custody then," he'd said.

"Very well. You go back to the island and hide away like you always do. I have a life to live."

He'd watched Sirena walk out of the hotel room, out of his life and out of Misty's life. Forever.

Now, he glanced around the cabin and wondered if Sirena had been right. Had he been hiding away all these years?

He sank into the armchair and stared at the blank canvas propped up on an easel in the middle of the room.

For the first time he couldn't think of a thing to paint.

Not one damn thing.

The following morning, Rhianna endeavored to focus on her lesson plan and Misty. She didn't want to think about Jonathan. She'd heard him sneak into the house well past midnight and go straight to his room.

She gave Misty a smile of encouragement. The girl was studying a worksheet. She'd look at each sign and try to form them with her small hands. When she was successful, Misty smiled. A few signs were more difficult and she made frustrated growling sounds.

Just like her father, Rhianna thought. *If he's not scowling, he's—*

A vision of Jonathan's lips came to mind.

Recalling his kiss, a surge of anger rushed through her. He'd taken liberties with her and she was confused by the feelings his kiss had aroused. Jonathan had managed to elicit a response from her, one she was unfamiliar with. No man had ever touched her the way he had, with a desire that her body answered willingly.

I want him.

She firmly closed the door on that thought. But it didn't stop the flow of other questions. Did Jonathan feel the same way? Did he want more than a kiss?

She was sure that Mrs. Atkinson knew something had happened. Every so often, Rhianna caught the housekeeper staring at her, smiling.

What if Mrs. Atkinson asked her again if Jonathan would be joining them for dinner?

Rhianna's mind conjured up a scenario.

Sorry, Mrs. Atkinson, she'd say. *Mr. Tyler has met with an unfortunate accident. He tripped over his inflated ego and hit his big head on a rock. He won't be joining us for dinner.*

"Ha!" Rhianna laughed aloud.

"I'm done," Misty signed. "Can you read me a story?"

Rhianna shot her a guilty smile. She'd have to wait for another time to continue imagining Jonathan's demise.

"A story?"

Misty nodded.

Suddenly, Rhianna's eyes widened. She'd been so distracted that when she repeated Misty's request, she hadn't signed. The girl could read lips.

"What would you like me to read?" she asked slowly, keeping her hands at her sides.

Misty grinned. "I'll show you," she signed.

As she raced upstairs to her room, Rhianna mulled over this new development. Jonathan hadn't mentioned that his daughter could lip read.

He doesn't know.

Thumping footsteps indicated Misty's return. She'd brought down three books, all fairy tales. She settled into a chair at the table, shoving the books eagerly toward Rhianna.

Misty handed her a book. "This one, Ms. McLeod."

Rhianna frowned. She was starting to feel like a drab spinster schoolteacher every time the girl addressed her so formally.

"Misty, you can call me by my first name," she signed. "I'm Rhianna." She spelled her name.

The little girl's eyes widened. Her hands flew into speech. "I can't do that. Daddy would be mad. He says I have to call my teachers by their last names. It's for…"

"Respect?"

Misty shrugged.

"That's all right, Misty. We don't have to tell your father. It can be our secret. We can even use a secret sign for my name. I'll teach you how, okay?"

Rhianna felt triumphant in the knowledge that she'd be going against Jonathan's rules.

"Rules, shmules!" she said with her back turned to Misty. "Rules are made to be broken. Anyway, your father broke the rules first."

The ASL course she'd taken a few years ago had taught her that to create special names for people, all one had to do was sign the first letter of the person's name and connect it to something special about them. In the class, a woman named Arlene was used as an example. She was a dentist, so the letter 'A' was signed with a brushing motion over the teeth.

"What do you like doing, other than reading and playing with Barbies?" Rhianna signed.

Misty pinched the sides of her dress and began twirling. "I saw this on TV," she signed when she'd stopped. "Daddy doesn't know the sign."

"Dancing." Rhianna spelled the word first, then showed Misty the sign. "I've got the perfect idea for your special name." She signed the letter 'M' rocking back and forth across her other open hand. "Misty the dancer."

The girl twirled and signed simultaneously. She grabbed Rhianna's hands and they spun in circles until they were dizzy.

Laughing, Misty flopped on her stomach across the bed. Rhianna followed suit. The girl's small hand caressed Rhianna's hair.

"Your hair is very pretty," Misty signed. "Your special name should be..." She signed an 'R' by crossing her index and middle finger and moved them in spirals from the top of her head to her shoulder.

Rhianna copied her, smiling. "I like it."

"How come my other teachers never taught me this?" Misty signed.

Rhianna rolled to one side and shook her head. "I don't know." She stared at the girl for a moment. "Why did your other teachers leave?"

"My first teacher made me memorize words all day. It was boring."

"What about your last teacher?"

"She always fell asleep at the table. She was a hundred years old."

Rhianna knew Misty was exaggerating, but it didn't change the facts. Jonathan had just assumed that these teachers would do their jobs. He'd also assumed that Misty was the difficult one, not the teachers.

"Did you tell your father about your teachers?"

"He didn't believe me. He thinks I'm stupid."

Rhianna blinked and unclenched her teeth. "Well, we'll just have to show him how smart you really are."

"Daddy has work to do," Misty signed, looking away.

"What kind of work?"

"Painting. Sometimes he lets me help him."

Ah, Rhianna thought. Maybe Jonathan was painting that cabin she'd seen, the one he'd warned her away from.

"How did you learn to lip read?"

Misty shrugged. "I don't know. I just know when someone is saying words I know. Can you teach me more? How to see more words?"

"I really don't know how to teach lip reading. Maybe your father can get you a special teacher for that."

Misty's eyes watered. "I don't want another teacher, Rhianna. I want you."

The girl's words hit hard. Misty would be heartbroken when Rhianna left the island.

But what about me? How will I feel?

She didn't want to think of that. Not now.

Stroking Misty's dark curls, she drew the girl close and hugged her. "Well, for now you're stuck with me, kiddo. I'm not a hundred years old and I won't fall asleep at the table. And if you promise to work hard on your lessons, I promise to make them as exciting as I can."

And I promise your father will know exactly what I think of him.

Rhianna didn't see Jonathan until nearly nine o'clock that evening. Mrs. Atkinson had already left for the night and Misty was tucked in bed and fast asleep. Earlier, Rhianna had read three stories, while they waited to see if Jonathan would put in an appearance.

Rhianna waited now, silently fuming.

Without acknowledging her presence, Jonathan entered the living room and poured a drink. He took a long swig, then his gaze caught hers.

"Misty says you think she's stupid," she blurted.

Jonathan lowered the glass. "Excuse me?"

"Her past teachers were the stupid ones," she said. "Your daughter is a very bright girl."

"I know that."

"Then maybe you should tell her once in a while." His calm demeanor infuriated her. "And maybe you should spend a little more time with her."

"I do spend time—"

"Not enough. Not for a child." Her nerves were on edge and prickly anger simmered on the surface. "Did you know Misty reads lips?"

"What?"

For the first time, Jonathan looked flustered.

"Your daughter can read lips. She's picked it up on her own. I'm not sure how good her comprehension is, but you can bet she understands more than what you've signed."

"So what do I do now?"

"Spend more time with her, talk to her."

"This is a bad time," he insisted. "I have to—"

"No, you don't." She pursed her lips. "You don't *have* to do anything. Whatever room you're painting can wait."

Jonathan's mouth twitched. "Can it?"

"Misty said you've been busy painting for the past few weeks. That you've hardly spent any time with her." Her eyes cut into him. "How can you be so selfish?"

Jonathan set his glass on the bar. "So I'm selfish now, am I?" He sauntered toward her. "Some people actually have to work for their money."

Rhianna blinked. "What's that supposed to mean? This is the first holiday I've—"

"I wasn't talking about your holiday," he snapped.

"Then what are you talking about?"

He glared at her. "I'm sure your employer—your *patient*—enjoys what you do for him, but some of us have real work to do."

"Real work? You call painting a room or furniture or whatever you're painting *work*? What are you really doing? Living off some rich trust fund your Daddy left you?"

"You don't know what you're talking about," he growled.

"Don't I?" She waved a hand. "Look around. You own a private island, yet don't go to work every day. So you either have a trust fund or no money at all."

"Or I made wise investments," he said dryly.

That he'd have money set aside hadn't even occurred to her.

"Look, Rhianna, I have until Roland comes back to finish what I'm working on. Then I'll be leaving for the mainland." He studied her for a minute. "You'll be leaving too. Until then, keep your thoughts about my relationship with Misty to yourself."

"Aye, aye, sir," she retorted, saluting him. "Is this why your wife left you? Because you're the big boss? Because you're always too busy?"

Something dark flickered in Jonathan's eyes and Rhianna knew she'd gone too far.

"It was the other way around," he said. "She was too busy for us."

Rhianna's heart sank at the pained expression in his eyes. When he turned on one heel and went upstairs, she stared after him.

Damn. What am I doing?

Chapter 14

Rhianna awoke with a start when something thumped deep within the house. She blinked at the clock on the bedside table. 4:38 AM.

What had awoken her?

As if in answer, a door squeaked downstairs. Someone was up, and they were moving in stealth mode.

Jonathan?

A soft crunching sound made Rhianna sit up. Flipping the sheet aside, she climbed out of bed and felt for her robe. Sliding into it, she tiptoed to the balcony.

She'd left the door open earlier, hoping the night air would cool the room. It hadn't. The night heat had brought with it a rise in humidity.

Rivulets of sweat tricked down the side of her face as she watched a shape move across the grass. It *was* Jonathan. A beam of light from a flashlight moved in front of him. Where was he going?

The cabin.

Curiosity made her do something foolish. Tying the sash of the robe tightly, she hurried downstairs, eased the door open and slipped outside. She'd follow him. Maybe then she'd see what he was up to.

Overhead, the sky was a midnight blue, hazy with clouds. The moon was nowhere in sight.

Led by the flashlight ahead, Rhianna passed through the trees. The path from the yard to the cabin was smooth, mostly flat rock and grass, which was a good thing since she'd forgotten to wear sandals.

She passed a long branch and it caught at her robe and snapped. She ducked out of sight as the sound echoed in the night. Peering from behind a coconut tree, she saw the light arcing toward her.

Crap!

She hid behind the tree, her heart stuttering a rapid beat. She'd have some explaining to do if he found her.

The light swept close, then disappeared.

She waited, fighting to keep her panting to a minimum.

What'll I do if he finds me?

She'd die of embarrassment, that's what.

Rhianna took another look. The light was gone.

Relieved, she continued down the path. Minutes later, a warm light appeared up ahead. It was coming from the cabin.

She moved around the side of the structure, away from the front door. She ducked under a window, then stood slowly and pressed her back against the cabin wall.

Okay, Rhianna. Take a quick look, then go home.

Grabbing the edge of the window frame, she pressed her nose against the cool glass. There was a drape across most of the window, but an opening in the middle revealed a small room, hidden mostly by shadows. Jonathan had set the flashlight on the table. The light pointed to something covered with a cloth. A piece of furniture, maybe.

Jonathan crossed in front of the window.

Rhianna jerked back.

Some time ticked by before she had the courage to look again. She blinked twice, wondering if what she was seeing was a dream.

What she saw made her heart race.

Jonathan stripped down to a pair of boxers. The damned heat was just too intense. He'd come to the cabin partly to cool off and partly hoping he'd be inspired by the serene solitude.

Standing in front of the easel, he wiped an arm across his damp forehead. Then he flipped the cloth and stared at the blank canvas.

What should he paint? A nature scene? The island?

No, he'd done those already. He needed something original. Something delicate, beautiful and full of mystery.

Rhianna.

He swallowed hard, unable to deny that ever since the woman had been dumped on the island, Rhianna McLeod was constantly on his mind.

Like a bad meal, he thought, even though it was untrue.

When he gazed at the canvas, all he could see was Rhianna. The brilliance of her auburn hair and jade eyes, the soft curves in all the right places, the tilt of her chin when she was pissed at him—which was often—and the fiery temper.

Jonathan grinned.

Yeah, Rhianna was a definite distraction.

Rhianna couldn't take her eyes off Jonathan. She watched through the window as he moved with a wild, almost feline grace. It did strange things to her. As did seeing him nearly naked. The boxers left little to the imagination, and she was having a difficult time keeping her mind from curiously wandering to his nether regions.

When she caught sight of the easel and canvas, she stifled a laugh.

"Oh my God," she whispered. "*That* kind of painting."

Jonathan Tyler was an artist—obviously a good one and definitely a messy one. This was how he made a living.

How could she have been so dense?

She thought of all the paint-stained shirts she'd seen him wearing. Mrs. Atkinson must have her hands full trying to get those clean.

Inside the cabin, Jonathan leaned forward, the fabric of the boxers stretching across his buttocks.

Rhianna could feel the heat rising in her cheeks. She'd never seen a man so natural in his own skin. Or one in such a state of undress.

Except Peter.

She sucked in a pained breath. She didn't want to think of Peter, but he continued to invade her thoughts and nightmares, filling her with self-loathing and fear. For years her secret past had controlled her.

Not any more, she promised. *I am going to exorcize you, Peter Waverley. One way or the other.*

And she knew just how to do it.

She peered through the window and watched Jonathan. He laughed at something. Then he picked up a brush and a palette, his face twisting into a frown.

Stepping away from the cabin, Rhianna bumped into a garbage bag. Something inside clanged, metal on metal. With a determined breath, she propped the bag against the cabin, then made a beeline for the trees.

Minutes later, she reached her destination.

The natural pool and waterfall waited for her, luring her close and inviting her into the cool depths. The rush of water soothed her. The perfumed air made her smile.

She could do this. She would conduct her own kind of exorcism ritual and destroy any last hold Peter Waverley had on her. She *had* to do it.

She hung her robe on a branch and peeled off her nightshirt and panties before she could change her mind.

I'm naked.

Rhianna shivered, knowing she was completely exposed to the elements. She folded her hands across her breasts and inched into the water. Its satin warmth enveloped her, the temperature only a few degrees less than the air.

The secrets—the mind numbing shame—had been pushed to the furthest recess of her mind, and it had been years since she'd replayed, by choice, the events of her past.

Peter Waverley had nearly destroyed her.

But I'm stronger than that.

Rhianna took in a long, steady breath. Releasing it, she did the one thing she'd been resisting all these years.

She remembered...

It had started with her head being forced underwater. Violent hands shoved her under and held her there. She tried not to panic but scented bath water crept up her nose, burning a trail down her throat. Then she was hauled upward, her lungs desperate for oxygen.

"This'll teach you for reporting me," Peter had screamed. "Don't you *ever* do that again! You hear me?"

He forced her underwater, again and again, until darkness threatened to overcome her. His menacing laugh was muffled, but audible.

"This is what you deserve, you stupid little bitch!"

He released her.

Air! She gasped at it between fits of coughing.

"We'll continue our discussion after you've dried off," Peter sneered.

"I won't let you rape me again," she rasped.

Under she went again.

I'm going to die.

Though she was only a scrawny teenager, she had fought back, kicking and slapping at his hands. But Peter was too strong. She held her breath until her head felt like it would explode. The pain in her throat and sinuses was agonizing.

But not as agonizing as when he rapes you.

She couldn't imagine going back to that hell. Always wondering if tonight would be the night he'd sneak into her room. Or if he'd find some other depraved act to use to humble her.

I can't do this any more.

Rhianna opened her eyes underwater and numbness settled over her. If she died, the pain and humiliation would be over. She'd be finally free.

She released her breath and inhaled water. Her body fought back, struggling anxiously to breathe. She clawed at the sides of the tub, wondering what she'd find on the other side.

Something better than the past sixteen years?

Freedom.

It was just after midnight when Rhianna drowned.

As Jonathan touched the brush to the canvas, ready to make a tentative outline, he heard a muffled clang. He'd tossed a garbage bag outside earlier. It was filled with old paint thinner and aerosol paint sealer cans.

He strode to the window, wondering if a bird had gotten into the bag. He surveyed the yard. Nothing. He expanded his search, peering at the tree line.

A flash of white caught his eye.

What the hell—?

He looked at the clock on the wall. It was just after four in the morning. Everyone should be sleeping.

Maybe it was a ghost.

He laughed at the thought.

I've been sniffing paint fumes too long.

Jonathan turned away from the window.

Since the Atkinsons weren't night owls and Misty would never leave the house at night, that only left one person.

His eyes fastened on the blank canvas.

Had Rhianna been spying on him?

With a sigh, Jonathan rested the paintbrush on the easel, wrapped the palette in plastic wrap and tugged the sheet back over the canvas.

Inspiration would have to wait. If that had been Rhianna in the trees, then she was heading in the wrong direction.

Flashlight in hand, he let out an irritated growl. "Why am I always running after you, Rhianna?"

Chapter 15

Rhianna waded into the pool, tears streaming down her face. She'd died in the Waverleys' bathtub. Peter, with his leering grin and grasping hands had revived her. She'd woken up in a hospital bed, alone and terrified. She recalled that early morning when Gwen, the silent accomplice who lived in her own world, entered the room. The cold expression on her face had been as far from motherly as a starving coyote eyeing its wounded prey.

Gwen had spat accusations at Rhianna. "Peter had to give you mouth-to-mouth, you ungrateful wretch. How dare you try to kill yourself in our house!"

"I didn't," Rhianna had said, her throat scratchy and sore. "He pushed me—"

"Liar!" Gwen had bellowed. "Lying's all you do. We've done everything to look after you, give you a good home. And this is how you repay us? By lying to Children's Services? By telling them my husband, the man who provides for us, did such unspeakable things?"

The look Gwen had given Rhianna was one of pure contempt. Then she'd spun on one heel and headed for the door.

"You're very lucky Peter heard you, or else we wouldn't be having this little talk. They wanna keep you here for observation, but I expect you to be home tomorrow." She paused. "If they want you to stay longer, you tell 'em you're fine, that you wanna go home. You hear? You have chores to finish."

The door had crashed shut. The sound was like a cell door slamming shut. To Rhianna, there was no difference.

Now, as she swam toward the deeper side of the pool, Rhianna felt a surge of inner strength. She could do this. And once she did, she'd be the one holding power over her own life. Not Peter.

"I won't let you win," she called out into the night. "I'm taking my life back. Every single part of it."

She tried to touch the bottom with her toes.

There was no bottom.

For a brief second, the old fear, the one that told her she would drown, resurfaced. After a near-death experience at sixteen, Rhianna had fled the Waverley's home. She found a part-time job cleaning tables at a café, in exchange for food and a small room in the back. Life was livable—until a worker from Children's Services caught up with Rhianna and threatened to send her back to the Waverleys. That night, Rhianna had hitched a ride south, from Bangor to Portland, and with help from staff at a woman's shelter, she started over.

And here I am, she thought. *Thank God for YMCA swimming lessons.*

Rhianna dove underwater, held her breath and counted to twenty. When she emerged, she smiled up at the brightening sky. "I'm alive."

She dove under again, this time holding her breath as long as she could. Seconds ticked by, but still she remained beneath the surface. Slowly expelling her breath, she relaxed completely. Finally, she rose from the depths and took in a labored breath.

One final test.

"You no longer have power over me, Peter Waverley."

Swimming to the base of the falls, she ducked under the pounding streams of water. The pressure was intense, as if tiny hands were pushing her under.

Break free!

Rhianna dove beneath the surface. She was slightly disoriented by the pressure of the falls, and when she emerged, she was surprised to find she was behind the waterfall.

Pale dawn light radiated through the curtain of water and illuminated a small cavern carved into the limestone knoll. The cave extended back several yards and there was a hole that let in more light situated on the left side of the ceiling. Light danced on the rock walls and the sound of the waterfall reverberated in the cave.

"Beautiful," she murmured.

She pulled herself up onto the smooth stone ledge that rose a foot from the surface. She sat with her feet dangling in the water, while an unfamiliar calmness washed over her. There was something about this pool, about Angelina's Isle. Something healing and promising. It teased the fragrant air, the powdered sand, the silky water. The island had started working its charm from the second she'd stepped onto it, bathing her in freshness. She'd never felt so clean.

"I wish I could stay here forever."

Sadness swept over her.

Soon, Roland would whisk her away in the boat. He'd take her back to the mainland and she'd fly back to Miami. Back to JT. And while she missed the old man dearly, she realized that going home meant leaving Angelina's Isle.

And Jonathan.

The thought sent a sharp pang through her heart.

Jonathan fingered the white bathrobe. Rhianna was here—somewhere—but the pool seemed undisturbed. Was she lying in the shadows, lids half closed, mouth partly open, with lips he wanted to kiss?

He wanted other things too. More skin on skin. The desire he felt for her had increased daily, making him crabby and uncomfortable. He could admit his flaws. And being tested by such a beautiful woman, being constantly reminded that she was out of his reach in every way, was enough to reduce any man to frustration.

"Rhianna?"

No answer.

She had to be here. Her clothes were still on the tree.

He tried another tactic. "If you're hiding because you're embarrassed, I'll have to come in and find you."

His threat resulted in more silence.

Damn, woman! Where the hell did you go?

He had a terrible thought. What if Rhianna had gone for a swim but had slipped and hit her head on the rocks? What if she was unconscious—or worse?

Jonathan waded into the water. With strong strokes, he swam around the pool's edge, into the shadows, but he came up empty. No Rhianna.

Flashes of memory besieged him. The day he'd found Rhianna sleeping on his dock, the smile on her face when she saw his home, her gentle encouragement with Misty, how she looked with her hair down…right before he kissed her.

I can't lose her now. I'm just getting to like her.

He dove now, panic overwhelming him. His fingers grazed the bottom. There was nothing there but rock and sand. He swam to the other side and searched the floor of the pool. Time after time, he came up empty.

Fear ate at him. What if he lost Rhianna?

Rhianna slid into the water. It was time to go. She pushed beneath the water and swam a few yards before surfacing in the center of the pool—a few feet from a shocked Jonathan. Not that she wasn't shocked too. Her pulse was beating so loudly she was sure even he could hear it.

"Where the hell were you?" he demanded.

"Why, did I scare you?" She could tell he was going to deny it, so she shrugged. "Now you know how it feels."

"I thought you were…" He looked away.

"You thought I was what?"

Jonathan's jaw flexed. "Never mind."

She stared at him for a moment. Then it hit her. He must have seen her clothes and gone looking for her, never suspecting she'd found the cave behind the falls.

"I was behind the falls."

Jonathan's head jerked up. "You found the cave?"

She nodded. "By accident."

"It's almost the only natural thing here," he murmured, gazing at the pool.

"What do you mean?"

He laughed, a rich sound that made Rhianna shiver. "Did you think this was a natural waterfall?"

Rhianna blinked. "It isn't?"

"We're on a small island that only has a few hills. You'd have to go to one of the big islands to see natural falls." He jerked his head. "I built this. The pool, the waterfall, everything except the cave."

"Wow. Who would've guessed?"

"There was a pond here, but it always dried up in the summer. That's what gave me the idea for this."

"How do you keep the water in it then?"

"Well water," he said. "The waterfall is rainwater driven, with pipes that create a circuit from the pool to the top of the falls. The well keeps it topped up."

"Your ex-wife must've loved it," Rhianna murmured.

He scowled. "Sirena and nature don't mix. Unless it's the wild jungle of Hollywood."

Silence.

"I think this place is unbelievably beautiful," she said.

"I think *you* are," he blurted, swimming up to her.

Jonathan's lips fastened on hers so quickly that she didn't have time to think or react. He didn't touch her anywhere else, just with his lips. A soft pressure, enticing her to respond.

And she did.

When she kissed him back, he gently pried her lips apart. The kiss deepened. She drew him in with an eagerness that surprised her. There was no holding back, no fear. Just this heavenly bliss that rushed through her body.

Jonathan touched her then. He wrapped his arms around her waist and drew her close. The satin boxers brushed against her. And something more.

He was rock hard.

When his chest met hers, Rhianna sucked in a breath. His tongue invaded her mouth. She let out a soft moan of pleasure, lost in the sensations, in the sweetness of his breath and the satin strokes of his tongue.

"Rhianna," he whispered, pulling away.

Reaching up, she drew his head down until his mouth met hers. She wasn't done. Not by a long shot. She had years to make up for, years to wash away, until there was only this—the most perfect, glorious kiss.

She slid her hands through his wet curls as he kissed her eyelids, her nose, her chin. She arched her back when his hot mouth moved down her neck.

Lost. That's how she felt when he kissed her.

"Jonathan..."

He kissed her lips hard, drawing out a moan of ecstasy. Then his mouth fastened on her shoulder and his tongue licked a line across the tiny beads of water that settled on her collarbone.

"I want to taste every inch of you," he said hoarsely.

She shivered.

Before she could say a word, a movement at the far end of the pool caught Rhianna's eye. She blinked, uncertain if she was imagining it.

She wasn't.

"Snake!" she screamed.

Chapter 16

A gray-black snake slithered across the surface of the water and moved slowly toward them.

"Get out of the water!" Rhianna shrieked. Swimming to the shallows, she glanced over her shoulder. "Hurry up! Why aren't you moving?"

Jonathan snorted. "It's an anhinga."

When she glared at him, he added, "A bird."

A raspy croaking erupted from the anhinga.

Crouching in the shallow water, Rhianna tried to ignore the heat rising in her cheeks. She'd nearly climbed out of the pool. Naked. In front of him.

"A bird," she said hesitantly.

"An anhinga is similar to a cormorant," Jonathan explained, wading toward her. "It has an elongated neck. When they swim, that's all you see. Locals call it the snakebird."

"Seems fitting to me," Rhianna said with a scowl.

"There are anhingas in Florida, you know."

"I don't get outside much."

"Why is that?"

"I like to stick close to home. In case I'm needed."

The anhinga raised its long, thin yellow beak and stared at them. Then, with a raucous croak, the bird swam toward the rocks, where it waddled ashore and spread its wings, standing motionless.

"What's it doing?" she asked.

"Drying his wings."

"Oh."

"They're also called water turkeys."

"Somehow I don't think he'll go too good with stuffing and mashed potatoes."

Jonathan chuckled. "You're probably right."

"How come you know so much about them?"

"Marvin's a walking encyclopedia."

She frowned. "Marvin?"

"Mr. Atkinson."

The anhinga let out a loud squawk.

"They're sure noisy," she said.

"In Brazil they're called devil birds."

"Great," she muttered. "We were swimming near that thing."

A smile tugged on the corners of Jonathan's mouth. "We were doing more than swimming."

Heat surged through her and she looked away.

Damn! Her robe and clothes were out of reach—too far to casually stroll up to them without Jonathan seeing every inch of her nakedness.

"What's wrong?" he asked, stepping from the water.

She swallowed hard. "I need you to look away."

"Oh, right. You're naked." He turned, his boxers clinging like a second skin.

"I thought I'd be alone."

It's what Rhianna had wanted. At first. Now she wanted nothing more than to feel his lips caress hers.

Did Jonathan feel the same?

In the glow of a rising sun, she studied his back. Jonathan looked like a cover model for People Magazine's Top 10 Sexiest Men, a magazine she'd discovered on Mrs. Fletcher's bookshelf. There was a difference, though, between flipping pages and staring at photos of gorgeous hunks and having one in the flesh only a few feet away.

A tremor raced up her spine.

Get a grip, Rhianna.

She blew out a slow breath and moved toward the rocky edge of the pool. She tugged the robe from the tree and watched as Jonathan leaned down to wipe the sand from his feet before slipping on his sandals.

Rhianna tried not to stare. It wasn't easy.

Jonathan gave her time to dress. He could afford to be a gentleman. He'd gotten what he wanted. The kiss. He did everything to convince himself that was *all* he wanted, but he'd be a fool not to admit that if Rhianna hadn't stopped things, he would have taken far more than he had.

"Okay," Rhianna said behind him. "I'm dressed."

"That was fast," he said, turning to face her.

With the robe tightly cinched around her small waist, Rhianna held a bundle of white in her hands and looked at him nervously.

Was she naked under the robe?

Don't think about that.

He stared at her, his desire mounting.

"I think we should go," she murmured.

"We should," he agreed.

She turned away and made for the path to the house.

"Wait up," he called after her. "I've got the flashlight. I should go—"

Suddenly, Rhianna stumbled, crying out in pain.

Jonathan rushed to her side. "Are you okay?"

"I think I broke my ankle."

"Let me take a look."

He handed her the flashlight, then knelt on the ground, easing her foot into his lap. There was already some swelling. His fingers gently prodded around the ankle bone.

She hissed in a breath.

"Sorry," he said.

"What's the verdict? Will I live?"

He smiled. "It's not broken, so you're in luck."

She tried to take a step and let out a yelp.

"Here," he said, scooping her up in his arms.

"What are you doing? Put me down."

"You need to stay off that foot."

"But—"

"No buts. Unless you want to land on yours."

"Ha ha," she said dryly.

"Put your arm around my neck."

She hesitated.

"I won't bite." He sighed. "I promise."

When she did as he suggested, he grinned. "Now isn't that better?" It sure felt good to him.

"Yeah. Thanks."

"No problem." He chuckled. "I'd say any time, but I think you have enough bad karma."

Rhianna looked away. "It does seem so, doesn't it?"

He laughed, then headed down the path. A few yards in, he veered off the trodden grass and followed a sandy path.

"Where are you going?" she demanded. "This isn't the way to the house."

"Trust me. We need to get some ice on that ankle right away. I have ice in my studio."

"Well, there's ice in the house too."

He let out a huff. "Are you going to argue with everything I say?"

Rhianna clamped her mouth shut.

When they reached the small cabin, Jonathan nudged the door open and strode to the sofa. Carefully easing Rhianna onto the cushions, he paused, his attention caught by her pouting lips.

God, he wanted to kiss them.

Ice, damn it! Get the ice.

But all the ice in the world couldn't cool the fire that was burning inside him.

When he released her, Rhianna bit her bottom lip and struggled to remain calm. She lost the battle.

Oh my God! What the heck is wrong with me?

Her pulse raced and a thin bead of sweat broke out on her forehead as she thought of the kiss in the pool. She'd responded in a way she'd never done before—carelessly, wantonly. She hadn't pushed Jonathan away like she had the handful of men who'd tried to get close to her in the past. Why?

Because she wanted him.

It was the only answer that made sense.

If the anhinga hadn't made noise in the pool, God only knows what would have happened. The bird had definitely dampened the mood, and she suspected she wasn't the only one unraveled by what had occurred. Jonathan had been uneasy too. It would explain their frivolous conversation about water turkeys and devil birds.

Now here she was, sitting on his sofa, alone with the man. No other distractions—except his hands on her ankle, his bare, tanned chest with its seductive contours and a smile that turned her into a molten mass of yearning.

How was she supposed to act now?

Jonathan took charge of the situation.

"Are you comfortable?" he asked.

She nodded, wondering if he regretted kissing her.

"You don't look so good."

"Thanks," she muttered.

He gave her a grim look, then grabbed a pillow from the armchair and tucked it under her foot. "Keep it elevated. It'll help relieve the swelling."

"What are you, Dr. Tyler M.D.?" she said wryly.

"I've learned to deal with small accidents." He strode toward the kitchen and tugged open the freezer door. "I pretty much have to out here. The closest doctor is almost an hour away." He popped ice from the tray onto a towel and rolled it carefully.

Returning to her side, he placed the makeshift icepack over her ankle. "This should help numb the pain."

"Aren't you worried about Misty?" she asked, trying to ignore the sharp sting of cold.

"Usually I have a radio for emergencies."

She blushed. "Oh, yeah…sorry."

Jonathan shrugged. "This isn't an emergency." He made a beeline for a kitchen cabinet. "Drink?"

"Sure." She took the opportunity to stuff her nightshirt and panties into the cushions behind her.

A few minutes later, Jonathan returned. "I hope rum and orange juice is okay. It's all I've got here."

"It's fine. Thank you."

As he passed the glass to her, their hands met. A spark of electricity shot between them.

"Sorry, it's the carpet," he murmured.

I don't think so, she wanted to say.

Jonathan's eyes flashed, as though he knew what she was thinking and was calling her on it.

Coward!

Unable to stand the tension, Rhianna blurted, "What were you painting?"

"What are you talking about?"

She pointed to the cloth covered easel. "That."

Jonathan frowned. "So you *were* spying on me."

"Not spying exactly, just…" She fumbled for an explanation. "Just checking to see if anyone was here."

"The fact that the light was on should've told you that."

She mentally kicked herself. "I guess it should've."

"Hmm…"

"What do you mean, *hmm*?" She gave him a mocking smile. "You think I'm some James Bond spy, here to steal your precious art so I can sell it on the black market?"

"The thought never crossed my mind."

But Rhianna could tell by his guilty expression it had.

"Listen, Picasso…I don't know the first thing about art or paintings, other than whether I like them or not. You can rest easy. I won't be making off with your treasures in the middle of the night."

"Of course you won't." At her questioning look, Jonathan added, "There's no boat. Remember?"

"How can I forget?" She paused. "You didn't answer my question. What are you painting?"

He grabbed a bath sheet from a hook and wrapped it around his waist before answering. "I haven't started it yet. I'm waiting for...inspiration."

"So is this what you do for a living? Paint?"

"You could say that." He sat down in the chair across from her and stared at the wall behind her head.

"Can I see some of your work?"

Surprise flickered in his eyes. "I never show anything until it's in a gallery. Call it superstition, but I don't need any more bad luck."

She raised her chin. "Are you saying *I'm* bad luck?"

"Rhianna, you're the queen of bad luck." He grinned at her. "Whether you're bad luck to me, we'll have to see."

Rising from the chair, he flipped the ice pack.

"God, that's freezing," she hissed.

"I can warm you up."

His gaze devoured her and she gulped in a breath.

"I should go back to the house," she said.

"Then I'll carry you back."

"No," she said quickly. "I'm sure I can walk now. It's not very far."

Rhianna made it three steps before her ankle gave out. Thankfully Jonathan was right behind her or she would have ended up on the floor. This time she made no protest when he lifted her into his arms.

Neither of them said a word as they approached the house. Jonathan carried her upstairs to her bedroom and set her down on the bed.

"Thank you," she said.

"For what?"

"For rescuing me. And carrying me here."

"No problem."

As he moved to the door, she said, "Lancelot's Landing is a very fitting name for this property."

"Why do you say that?"

"You know," she said with an awkward laugh. "Sir Lancelot, brave knight rescues the maiden and all?"

He bowed low, the towel threatening to slip off. "At your service, milady."

She let out an unladylike snort. "Somehow I don't see Lancelot in a towel.

Jonathan's eyes narrowed. "What *do* you see him in?"

There was no way Rhianna was going to touch that.

"Good night, Jonathan."

"Sleep well...milady."

When the door closed behind him, she let out a pent up breath.

"I can warm you up," he'd said.

"I bet you can," she murmured.

Chapter 17

Rhianna awoke to the chatter of tropical birds. She glanced at the clock on the nightstand. It was after ten in the morning. She'd slept in.

"Damn!" she muttered. Misty must be wondering where the heck she was.

She threw off the covers and tentatively tested her foot. A dull ache settled around her ankle, but it was bearable. The good news was she could walk.

Quickly dressing, Rhianna went downstairs in search of her young charge and a pot of coffee.

"Misty?"

The house was unusually quiet.

As she entered the kitchen, she expected to see Misty at the table, coloring or playing with her Barbies. But the table was empty except for some fresh flowers in a vase, a carafe of steaming coffee and a clean mug.

"Bring on the caffeine," she mumbled.

She caught sight of a note on the fridge door.

Rhianna, I hope your ankle is better. I decided not to wake you this morning. Take the day off. The Atkinsons are looking after Misty, so put your foot up and relax. I'm taking my easel down to the beach. See you later tonight. By the way, thanks for the mementos. Jonathan.

Mementos? What the heck was he talking about?

Something twinged in the back of Rhianna's mind and a sinking feeling in the pit of her stomach made her moan.

"Oh no…I left my panties and bra in his studio."

Chewing her bottom lip, she thought of her options. She could wait for Jonathan to return her clothes. That would turn her a few shades of red. Or she could sneak into the cabin while he was painting at the beach.

He'll never know I was there.

Slipping her feet carefully into a pair of sandals, she headed for the door. As she limped across the lawn, mindful of her sore ankle, her head bobbed left, then right. God, she hoped no one would see her entering Jonathan's cabin.

At the cabin door, she hesitated.

What if he's still inside?

She knocked. "Jonathan? You in there?"

Silence.

Relieved, she eased open the door. The easel was gone.

"Okay. Do this before he gets back." She frowned. "So where are my clothes?"

She checked the kitchen area, the floor, even the bathroom. Her clothes were nowhere to be seen. The only thing she could think of was that perhaps Jonathan had already brought them back to the house.

With a moan, she slumped into the armchair. "Why couldn't I have left behind a ratty sweater—or socks?"

Heavy footsteps sounded on the porch.

Her heart did a back flip. *Oh crap.*

Jonathan stomped into the cabin, muttering under his breath. He shoved the easel and canvas against the wall by the door and dropped a tool box on the floor.

He straightened, finally noticing her.

"Jesus Christ, Rhianna!"

She gave him a coy smile. "Did I startle you?"

"What are you doing here?"

"I, uh, came to get some things I left behind."

"Ah," he said, his pinched expression relaxing. "I almost brought them to the house this morning."

"Why didn't you?"

He smiled. "I knew you'd come get them."

The air was charged with electricity. Rhianna could feel the sparks on her skin.

"So where are they?" Her voice was raspy.

"Hanging on the back of the bathroom door."

"I didn't put them there," she said, her cheeks aflame.

Jonathan shrugged. "I didn't want your lingerie to get covered in paint."

"I'll get them and be out of your way."

Rhianna disappeared into the bathroom, returning a few minutes later with the nightshirt and panties balled up in her hands.

"Bye," she mumbled.

"Wait."

When she turned, she was shocked by the conflicting expressions in his eyes. Frustration mixed with hunger lurked beneath the surface. Both were dangerous.

She should leave. *Now!* Otherwise, he was going to take what he wanted. She could see it in the way he stared, the way he clenched his hands at his side, as if afraid he'd touch her.

She held her breath.

"I knew you were naked under that robe," he said, wiping his forehead with the back of a hand.

She gulped in a breath. "I don't think—"

"When I look at you," he interrupted, "I feel I can paint anything."

"Then what's stopping you?"

"You."

"Me."

Jonathan took a step closer. "You're all I've been able to think about lately. And now I know what I need to paint."

"What?"

The corners of his mouth lifted. "You."

She gaped at him. "Why would you want to do that?"

"Because you're beautiful."

At first, she didn't know how to reply. In a small voice, she said, "You need glasses."

"Don't you know how beautiful you are?"

She snorted. "I bet you say that to all the ladies."

"There's only you and Mrs. Atkinson around," he said dryly. "And somehow I don't think Marvin would appreciate me hitting on his wife."

"Is that what you're doing? Hitting on me?"

The words were out of her mouth before she could contemplate the ramifications.

Jonathan's eyes narrowed. "If I were hitting on you, I'd give you more than a bad line."

There was no breathable air in the room.

Rhianna stood rooted to the floor as he approached her in slow, deliberate steps, his eyes locked on hers and filled with smoldering passion.

"If I were hitting on you," he said, "I'd tell you how stunningly beautiful you are, that you have the most amazing green eyes I've ever seen."

Warm hands caressed her face as he lowered his head.

"If I were hitting on you," he whispered, "I'd kiss you again and again."

And he did.

Jonathan's lips met hers with an urgency that scared her. But this time Rhianna didn't pull away. When he moved closer, she met him halfway. Their lips locked in a passionate kiss that took away all sense of time and place. There was only now. *This* time. *This* place.

Jonathan tasted of strawberries. His mouth devoured hers, drawing her away from her skin until she was a quivering mass of desire.

He groaned. "What do you want, Rhianna?"

I want you...

She parted her lips, inviting him in.

"I can't stop thinking of you," he whispered against her throat.

She moaned as his lips drifted lower, teasing her, while his fingers flipped through the buttons of her shirt and peeled it away. Her bra quickly followed, along with the clothing in her hands.

Sapphire eyes caressed her.

"You're so beautiful," he said.

In a moment of shyness, Rhianna tried to cover her breasts, but Jonathan caught her hands and kissed her hard.

"I want you," he said, nipping at her lower lip.

Old fears resurfaced, but she pushed them aside. This was *her* time. Time to experience passion the way it was meant to be experienced. Time to take that final step, to learn what she'd been missing all these years.

He stared deep into her eyes, an unspoken question on the tip of his tongue. When his mouth claimed hers in a breathless kiss, she gave him his answer.

Yes...

Wasting no time, Jonathan swung her into his arms and carried her to the sofa where he eased her onto the cushions. Hovering over her, he said, "Are you sure?"

In answer, she reached up and drew him down, her gaze never leaving his. What she felt now couldn't be wrong. She felt beautiful, desirable...whole.

"Yes," she whispered.

He bent his head and kissed the inside contour of her breasts. Hot kisses rained over them, searing them. Then he blew across one nipple, causing it to go rigid.

Rhianna gripped the cushions beneath her.

"Please..." she moaned.

Jonathan's mouth captured a nipple and she cried out. The sensation of his wet mouth and soft tongue on her sensitive nipple made her gasp and arch her back in response.

Had she died and gone to heaven?

The throbbing between her legs intensified until she couldn't stand it any longer. "Oh God..."

He moaned against her breast.

Jesus! What was he doing to her?

Shivers of intense pleasure raced through her. She was adrift on a sea of ecstasy that pushed her higher.

Jonathan reached down, one hand sliding between their bodies. Heat radiated from his hand through her jeans, scorching her skin. When he cupped the source of her frenzied yearning, she knew she was at the peak of something wonderful.

"I want to touch all of you," he said hoarsely.

When Rhianna was completely naked, Jonathan studied her with an intensity that bewildered her.

She had never felt so exposed.

Jonathan peeled off his own clothing, unable to calm his racing thoughts. This was what he'd been waiting for. *Rhianna* was what he'd been waiting for.

My muse.

Heart pounding, he studied her. He took in the luxurious locks of auburn hair that partially covered her breasts. Her stomach was flat and smooth, her hips gently rounded.

She reached up. "I feel self-conscious."

"You're perfection."

He lowered himself until her feverish skin connected with his. She hissed in a ragged breath, her eyes reflecting wonder and nervous anticipation. Then she took a small breath and held it.

Jonathan chuckled. "What are you doing?"

"Waiting."

"It would be rude of me to keep a lady waiting."

"I don't know how—"

"Shh." He grazed her lips with his thumb. "No talking."

He claimed her mouth. It started as a sweet kiss, but swiftly ignited a fire that neither of them could extinguish. Her tongue entwined with his and he groaned.

God, how he wanted her. That was evident by the hardness between his legs.

"See how much I want you?"

He moved his hips in small circles and Rhianna's eyes flared at the sensual contact. Releasing her, he shifted to one side and leaned against the back of the sofa. With one hand he traced a path from her neck to between her breasts to her stomach. She quivered under his touch. He leaned down to kiss her, his fingers wandering lower.

She was hot. And wet.

"Wait." But even as she said this, she moved against him.

He parted her legs and continued touching, caressing, exploring. Her breathing quickened and she arched her back, crying out his name. Positioning himself above her, he prodded at her opening in teasing movements. She squirmed beneath him, panting, her eyes half-glazed.

If he didn't get inside her now, he'd explode.

"Are you ready?" he whispered, biting her lip.

She bucked beneath him and bit him back. "Yes."

In one fluid movement he was inside her, trapped within satin depths. She was so hot, so tight, he could barely hold back. He groaned and kissed her hard, afraid to move, afraid he wouldn't last.

Something wet touched his cheek.

He raised his head. And froze.

"What's wrong?" he asked. "Did I hurt you?"

Rhianna couldn't stand the pained expression in Jonathan's eyes. "It's not you."

"Then what?"

She closed her eyes. How could she tell him? How could she possibly explain to him that she'd been violated by a disgusting excuse of a man for so many years that it made her feel dirty, used...unworthy.

Damn you, Peter Waverley!

She'd done everything to put Peter out of her mind. The sensations she felt with Jonathan were so different, so exciting. She wanted more. But when he'd entered her, it brought everything crashing down around her.

Jonathan waited patiently.

"I can't do this," she said, crying softly. "I'm sorry."

"Tell me what's wrong, Rhianna."

"I...I can't."

He withdrew from her, visibly confused and deflated. She was barely able to look at him.

He'll never want me now. Not after this.

Rhianna recalled her little ritual at the pool. How stupid could she be? How could she possibly think that a few words and holding her breath underwater could cleanse her and make the nightmares go away?

Maybe she should just accept this as her life.

Maybe I'll always be damaged goods.

Outside, the sun spread radiant rays across the land and sea, but inside the cabin an invisible cloud of gloom had invaded the room.

While they dressed in awkward silence, Rhianna tried not to think of what had just happened.

Oh my God. I let him—

No, she couldn't go there. Not now.

Jonathan smoothed a t-shirt over his chest, his eyes searching hers. "We're both adults, Rhianna. I've let you know how I feel. I want—"

"Let's not talk about it," she cut in. "Please. I feel humiliated enough."

"Don't. We did nothing wrong."

She didn't reply.

With a sigh, he said, "I should go."

"No, I should," she argued. "This is your studio."

He gave her a half-smile. "Yeah, I guess you're right."

She paused in the doorway. She wanted to say something—explain why she couldn't give that part of her to him—but the words wouldn't come.

"I guess I'll see you later tonight," Jonathan said.

She could feel his stare burning into her back as she hobbled across the yard. He still wanted her. She knew that. What was worse, she wanted *him*, and the only thing standing in the way was her past.

How was she ever going to rid herself of that?

Chapter 18

Rhianna spent most of the day in bed. She stared up at the ceiling and played out variations of an imaginary conversation with Jonathan—where she revealed what had happened in her youth. No matter how the conversations played out, she was left with the same results. Jonathan would storm out of the house, unable to look at her, sickened by her...blaming her.

He's not like that.

But how could she be sure? She didn't know much about the man. She knew nothing of his history, where he came from, his youth. He'd probably had the perfect upbringing and never had to face such vile ugliness.

Do you want to bring that into his life? Into Misty's?

They deserved better.

She threw one arm across her face. "Just finish your time here and leave. You'll forget about them after a while."

But would she? How could she possibly forget the gentle caresses of Jonathan's hands on her body or his soft lips on her breast? Even now, she wanted more.

Rhianna let out a moan. "Don't think of that."

Turning on one side, she caught sight of the framed photograph of JT. It had fallen into the open drawer of the nightstand. Jonathan must have knocked it over when he'd carried her to her room.

"JT, why did you send me here?"

Higginson must have allowed JT to make the arrangements. Still, it was unlike the butler not to confirm everything. JT's memory was not the best.

She placed the photograph back on the table. Closing the drawer, she saw her cell phone on the floor. Something else Jonathan must have knocked over. She picked it up and flipped it open, knowing there'd be no signal. And there wasn't.

No phone. No radio. No way to contact anyone.

Rhianna released a frustrated groan.

It hadn't been her idea to get stranded on this blasted island. Fate had intervened, however, and now she was stuck here, but one day Angelina's Isle would be a past memory.

Would she view it with relief or regret?

By late afternoon, Rhianna decided she'd spent enough time sulking and wishing for something she couldn't have, so she headed downstairs. Surprisingly, her foot didn't hurt at all. Or maybe she just couldn't feel it because of the sharp pain she felt in her heart.

As she reached the bottom step, she heard Mrs. Atkinson's familiar whistling coming from the kitchen. She found the housekeeper chopping potatoes, while Misty sat at the table and rolled a large carrot between her palms.

"Hello, dear," Mrs. Atkinson said. "How's your foot?"

"Much better, thank you." Rhianna inhaled deeply. "Something smells fabulous. What is it?"

The older woman smiled. "Your supper."

"We grew everything in the garden," Misty signed. She pointed to a basket filled with various vegetables. "Mrs. Atkinson let me help her pick them. We're making chicken soup."

Rhianna smiled. "So you had a good day?"

"A *great* day."

Misty skipped around the kitchen, a grin plastered on her face. Suddenly, she stopped and looked up at Rhianna with innocent blue eyes. "What did you do today?"

Rhianna stifled a cough. "Well, I…"

She didn't know what to say. It's not like she could tell the child she'd been making out with her dad.

Making out? What are you, a teenager?

"I hurt my foot," she said. "So I spent most of the day in my room, resting it."

She caught Mrs. Atkinson looking at her. There was an odd expression in the woman's eyes. Suspicion.

For a moment, Rhianna wondered whether Mrs. Atkinson knew what she'd been up to earlier that day. If she did, did the housekeeper approve?

For some reason the thought that Mrs. Atkinson might judge her harshly for getting romantically entangled with Jonathan saddened Rhianna. She liked Jonathan's housekeeper.

"Can I help you, Mrs. Atkinson?"

"That's okay, dear. I've got it covered."

There was a knock on the back door. Mrs. Atkinson opened it and beamed a smile at the thin man standing on the porch.

Rhianna had met Marvin Atkinson shortly after arriving on the island, but the man rarely left his home, except when he was repairing something or doing yard work. He probably hadn't said ten words to her.

Marvin gave Rhianna a shy nod.

"I fixed the washing machine," he told his wife. "Will you be home soon?"

Mrs. Atkinson surveyed the potatoes she was chopping and the basket of vegetables. "I have to finish making the soup."

"I can do that," Rhianna offered.

Mrs. Atkinson's dark eyes widened. "Thank you, dear. Are you sure?"

Rhianna threw her a wry grin. "If I can't make chicken soup I'd be pretty useless, wouldn't I?"

"I'm sure you're anything but."

The Atkinsons left the house together, hand in hand.

Watching them, Rhianna's stomach churned. She wondered if she'd ever have what they had. A joyous love, simple and uncomplicated.

She turned back to her charge. "Let's make soup."

Misty grabbed the basket from the table and carried it to the counter. "Can I cut the carrot?"

"I think you should be in charge of washing them." At the pout on the girl's face, Rhianna added, "After I cut them, you can put them in the pot."

Misty nodded, then signed, "Daddy's going to love our soup. He's going to be very happy."

Rhianna sighed. *Well, at least one of us will be.*

Soon, the potatoes, carrots, onion, zucchini, peas and chicken were simmering in a pot on the stove, while Misty sat at the table, swinging her short legs under the chair. She'd been a great helper, but it appeared Rhianna now had a problem on her hands.

"I'm bored," Misty signed.

"What do you want to do?"

"I don't know."

"Do you want to walk on the beach?"

Misty gave a shake of her dark curls.

They sat for a moment in silence.

The house is too quiet, Rhianna thought.

She reached across the table and turned on the portable radio. Turning the dial, she found a station with current pop hits. She opened her mouth and began to sing along.

Misty's eyes widened. "What are you doing?"

"What?"

"Why is your mouth moving like that?"

"I'm singing," Rhianna signed. "Don't you know what that is?"

"No. No one's done that before."

"Do you like music?"

Misty frowned. "What's that?"

Rhianna was shocked. Why hadn't someone taught Misty about music? Or shown the girl how she could *hear* in a different way than hearing children? Surely Jonathan and Misty's other teachers knew that a deaf person could enjoy music too.

Rhianna let out a sigh. "Misty, even deaf children can hear music. You just need to learn how. I'll show you."

She took Misty's small hand and placed it on top of the radio. Then she turned the volume up. Misty jumped back in surprise.

"It's okay," she reassured the girl.

Misty touched the radio again. The smile she gave Rhianna transformed her, and whatever boredom had been lurking behind her blue eyes instantly vanished. Misty turned the dial up as far as it could go. For a small radio it thumped out a decent volume, but Rhianna knew Misty needed to experience more than the moderate vibration from the old radio.

"Misty, let's go in the living room."

"But I like this."

"Trust me. I have an even better way for you to hear."

When Rhianna had first arrived, she'd noticed an ancient stereo system, complete with record player, tucked into the back corner of the living room. It didn't take her long to unearth the four speakers that were hiding in the corners of the room. From the amount of dust on the equipment, she surmised that the stereo hadn't been used in a long time. Hopefully, it still worked.

"This plays louder music." Rhianna pointed to the stereo. "You'll be able to hear it with your feet."

Misty let out a raspy laugh. "My feet?"

Rhianna flipped through a pile of old record albums that were in the cabinet under the stereo. "There's got to be something suitable for a six-year-old." There was. *ABBA's Greatest Hits.*

She placed it on the turntable and showed Misty how to work it. "See? It's easy. Now we'll turn up the volume."

Misty stood beside her, with her hands clasped as if receiving the most precious gift, as Rhianna cranked up the volume and the bass. Music pounded into the room and the hardwood floor vibrated with the beat.

"I can feel it," Misty signed, her eyes filled with amazement. "It's in my toes." She ran from speaker to speaker, touching the sides, feeling the vibrations.

When Rhianna began to dance, Misty stopped in the middle of the room, her eyes wide. "What are you doing?"

"Dancing."

"Why would you do that…dancing?"

"Because it's fun." Rhianna twirled. "You try it."

Misty attempted to mimic her. She hopped and swayed, giggling the entire time. Every now and then she'd sign, "I'm dancing."

It was a Hallmark moment, one Rhianna wanted to freeze and take with her when she left. She closed her eyes and swayed to the music. Lost in thought, she didn't hear the front door open. Or the footsteps approaching.

"What the hell is going on?"

Furious, Jonathan strode over to the stereo. He turned it off, then slowly turned toward Rhianna. He had to take a couple of deep breaths before he found his voice.

"What are you trying to do? Destroy Misty's eardrums completely?"

"It won't destroy her ears," Rhianna argued. "I was just showing her how she can hear music."

"In case you haven't noticed, Ms. McLeod, my daughter is deaf. She can't hear anything."

"Well, in case you hadn't noticed, Mr. Know-it-all, your daughter is having fun. From the look of all the dust on that stereo, fun is something you don't know much about. Don't you ever listen to music? Or are you too busy painting?"

When Rhianna came up for air, he said, "The stereo belongs to my ex-wife."

"So?"

He shrugged. "So I don't use it. I should've thrown it away. Or shipped it to her."

She gave him a smug look. "Oh, so you're just a natural music hater."

"I don't hate music," he said in a tight voice. "I—"

A blast of music cut him off.

Jonathan spun around, his breath catching in the back of his throat. Misty grinned back at him as she placed both hands, palms flat, on a speaker that was pumping out "Dancing Queen" lyrics. The smile that radiated from her was one of unmitigated joy.

"Look, Daddy! I can hear the music." She stomped her feet to the beat.

He swallowed hard, unable to speak.

"Dance with your daughter," Rhianna said.

With a little prodding, he caught Misty's hands and spun her around in wobbly circles until they were both laughing and dizzy. When the music slowed, he lifted Misty until she was standing on top of his feet, and they danced slowly, without a word.

God, it had been years since he'd danced.

"You two look…perfect," Rhianna said quietly.

The music soon kicked into high gear again and Misty tugged at his hand. He tried to teach her a few dance steps—the few he could remember—but he ended up tripping over his long legs and clumsy feet.

"Not exactly Dancing with the Stars," he said, grinning at Rhianna.

She smiled back. "No. It's far better."

"You've turned her into a dancing maniac," he said as he dropped into a chair, exhausted. "I knew I'd regret leaving Misty with you."

She gave him a hurt look. "What do you mean?"

"I'm joking." He chuckled wryly. "Sorry for barging in and yelling at you."

She shrugged. "It's okay. This is all new for you. I understand."

"I don't think you do," he said with a sigh. "Not completely. When Sirena left us, I had a lot of resentment toward her."

"I'm sure you did. She never wanted custody of Misty?"

He shook his head. "No, and I never pressure her about that either. To tell the truth, I was afraid."

"Of what?"

"Losing Misty." He chewed his bottom lip. "Sirena is…flighty. She can't sit still in one place for long. Eventually she would've disappeared. And taken Misty with her. I was relieved when she didn't want custody. But I also felt guilty for being relieved."

"Jonathan…"

The way Rhianna said his name made him look away.

"You did the best under the circumstances," she said, touching his arm. "You're a great father and Misty loves you."

"I know. But I can't help thinking I should've done more to keep Sirena in Misty's life."

"That's Sirena's choice. It always has been."

Rhianna was right. His ex-wife had made her choice.

Jonathan glanced at Rhianna. *And I've made mine.*

Chapter 19

Back in his Miami home office, JT Lance sat behind a mammoth oak desk and thought about all the tough choices he'd made over the decades—some that had resulted in something positive and some that had ended with tragic consequences.

And too many regrets.

The phone gave a shrill ring, jarring JT from his thoughts. *Winston Chambers*, the call display read.

He picked up the receiver. "You got your money, Chambers. We have nothing left to discuss."

"Well, actually...we do."

JT hissed in a breath. "We had a deal. I paid you what you asked for and you were supposed to go your own way. You swore you would."

Chambers let out a taunting laugh. "And you believed me?" There was a tense pause. "I've run into a bit of a problem and I think you can help me fix it. Two hundred thousand should suffice."

Shocked, JT closed his eyes. He'd never be rid of Chambers at this rate. The man would drain him dry.

"I can't pay you any more," he said, seething. "I won't. Whatever you know, it's not big enough to warrant being blackmailed like this."

"Then I'll tell her. Rhianna will know your secret."

JT swallowed a lump of guilt. "Then it's time she does. I'll tell her myself."

He glanced up as Higginson entered the room. On the pad on the desk, he wrote: *Chambers wants more $!*

Higginson silently read it, then patted JT's arm.

"I'll tell her tonight," JT told Chambers.

Another laugh from the private investigator.

JT scowled. "What's so funny?"

The line went silent. Then he heard the click of a lighter. The sound of inhalation confirmed JT's thoughts that Chambers had lit up a cigar. The man was taking his time, torturing JT—and enjoying every minute.

"I know Ms. McLeod has taken a little trip," Chambers said finally. "Wire the money to me by the end of the week. If it's not there, I'll make you very sorry you crossed me."

Chambers hung up, leaving JT staring at the receiver.

"He knows Rhianna's not here."

"Does he know where she went?" Higginson asked.

JT shook his head. "I don't think so. Not yet."

"How much does he want?"

"Two hundred thousand."

Higginson slumped in the chair across from JT. "Do you think he'll follow through with his threat?"

"I don't know." With tear-filled eyes, JT stared at Higginson. "But I do know I don't want that bastard anywhere near Rhianna."

"What do you want to do?"

"I can't pay him. If I do, he'll keep wanting more." A steely determination gripped JT. "He gave me until the end of the week."

"What can you do in four days?"

JT groaned. "I'm not sure."

"The man is slime," Higginson said, his jaw clenched.

"Lower than slime. But it's my fault he's doing this."

"JT—"

"Everything bad that's happened is the result of one stupid choice." A tear escaped and JT batted it away. "My past is catching up to me, but I have to make this right. For everyone."

Higginson sighed. "Tell me what I can do to help."

"You're a good friend, Higgie."

A slow chill of weariness settled into JT's old bones and his mind wandered into the ominous gray fog that lured him in like a mythical sea siren calling a ship to its rocky doom. It confused him, this fog, this callous disappearance of thought and struggle for names or events.

He eyed Higginson in bewilderment.

What were we talking about?

Winston leaned back in his extra-wide chair and sucked thoughtfully on a slender cigar—a bargain brand, only forty bucks a pack. The taste was darker, muddier, nothing like his precious Cohibas. But he only had one of the hefty beauties left, and he was saving it for a special occasion.

Would Lance pay?

He'd better, or Winston would make his life—what was left of it—a hell on earth. The reticence he'd heard in Lance's voice suggested the old guy wasn't feeling the pressure. *Yet.*

The computer monitor in front of Winston displayed his withering bank account. His client list had diminished to Lance and two others he'd milked *bonuses* from. Blackmail was far more lucrative than tracking down deadbeat dads or following cheating spouses, although he did enjoy taking photos of their sexual exploits.

He swiped his receding forehead with the back of his arm and it came away covered in a thin sheen of sweat. Outside the dingy one-room office, the sun was in sizzle mode, but it wasn't the heat that was getting to him. Fear was eating away at his churning stomach. Popping three extra strength Rolaids into his mouth, he chewed quickly and drowned the chalky taste with a brandy chaser.

"It'll all work out in the end," he muttered.

But would it?

He'd put down a large chunk of Lance's last payout at the race track. He nearly had a heart attack when he lost it all. Now he had debts to pay. Some of the guys he owed wouldn't wait much longer. Last time they paid a visit, he'd ended up in the hospital with two broken ribs and a mild concussion.

Winston picked up the photo of Rhianna McLeod.

"I'll make him pay me. One way or the other."

A devious plan began to percolate. There *was* a way for Winston to get a gigantic payout, easily a cool million. Threatening the old guy that he'd tell JT's secret would only get him so far. This new idea would secure his future someplace overseas where no one could track him down.

"JT'll beg to pay me anything," Winston said, kissing Rhianna's likeness. "You'll beg too, my dear. For something far different."

Chapter 20

That night, after Misty went to bed and Mrs. Atkinson returned to her cottage, Jonathan coaxed Rhianna into the living room with the promise of an after dinner drink. He was craving her company, and he needed someone to talk to about Misty.

"I can't thank you enough for everything you've done for Misty and me," he said, handing Rhianna a glass of Merlot. "She's been less irritable."

"That's because both of you have learned to sign more effectively."

"I know. But neither of us would be signing so easily without your help. Thank you."

Rhianna shifted and looked away. "I'm glad I could help. That was the agreement after all."

"Agreement?"

She glanced at him. "For staying here."

He laughed. "Well, it's not like you can leave."

"No, I can't."

A strained silence filled the room.

Finally, Rhianna said, "I hope it hasn't been too difficult having an unwanted guest."

Unable to form a single word, Jonathan remained silent. A waft of Rhianna's perfume, with delicate notes of spice, vanilla and seduction, made him dizzy and he struggled to take his eyes off her moist, slightly parted lips. He wanted nothing more than to crush them with his, to taste her sweetness again. Earlier that morning, he'd seen apprehension in her eyes and it incensed him that he had caused it. But she didn't look afraid now. Just nervous.

"What?" she asked. "Why are you looking at me like that?"

"Because you're beautiful," he said. *And I don't want to let you go.*

That sudden realization smacked him hard.

Damn, Rhianna was getting to him.

Rhianna could barely breathe. In all these years she'd never felt so tempted. No other man had made her feel this...safe. And there was enough sexual chemistry between them that it was impossible to deny she was attracted to Jonathan.

What the heck was she going to do about him?

She didn't have time to pursue that train of thought because Jonathan gently pried the wineglass from her fingers, set it on the bar and pulled her into his arms.

"What are you doing?" she asked, stunned.

"You wouldn't deprive a man of a dance now, would you?" He pointed a remote at the stereo and smooth, sultry jazz filtered into the room. "I hope you like this."

She swallowed. "Jazz is one of my favorites."

Jonathan twirled her into the center of the room, then reeled her back in, catching her around the waist. With a breathless laugh, she stared into his sea-blue eyes and was immediately caught in a tidal wave of emotion. She didn't know what to say. Every thought seemed juvenile and silly.

He reached up and released her hair from the ponytail.

"I like it down," he said, drawing her closer.

His rough cheek grazed hers and she stifled a gasp. She tried to focus on the music, but all she could hear was his steady heartbeat. As the heat of their bodies melded, her pulse raced.

"Relax," he whispered. "I don't bite."

"Right."

He chuckled. "Not unless you want me to."

The thought of Jonathan's teeth nipping at her flesh nearly made Rhianna moan out loud.

What was he doing to her?

With a ragged sigh, Rhianna curled into Jonathan, her head tucked under his chin. He smelled of sandalwood, vanilla and paint, a heady combination that was soothing, yet stimulating.

His breath breezed across her hair.

She shivered.

How long could she fight these feelings?

Don't fight them.

Jonathan's hand caressed her lower back. The fabric between them seemed nonexistent, as though they danced naked, her feverish flesh on his. His slow, sensual moves sent tiny flutters throughout her body.

Did he feel her treacherous response?

She didn't know how long they danced. Or how long he held her. She only knew that she wanted it to go on forever.

"I could do this all night," he said, reading her mind.

His admission caught her off guard.

"Why would you want to do that?"

"Because you feel good in my arms."

"Oh."

"I want to kiss you, Rhianna."

She took a deep breath. "Kiss me then."

Without hesitation, Jonathan bent his head and captured her lips. She gasped and he took full advantage, his tongue entwining with hers. A powerful longing grew deep within her. She wanted more.

So did Jonathan.

When he swept her up in his arms and carried her upstairs, Rhianna didn't fight him.

She trembled, aware of her own mounting need. There was only one way to fight her inner demon, and that was to conquer her fear of the past.

"Your room or mine?" he asked.

If she'd been thinking clearly, Rhianna would have laughed. But she wasn't thinking clearly. All she knew for sure was that she had to quell the desperate throbbing that pounded through her body.

"I don't care," she murmured.

The décor in his room was dark, with warm, masculine tones and rich cherry furniture. A king-sized bed waited at the far end of the room.

That was all Rhianna had time to notice because Jonathan slowly slid her down his body until her feet reached the ground. His fingers drifted to the buttons on her blouse. In seconds, it was on the floor. The rest of her clothes followed as he bared her, body and soul, his hands caressing every inch of her until she couldn't stand it.

He backed her against the door and his hands clasped hers, pinning them just above her head. A flicker of panic gripped her, but when his tongue found her nipple and teased it to attention, all fear was erased. She trembled when his lips coaxed a response. Then she gave in to the sizzling thrill of his mouth.

"Do you want me to stop?" he breathed into her ear.

"No."

"Are you sure? Because I will if you want me to."

She sighed. "Just shut up and kiss me."

Jonathan kissed Rhianna fiercely, ravishing her until she clung to him, breathless, her skin burning.

He craved her touch.

Carrying her to the bed, he swiftly undressed and stretched out beside her. He was rigid and pulsating with need. There was only one way to satisfy his lust.

Lust?

No, what he felt was much more than that. But he had to be gentle. He didn't want to hurt her. He was pretty sure she'd been hurt enough in the past.

Although the shadows hid her, he found Rhianna's lips. Only their mouths touched.

Lightly…persuasively.

Then, reaching for the lamp, he turned it on low. The golden glow illuminated Rhianna's curves as she lay on the bed, one arm draped across her breasts. Her eyes shone, expectant and nervous.

"Trust me," he said, lifting her arm to her side.

"I do."

He swallowed hard at her admission. She'd just handed him a precious treasure to guard. His throbbing desire intensified at the thought.

Leaning over her, he cradled her face in his hands. "I want to see *all* of you."

He felt her hesitation.

Kissing each eyelid, he said, "You're so beautiful."

"No, I'm not."

He placed a finger against her mouth. "Yes, you are."

Jonathan brushed her face with his fingertips and trailed them down her neck to the valley between her breasts.

She arched toward him. "Jonathan…"

Hearing his name on her lips, made him shiver.

Rhianna knew she was heading for trouble with Jonathan, but all that mattered was finding release from the agonizing desire that consumed her. She'd never felt this way before, so physical, so sexual…

So out of control.

God, how she ached for him.

Their lips met in a tender kiss and Jonathan's calloused fingers skimmed all over her. Stroking her, squeezing her, until her entire body tightened. When his mouth touched her breast, she let out a moan. His lips brushed a nipple and she thought she'd crawl out of her own flesh.

Finally, he reached lower, in search of the one place she needed him to touch. She sucked in a breath when he found it. Hands entwined around his neck, she drew him back to her mouth as he straddled her.

There'll be no going back after tonight.

She didn't care. Jonathan had opened the floodgates. Only he could close them.

"What do you want, Rhianna?"

"I don't know."

"Yes, you do," he said, nipping at her bottom lip.

"I want...I want you inside—"

Jonathan entered her swiftly. There was no pain, only a quivering that left her breathless. When he pulled back, she bucked against him.

"Don't stop," she hissed.

"I wasn't planning on it."

As Jonathan moved between her thighs, Rhianna felt more disconnected from her past and more in tune with a wondrous soaring sensation. Every synapse fired, every nerve quivered as she climbed higher. And higher.

A searing tremor of pleasure shot through her. Hot tears formed in her eyes and her raspy breath mingled with Jonathan's. She dug her nails into his shoulders and clung to him, half-sobbing, while delicious, mind-numbing spasms wracked her body and shook her to the core.

Rhianna awoke hours later, at first startled by the unfamiliar room draped in shadows.

Then she remembered.

Jonathan.

He had made love to her, and she'd enjoyed every minute of it.

Rolling slowly to her side, she reached for him, but the other side of the bed was empty.

"Jonathan?"

There was no reply.

"Where are you?" she whispered in the dark.

She recalled his kiss and touched her lips. She thought of his hands on her, every moment leading up to a culmination that rocked her world.

Now he had vanished.

Swallowing hard, she sat up and turned on the lamp.

His clothes were gone too.

Rhianna moved from the bed, ignoring the dull throbbing of her body. Dressing hastily, she ran to her room and closed the door.

Seeds of doubt sprouted.

Did Jonathan regret what they'd done?

Tears sprang to her eyes. "Of course he does." She moaned. "What have I done?"

Sitting on the bed, she released a pent up breath. There was still a couple of weeks left of her stay here. How was she supposed to face him now?

She fell back. "Way to go. Your first *real* experience and you've scared him away."

Glancing at the clock, she saw it was just after three in the morning. The sun hadn't even struggled to make an appearance yet.

There was no way she could sleep now.

Not with Jonathan out there some—

She sat up. "I know exactly where you are."

Moving to the window, she peered through the glass.

There was a light on in Jonathan's studio.

He's painting.

"Great job, Rhianna. You've driven him to work."

Her breath fogged up the glass. With one finger she drew four vertical lines.

"Prison bars," she muttered, though she suspected she wasn't the only one feeling imprisoned.

She had to get away. Think about things. She needed someplace quiet. Peaceful.

Where could she find that?

She smiled. *The pool.*

Grabbing a towel from the bathroom, she slipped quietly downstairs and out the door. She followed the path instinctively, her desire for calm leading her.

She heard the falls before she saw them. Without pausing, she peeled off her clothes, leaving a trail behind her. She stepped into the water and waded toward the center of the pool. Cupping her hands, she poured water down her neck. She sighed and closed her eyes.

Then her calm was interrupted.

She didn't hear him approach as much as she sensed it. When she opened her eyes and turned, Jonathan stood on the shore, watching her.

"I thought you'd be sleeping still," he said.

She shrugged. "I woke up."

"I can see that. Sorry, I felt an urge to paint."

"I guess you have to give in when it hits you," she said dryly.

"I have another urge now," he said in a low tone.

She blinked. "I thought, maybe, you didn't—"

Jonathan stripped in the dark and waded out to her. "But I do."

She trembled when he reached for her. He tasted her skin, tracing feathery kisses along the side of her neck.

"I want you, my little castaway." He kissed her hard. "I want to take you behind the falls."

And he did.

Chapter 21

The following day passed by quickly. In the morning and afternoon, Rhianna taught Misty new signs and tested the girl's conversation skills. That night, Jonathan taught a willing Rhianna a few things—about the ancient art of lovemaking.

Now, stretched out on her stomach in Jonathan's bed, she was fulfilled like never before. It was like someone had climbed inside her head and swept away the cobwebs, then moved to her heart and flipped a switch.

Something had changed. *Everything* had changed.

Rhianna studied the man beside her. Jonathan was lying on his side, facing her, eyes closed.

Did he feel the change too?

She sighed and hugged the pillow.

Jonathan had never mentioned a future together and she had no idea what to expect from him—or if she had the right to expect anything. For all she knew, this was a summer fling, a simple distraction. He'd forget all about her once she was gone.

Of course, he's not looking for anything permanent, she berated herself. *He lives on a blasted island in the middle of nowhere and you have a job and life back in Miami.*

Now she was pissed.

She caught Jonathan staring at her.

"What are you thinking?" he asked.

"Nothing."

He propped his head up on one hand. "Liar."

"I'm just wondering where this is leading."

"By *this* you mean...*this*," he said, trailing his hand across her back.

"That tickles. Stop it."

His eyes narrowed. "What if I don't want to?"

"Then we'll never get any sleep."

He kissed the back of her neck. "Sounds like a plan."

"I'm starting to wonder if this is all you want," she blurted.

Jonathan froze. "You think all I'm after is sex? You should know me better than that."

Rhianna rolled to one side, pulling the sheet up to her chest. "Why would you think that? I don't see you until after supper, then we're with Misty, and then after that we're…here. We never just…talk."

"We can talk anytime you want," he said.

For some reason, this angered her even more.

"What part of *you aren't around to talk to* don't you get?"

She knew she sounded like a disgruntled wife.

"I've been a bit busy," Jonathan said. He smiled. "I finally had an idea for a new painting. I think it'll be one of my best."

Rhianna let out a huff. "Great. I'm happy for you."

She moved from the bed and began collecting her clothing.

"What are you doing, Rhianna?"

"Going back to my room."

"Don't. Come back to bed and we'll talk."

She eyed him suspiciously. "Talk."

"I can do that you know. I'm not just a sexy guy after your body, you know."

She arched a brow. "So you're sexy now, are you?"

"That's what you told me an hour ago," he said, grinning.

"Maybe I should've kept that to myself. Wouldn't want it to go to your head."

He patted the bed. "Come on. I promise I'll behave. We'll talk and I'll keep my hands to myself. I won't even kiss you."

Rhianna felt a twinge of disappointment.

Jonathan watched as Rhianna slipped into her bra and panties. *Don't touch,* the action warned him. His fingers itched to do just that.

"Fine, we'll talk," Rhianna said with a sigh.

When she slid beneath the sheet and pulled it up to her neck, he almost laughed.

"So," he drawled. "Where do we begin?"

"Tell me about your childhood. Where were you born? Do you have any siblings?"

"I'm an only child, born in New York, in the Big Apple."

"And your parents? Where are they?"

"My mother died almost five years ago."

She touched his hand. "Sorry. Maybe we shouldn't—"

"Hey, you wanted to know more about me," he said. "My mother is dead and my father's an asshole." He tried to keep the bitterness from his voice. "It's been years since I last saw him."

Rhianna's eyes widened. "You mean he's never seen Misty?"

"Nope. And it's better that way."

"But she's his granddaughter. His only grandchild."

"Let me tell you about the man that is Misty's *grand*father," he said, seething. "He's a rich, powerful man who doesn't care one bit about family. When I was about seven, I overheard my parents arguing about a woman's photograph my mother had found in one of his jacket pockets."

"Your father was having an affair?"

"He always denied it, but yeah. He was messing around on my mother."

"That's awful."

"My old man would yell at my mother, stay out all night doing God knows what, then creep into the house the next morning." Jonathan flicked a look at the window, his voice softening. "I couldn't wait to leave. I moved out the day after I turned eighteen. He called me after I went into art school. When he found out what I was doing with my life, he nearly had a heart attack. Said I was wasting my potential."

Jonathan remembered that call so clearly. His father had yelled at him, called him crazy and irresponsible. Jonathan had hung up on him.

"And you haven't been back?" Rhianna asked, her eyes luminous.

He shook his head. "I kept in touch with my mother. But I never went to see him."

"Did your mother ever see Misty?"

"When they moved south after my mother's diagnosis, Misty and I would go visit her every couple of months. We'd meet at a restaurant. My father never knew."

"It's been a long time, Jonathan. Maybe he's changed."

"I doubt it. The last time I saw him was the day I married Sirena. He walked into the back room where I was getting ready and told me my marriage was doomed from the start. Called Sirena a gold-digging wannabe movie star with no talent." Jonathan smiled. "He was right about that."

"I still can't believe she'd walk out on Misty. Just give her up like that."

"Sirena only cares about her career. Everything else just got in the way. Including me and Misty." He stared at Rhianna. "I don't know why it took me so long to realize Sirena wasn't the one."

"Sometimes it's hard to face reality," she said in a quiet voice.

Rhianna wanted to comfort Jonathan, but she sensed now wasn't the time. He was too angry, too hurt by his past. If there was one thing she knew well, it was that past hurts don't heal overnight. Fixing what was broken took time—and a lot of soul searching and persistence.

"My reality was that the three of us didn't work," Jonathan told her. "We used to come to Angelina's Isle to get away from winter. Misty and I fell in love with it, but Sirena hated it from the start. I built the pool for her, thinking it would make her happy."

"But it didn't."

"No. Sirena can't cope without her weekly spa days and her morning Starbucks cappuccino." He chuckled. "And she would've hated having you stranded here."

Rhianna shot him a scornful smile. "Gee, thanks."

"She hated other women. Everyone was competition to her."

"But you loved her."

He shrugged. "I thought I did. But hell, what did I know about love?"

Rhianna didn't want to contemplate the topic of love, so she changed the subject. "Did your parents get a divorce?"

"No. My mother forgave him and stuck by him to the bitter end."

Unable to stand the pain in his voice, she wiggled closer and eased one arm across his chest. "She loved your father very much."

Jonathan said nothing.

She took a deep breath. "If she could forgive him, why can't you?"

He glared at her. "Because he always carried around his lover's photo. I caught him staring at it every time he thought he was alone."

She didn't know what to say.

"It was as though he just couldn't live without this woman," he continued. "He'd storm out of the house and into a bar nearly every night. One time he was so intoxicated the bartender took away his keys and called the house. My mother was out somewhere, so I had to get him." He let out a huff. "My old man bawled like a baby all the way home."

"That must've been very difficult," Rhianna said, picturing a young man looking out for his father. "He was lucky to have you."

They drifted into silence and listened to the sounds of the night birds.

"What about you?" Jonathan asked finally. "Where's your family?"

Rhianna rested her chin on his chest. "My parents died in a car crash."

"How old were you?"

"I was born that same night." She swallowed hard. "When they arrived at the crash, paramedics found my father dead and my mother barely holding on. She was pregnant. With me. They took her to the hospital and performed an emergency C-section." She looked away. "I was the result."

Jonathan stroked her hair and it felt comforting.

She faced him. "My mother died on the operating table. They said it was a miracle she'd even survived the crash."

"She was holding on for you. She wanted you to survive."

A tear trickled down her cheek. "I guess."

Jonathan lifted her chin. "I *know*. And so should you."

Rhianna tried to smile through the tears. For years she'd told herself it was her fault that her mother had died. That maybe she would've survived if she hadn't been pregnant.

Yet, Jonathan had put everything into perspective.

Her mother had wanted her, loved her.

Jonathan gently wiped away her tears. "We're a sad pair, aren't we?"

She nodded. "I'll say. Fate dealt us both a cruel hand and tried to squash us like bugs."

"But we're survivors," he reminded her.

"Yes, we are."

And she'd survived far worse than her mother's death.

Jonathan stared into her eyes. "Someone else hurt you bad, didn't they?"

She gasped. *How did he know?*

"I've seen fear in your eyes," he explained. "And that first time…when I wanted to make love to you, I knew someone had hurt you terribly."

She couldn't breathe. This wasn't a conversation she wanted to have. Not with anyone.

"You can tell me," he whispered.

She buried her head into his arm, unable to face him. Should she tell him? Would it change things between them if he knew how her body had been abused and used? Would he be disgusted with her?

Tell him. He has to know.

"After my parent's died," she began, "I went to live with my aunt and uncle. Until they died in a boat accident. Then I went into foster care. The first two families I stayed with were short term, nice people, even though I was a basket case at the time. Then Children's Services found me a more permanent home, a couple who claimed they might even adopt me. If I worked out."

She paused, gathering her strength.

"But I wasn't the problem. My foster father was. He…" She nearly choked on the next word, "*abused* me." Tears pooled in her eyes and she let out a sob "He raped me every time his wife left the house, and I was powerless against him."

Jonathan pulled her into his arms, rocking her like a child as she cried for her stolen youth. For the lonely child who had felt so trapped, so used. For the young woman who had been afraid of human contact. She wept until her throat ached, until she couldn't shed one more tear.

Finally, she lifted her head and gazed into his eyes, fearful of what she might find there. It wasn't what she was expecting. Instead of horror and disgust, she saw compassion and understanding.

"You're safe now, Rhianna," he whispered, his eyes wet. "Nobody can ever hurt you like that again. I won't let them." He leaned forward and kissed her lightly on the lips.

"You said you wouldn't touch or kiss me," she said hoarsely.

"I said not while we're talking."

"But—"

"Rhianna, we're done talking," he said, kissing the corners of her mouth as if he wanted to kiss away every invisible, painful scar.

With a sigh, she gave in and his hands whispered against her flesh, giving her goosebumps.

There was no question that Jonathan cared for her. But did he care for her as much as she was beginning to care for him?

Chapter 22

JT took a deep breath before picking up the phone and making the call.

"Mr. Chambers," he said when the private investigator answered, "let's get this over with."

"You make it sound like a root canal," Chambers replied. "This isn't personal. It's just business."

"It *is* personal. Especially when you threaten someone I care about."

"I didn't really threaten her. Just thought she should know why you—"

"Listen, Chambers," JT cut in, "I'll tell her on my own terms. Got it?"

"Okay, okay. Don't blow a gasket, old man." Chambers paused. "What about my money?"

"I've considered your demands."

"And?"

"And I've decided to pay you."

"That's a smart thing to do, Mr. Lance."

JT rubbed his brow with a shaky hand. "You'll get it tomorrow afternoon. But it will be the very last time. Understand?"

"That I do."

"I'll need some kind of commitment on your part that you'll leave us alone after this."

"You have my word." Chambers chuckled. "Yeah, I guess that doesn't mean much to you. What do you have in mind?"

"I want you to leave town."

"Leave Miami?"

"Miami, Florida, the entire United States! I want you gone, out of my life. And I'll throw in an extra fifty thousand if you do this right after you get the wire transfer. I'll pay you the fifty when you send me a postcard from wherever you end up."

Hopefully in hell, he thought.

"I'll book a flight first thing in the morning."

"You do that, Chambers."

JT hung up the phone.

Could he trust the man? No. There was no trusting a guy like Winston Chambers. And no predicting his next move either.

Will Chambers take the money and disappear?

God, he hoped so.

On the floor above his office, Winston paced the dirty linoleum hallway of his cramped one-bedroom apartment. Outside the grimy window, a red neon sign buzzed and flickered, annoying the hell out of him. He'd wanted to shoot the damned thing since the day he'd moved in. Now he was wondering why he hadn't.

From the half-open window, the sounds of dwindling traffic could also be heard. Somewhere in the night, a siren wailed and a horn blasted. No peaceful serenity here. Not in the seedy district of Miami.

Inside the apartment, month old newspapers and well-thumbed girlie magazines covered the sagging couch and stained carpet. A broken laundry basket heaped high with dirty clothes sat neglected on the floor near the bedroom door. It had been a few weeks since he'd taken a trip to the basement laundry room and now his apartment smelled like rotten seafood and cat piss. Except Winston didn't own a cat.

A scurrying movement caught his eye.

A plump cockroach poked its head from beneath a pizza box. Hurrying toward it, Winston flattened the roach with his fist, then glimpsed his contorted reflection in the cracked mirror above the table.

He grinned. "Winston Chambers, roach hunter."

Roaches weren't the only thing he liked to hunt. That's why he'd gotten into the PI game.

He wiped the remains of the roach on a napkin and surveyed the room. "I certainly won't miss this place."

There was nothing here he wanted. What he *did* want was somewhere in the Bahamas.

How hard can it be to find her?

He laughed so hard he started to wheeze.

"Okay, Win. Let the hunt begin."

An hour later, he emerged from the bedroom, a bulging gray suitcase in one hand and a brown leather briefcase he'd bought online in the other. Over his left arm, he'd flung his only good suit. He set the suitcase near the door and hung the suit in the closet. Then, with a sweep of one arm, he cleared the kitchen table.

Drenched in sweat, he set the briefcase on the table and opened it. He extracted a large manila envelope. Inside were his treasures—more than fifty photographs of Rhianna McLeod, taken at different intervals in her life.

Winston had tracked the girl down after she'd left nursing school. He'd found her living with a deaf lady who was getting on in years. That made it all too easy for Winston to sneak in and take pictures of Rhianna. He'd hidden in closets, the basement and the old lady's bedroom.

It was amazing the quality one could get with a decent camera and a zoom lens.

He carefully spread the photos out on the table.

"There you are, my dear." He smiled and fingered a photo of Rhianna having tea with her patient. "One lump or two?"

The next photo was of a sad Rhianna. Tears streamed down her cheeks as she said a few words at the old lady's funeral. Winston had sat in the back row, as bold as could be. He'd even offered her his condolences.

"I'll take care of you," he said now, pulling a wad of cash from the briefcase pocket.

He had enough money to get him to the Bahamas and then on to his permanent destination. Morocco, perhaps. He would've gone to Haiti, but it was still in ruin after the earthquake.

It didn't really matter where he went, as long as no one could find him. Once JT Lance paid him, he could live comfortably overseas. Winston would be able to start over, with his new life.

And my new wife.

"Our wedding night will be one you'll never forget."

Though he would've loved to sit back and fantasize about Rhianna's naked body under his, he had work to do. He collected the photos of Rhianna and placed them back in the envelope. With the briefcase in hand, he left his apartment and clambered downstairs to his office. Panting, he flipped on the light and headed directly to his paper-littered desk. A few taps of the keyboard and his flight was arranged and he'd booked a hotel.

"One more thing," he muttered as he printed off the boarding pass.

He waddled toward an abstract painting and swung it to one side, revealing a wall safe. He entered the combination and the safe popped open. He withdrew a shoebox containing several fake passports he'd obtained over the years. He shoved the passports into the briefcase.

There was one other item in the box, something that would assure his success.

An unregistered Glock-17.

Winston picked up the gun and caressed it against his cheek. He couldn't take it on the plane, of course, so he did the next best thing. He wrapped the gun in bubble wrap and placed it back in the shoebox. After he securely taped the box, he addressed it to himself, care of the hotel in Nassau. He'd overnight the package.

Then tomorrow, he'd find out which hotel the lovely Rhianna McLeod was spending her vacation in and do a little recon visit. And when the Glock arrived, he'd go after her.

Just don't make me shoot you.

Chapter 23

Rhianna awoke the next morning in her own room. She had insisted on it, even though Jonathan had asked her—begged her—to stay.

"I don't want Misty to walk in and see me in your bed," she'd told him firmly. "It would just confuse her."

Still, she wondered what it would be like to wake up in his arms in the morning.

She shook her head. Nothing good could come of a thought like that.

After brushing her teeth, she eyed the bathroom mirror with disdain. "This is only temporary," she told her reflection. "Nothing more than a summer fling."

But it sure didn't feel that way to her.

She dressed, brushed her hair into its usual ponytail and went downstairs to get ready for the day's lessons with Misty.

"Hi, Rhianna," Misty signed from the kitchen table. "I've done one worksheet already."

Rhianna flicked a look at the clock on the wall. It was after nine. She'd slept in. Last night's energetic extracurricular activities had exhausted her.

"Let me see," she said, ignoring the heat that seared her cheeks.

She checked the page Misty had worked on and was surprised to find the young girl had correctly identified all of the signs.

She smiled and gave Misty a hug. "Great job. You got them all right."

"Daddy said if I did a good job this morning, he'd have a surprise for us later."

"Really? What kind of surprise?"

Misty rolled her eyes. "I don't know," she signed. "It's a surprise, remember?"

"Ah, of course," Rhianna said, laughing. "A surprise."

She grabbed a coffee and muffin, settled into a chair and quickly got Misty onto the next project. Though Rhianna did her best to stay focused on the day's lessons, it was difficult. Her mind kept straying to her charge's handsome father, and his strong yet gentle hands and sensual mouth. Every time she thought of Jonathan, her hands grew clammy.

Don't think about him!

Before lunch, Jonathan made an appearance. He was dressed in a white muscle shirt and beige Bermuda shorts, and he seemed to be in a very good mood.

"What's going on?" Rhianna asked.

"I'm taking a break from painting. You've got me for the rest of the day."

"That's our *surprise*?"

He arched a brow. "Are you telling me you'd pass up a picnic lunch and swimming with me and Misty?"

She giggled. "Well, since you mention swimming, I guess I'll go."

Caught up in the moment, Jonathan leaned down and planted a kiss on her lips. Right in front of Misty.

Rhianna stifled a gasp. "Are you sure you should be kissing me—"

"Of course I'm sure," he said, kissing her again.

He caught his daughter's eye and signed, "Every beautiful girl deserves a kiss." He leaned down and kissed her cheek.

Misty wrapped her arms around her father's neck, and Rhianna couldn't help but notice how happy they looked. Happy and complete. The perfect picture—father and daughter.

She sighed.

Did she really want to disturb their perfect world?

The question haunted her until it was time to head for the beach. The picnic lunch Mrs. Atkinson made them was superb. They ate on the dock to avoid getting sand in their food, although Misty argued that *sand-wishes* should be eaten on the sand. She made Rhianna and her father make a wish before taking the first bite.

"Then your wishes will come true," Misty signed.

"Don't know where she got that from," Jonathan said, shaking his head. "She's always called them sand-wishes."

Rhianna grinned. "I think it's cute."

After lunch, they swam in the ocean. Misty proved to be a very good swimmer, a natural little fish in the water. But it was Jonathan who impressed Rhianna most. She couldn't take her eyes off him. His face had relaxed into a permanent smile and he laughed with ease. His tanned muscles rippled as he swam out to a buoy, then back to the dock.

Later, they stretched out on towels on the dock.

"I could stay here forever," Rhianna said with a sigh.

Jonathan's brow arched. "Really?"

She blushed. "It's peaceful here. And beautiful."

He opened his mouth to reply, but Misty tugged at his hand. "I'm sleepy, Daddy."

"Nap time," he signed back.

Rhianna gathered the remnants of their lunch and packed the basket, while Jonathan shook off the beach towels and tucked them under his arm.

"Let's go home," he said.

Rhianna's heart did a peculiar flip-flop. *Home?*

When they arrived at the house, she followed Jonathan and Misty upstairs. She hung back in the doorway and watched Jonathan tuck his daughter into bed.

"Bear hugs," he signed, opening his arms.

Misty squeezed him tightly and he made funny gasping sounds.

"Help me, Rhianna," he pleaded.

"No way I'm getting in the middle of this," she said with a laugh.

After Misty released him, Jonathan moved toward the door. "Have a good sleep, sweetheart."

Misty clapped her hands twice. "Wait!"

"Do you want a glass of water?" Rhianna asked.

The girl gave her a shy smile. "I want a kiss. From *you*."

Rhianna crossed the room, trying to appear nonchalant. She leaned down and kissed Misty's cheek. In return, small arms wrapped around her neck, tugging her down until she had to sit on the bed.

Misty cocked her head to one side. "I'm glad you ended up on our island."

"Me too."

"I love you, Rhianna."

Rhianna was stunned. "I love you too. Sweet dreams."

She lowered her head and made a beeline for the door. Squeezing past Jonathan, she slipped into her bedroom and with her back against the door, she stared up at the ceiling and blinked back the tears that had nearly betrayed her.

She was far too close to Misty. And Jonathan. He was making her want things she shouldn't want. Impossible things. No matter how much she wanted to go home and see JT, she couldn't fight the yearning of her heart. She'd give anything to be more than Misty's teacher, more than Jonathan's short-term guest and his summer fling.

"I want what I can't have," she whispered.

Every day she stayed on Angelina's Isle would make it that much harder to leave, but she had to get away from Jonathan Tyler and his seductive charm. Before it was too late. Before her heart was permanently crushed.

She let out a soft sob.

The thought of leaving was almost too much to bear. She'd fallen for the place—and the people. Including Jonathan.

That sudden realization made her gasp.

I'm in love with Jonathan.

A knock on the door startled her.

She wiped her eyes and pasted on a smile. "I'll be downstairs in a minute."

The door cracked open. It was Jonathan.

"Are you okay, Rhianna?"

"I'm fine." She turned away so he wouldn't see her red eyes. "I need a shower and a change of clothes. I've got sand all over me."

"All right. I just thought..." His voice faded. "Never mind."

The door closed.

Twenty minutes later, Rhianna emerged from the bathroom in her robe, refreshed—in body and mind. Now she had to make a decision. Give her heart to Jonathan on a silver platter, or maintain a safe distance. Either way, she knew she had to face him and find out where he thought this *whatever-it-was* was leading.

She dressed in an aqua and white summer dress and blow-dried her hair, clipping it back this time in a silver barrette. After applying a pale copper lip gloss, she went downstairs.

When she reached the kitchen, she was surprised to find only Mrs. Atkinson there. Savory smells came from the oven and stove top, and a pie rested on the counter.

"I'm making a roast chicken dinner tonight," the housekeeper said as she sliced carrots. "Mashed potatoes, fresh carrots and peas from the garden, and a strawberry pie for dessert."

"Sounds delicious," Rhianna said. "Would you like some help?"

"I've got it covered, dear, but thanks for the offer." Mrs. Atkinson raised her eyes and studied Rhianna before saying, "Why don't you relax for the rest of the afternoon? I'll be here for Misty when she wakes up."

"Do you know where Jonathan is?"

"He went back to his studio."

A wave of disappointment swept over Rhianna. "Oh."

There was a long moment of awkward silence.

Mrs. Atkinson set the knife on the cutting board. "Rhianna, dear, can I make an observation?"

"Of course."

"I've known Mr. Tyler for a number of years. I've watched him convince himself he loved a woman who only thought about herself. He did everything he could to make his marriage work. And he was miserable."

"Why are you telling me this?"

Mrs. Atkinson sighed. "I've seen how he looks at you. And how happy you make him."

"What do you mean?"

"Our Jonathan has very strong feelings for you. I suspect you feel the same about him."

Rhianna opened her mouth to argue, then snapped it shut.

"I've never seen him this relaxed," Mrs. Atkinson added. "Or happy."

"Maybe he's just been alone too long."

"Perhaps. But that doesn't change how you two feel about each other. Does it?"

"You're an observant woman." Rhianna said self-consciously. "Maybe too observant."

"With no TV here, what else is there to do?" Mrs. Atkinson smiled, then picked up the knife and resumed her chopping.

"So what do you suggest I do about these...feelings?"

"Well, first thing you do," the housekeeper said, wiping her hands on her apron, "is drop in on Mr. Tyler. He promised you the rest of the day, right?"

"He did."

"Never let a man get away with not keeping a promise."

"I'll remember that," Rhianna said as she strode toward the front door.

"One more thing," Mrs. Atkinson called after her.

"What's that?"

"No matter what has happened in the past, there's no future without a certain amount of risk. If you want something badly enough, go after it."

Rhianna thought about Mrs. Atkinson's words all the way to Jonathan's studio.

Could she risk heartbreak?

Jonathan paced the cabin floor, frustrated by the conflicting feelings he had for Rhianna. No other woman since Sirena had made him feel the way he did now. His little castaway was nothing like Sirena. His ex-wife only knew how to take. Rhianna did the opposite.

At first, it was all about the chase. He'd be the first to admit that. Hell, it had been a long time for him. But now? He felt more than just physical desire for Rhianna. What he felt was seductive and dangerous.

One part of him told him to view things as a brief fling. Another part couldn't bear the thought of watching her leave.

What the hell was he going to do?

He strode toward the painting he'd been working on. It was veiled with a white sheet. When it was complete, this painting would be his best work. He knew that without a shadow of doubt. His newest creation could bring in a hundred thousand easily, thanks to Rhianna.

He reached for a brush just as the door behind him opened. He turned and his heart did a little skip. Rhianna, looking fresh and beautiful, stood in the doorway.

"You found me," he said.

"You're not a hard man to find."

He shrugged. "I figured I might as well come back here and tidy up, since you were busy."

"Are you painting?"

"No." He turned toward her, brush in hand. "I don't think I'm in the mood to work on this."

"What are you in the mood for?"

He frowned. "Are you trying to tempt me?"

"I don't know."

He took a step closer and watched her from hooded eyes. He wanted nothing more than to take her, right there against the door, but something held him back. Perhaps the slight tremor of her hands. Or the barely concealed fear that haunted her eyes.

Go slow, he reminded himself.

A glimmer of a thought teased his mind. "I know what I'm in the mood for."

She waited silently.

Jonathan cocked his head to one side. "I want to paint you."

Rhianna laughed. "Me? I'm hardly a model."

"Do you trust me?"

Her smile faded. "Yes."

Jonathan placed the paintbrush on the table by the easel. Then he took both her hands and led her to the sofa. Reaching for the barrette in her hair, he unclasped it. As Rhianna's long tresses fell about her shoulders, he reached for the hem of her dress and pulled it over her head. Rhianna shivered when he wrapped his arms around her and unclasped her bra.

"What are you doing?" she asked, breathless.

"I want to paint the beauty I see in you. The part you try to hide, but can't."

He slid the bra from her arms and flung it to the floor. Then he hooked his thumbs into her panties and slowly peeled them down her long legs.

"I didn't come here for…" Her voice faded as he knelt on the floor.

"I know."

Rhianna's green eyes flickered between uncertainty and yearning. "I came here to talk."

"Later."

He wanted to kiss her. Everywhere.

Not yet.

Rhianna could feel his breath on the place where her legs met. It sent tingles through her body, and all her thoughts of confrontation flew out the window. How could she possibly think with Jonathan kneeling before her, asking her to trust him?

"Lie down on the sofa," he told her.

When she was positioned on her back, he studied her. Then he raised one of her legs.

"Like that," he said.

She watched him move to the table by the easel and squeeze various paint tubes onto a wooden palette. With three brushes in his hand and the palette, he approached her.

"What are you doing?" she asked, confused.

He smiled. "I'm painting you."

"Shouldn't you be working on canvas?"

"You're my canvas."

Rhianna's heart fluttered. "You can't put paint on me. I'll never get it off."

"These are watercolors. Very safe on the skin and they'll come off in the shower."

Her eyes widened. "But—"

"You said you trust me, Rhianna."

"I do."

"Then close your eyes and be my canvas."

She did as he asked, holding her breath, waiting for the first touch of paint.

"This is a wandering vine," he said as the cool tip of a brush moved down the side of her neck in flowing swirls toward her right breast.

Rhianna quivered when another brush stroke slid under her breast, then upward very slowly, ending just below her nipple. She gasped at the erotic sensations it caused. The soft strokes reminded her of his tongue caressing her skin.

"This is a hibiscus, just opening to the sun," Jonathan said, his voice hoarse.

The brush swirled over her breast and a moan escaped. When cool paint circled the tender nub, she clamped her legs together in response.

"Be still," he whispered.

He added curves and curls in agonizingly fluid motions, until she was nearly going out of her mind. What she wanted—what she needed—had nothing to do with paint and brushes.

A warm hand slide up her thigh.

"Relax," he murmured. "Trust me."

Another swipe of paint left an icy trail from her breast down to her belly button. She thought he'd stop there, but he didn't. The tip of the brush swirled lower, then veered off to one side before curling inward along the inside of her thigh. He did this on the other side, then slowly parted her legs.

She heard a hiss of breath. Not hers. Jonathan's.

"I trust you," she said. "Completely."

With her eyes still closed, she imagined him staring down at her, watching her every response as he painted her body. Her heart beat quickened. She'd never felt so liberated, physically or emotionally. Or so turned on. Every muscle in her body begged for release, and in that moment she knew that she'd take anything Jonathan gave her. Even if it meant leaving with a broken heart.

"I want you, Rhianna," he whispered in her ear. "But this time I'm going to give you what you need."

Before she could say a word, something wet whispered against her, between her legs. At first, she thought Jonathan was painting her there.

Then she realized he wasn't using a brush.

Chapter 24

Winston spent most of the hour-long flight to Nassau in the washroom at the front of the plane. The three glasses of red wine had done nothing to calm his nerves. The turbulent flight had him holding his breath and clenching the armrests until his knuckles turned white. It also didn't help that he had to suck in his stomach each time he passed in front of the middle-aged woman seated beside him. She was so engulfed in some trashy romance novel—like the ones Winston's mother used to read—that she barely moved her legs. Maybe next time he got up he'd step on her toes.

His stomach gurgled loudly.

"Gravol," the woman said without looking up.

"Excuse me?"

"That's what I take before a flight. Settles the stomach."

"Thanks for the advice," he said dryly.

The woman resumed her reading.

As the plane circled for the final approach, Winston's gut churned and he was sure he'd vomit this time. He staggered to his feet, planning to get to the bathroom before the seatbelt light flashed, but he was too late. The flight attendant was shaking her head and motioning for him to fasten his seatbelt. Returning to his seat, he gritted his teeth against a wave of nausea.

"There's a barf bag in the pocket in front of you," the woman beside him said.

Winston wanted to strangle her right there. Erase that self-righteous smirk off her face.

Instead, he smiled. "I'll try not to get any on you."

The woman's eyes widened in horror and she shifted as far away from him as possible.

In the end, he had no need of the paper bag. The plane landed smoothly and he was the first one out the door and into the airport. He made a beeline for the men's room and emptied his breakfast and lunch into the toilet. He felt much better after that.

A long lineup of taxis waited outside the airport, and Winston settled on a black vehicle with an equally black driver. Both suited his dark mood. The driver took him to the Nassau Palm Hotel, a few blocks from the downtown core. It wasn't a four-star hotel, but it would do. The main attraction for Winston was that the famous Paradise Island casinos were only a short ferry ride away. Since he had to wait for his Glock to arrive tomorrow, he'd wile away the hours at the casinos.

Maybe his luck would change.

In a small room on the third floor, Winston unpacked the few pieces of clothing he'd brought and hung them in the tiny closet. Then he stripped off the suit and carefully placed it in the laundry bag, readying it for the hotel staff to send it out for dry-cleaning. He'd need the suit tomorrow in order to pull off his act.

Dressed in a pair of baggy shorts, a Red Sox t-shirt and a sun visor from his last trip to Mexico, Winston added a pair of reflective sunglasses to finish the look. He resembled most of the men he'd seen in the hotel lobby. Nondescript. Average. Forgettable.

"You look like a tourist, Win," he said to his reflection in the dresser mirror.

If he could mingle with other tourists in Nassau and keep a low profile, no one would remember him. Or be able to describe him to the cops.

That meant no one could find him later—or Rhianna.

Winston set his laptop on the dresser and plugged it in. He'd have to pay for Internet access, but that was fine. He was using a stolen VISA. It belonged to Charles Duke, a wealthy client who suspected his wife of being unfaithful. And she was—with Winston. With her desire for bondage scenarios, she'd made it easy for him to confiscate the credit card and her husband's passport during Winston's last visit.

Signing in to his Miami bank account, he released a slow whistle when he saw the balance. Lance had been true to his word. The five hundred grand had been deposited, bringing his "escape" account over the one million mark.

You've made me a rich man, JT.

To celebrate, Winston called down to room service and ordered a steak dinner, rare, with fries. And banana cream pie for dessert. He also asked for a bottle of champagne and two glasses. Tomorrow, he'd have a special toast with his fiancé.

Half an hour later, a room attendant knocked on the door and wheeled in a cart with dome-lidded plates. The man handed Winston an ice bucket containing a champagne bottle. "I hope this'll be okay," the attendant said. "It's our finest."

Winston gave a nod and tipped the man. Not too much, not too little.

When he was alone, he sat at the table. It was barely big enough for the two plates. The steak was a bit overcooked, but other than that, he had no complaints. He switched between bites of fries and pie and devoured everything in twenty minutes.

"Time to do some creative financing," he said, opening his laptop on the table.

Within a half hour, all the funds were transferred from his Miami account to his Zurich account. From there the money was sent through various untraceable networks until it reached an obscure bank in Morocco.

Then he constructed an email.

Dear Mr. Lance, I've moved overseas to Switzerland. You can confirm that by stopping by my former office. I've mailed you a postcard, but it'll take a couple of weeks. Please have my bonus sent to the Credit Suisse in Zurich, Switzerland, immediately.

He included the pertinent banking information, then hit 'send'. When the extra fifty thousand arrived in Zurich, he'd reroute it to Morocco as well. All traces of Winston Chambers would end in Switzerland and Lance would have no reason to suspect Winston was anywhere else, especially since he'd cleaned out his office and left a false forwarding address with his landlord.

He leaned back in the chair and cracked his knuckles. "Now for the next order of business—locating the elusive Ms. McLeod."

Opening the nightstand drawer, he shoved aside a nearly new Bible and grabbed the phone book. He flipped the pages until he came to the heading he was seeking. *Hotels.* He spent nearly three hours calling hotels and inns in the Nassau area.

No luck.

"You have to be staying somewhere," he muttered.

Next, he tried some of the other islands, each time professing to hotel clerks that there had been a family emergency and that he had to reach his *niece* immediately.

But Rhianna wasn't on any of the other main islands.

So where the hell was she?

With the suit in hand, Winston took the elevator down to the lobby. At the front desk, he flagged down an attractive, blond-haired desk clerk in her mid-twenties. She'd be more receptive to his story.

"Can I help you?" she asked pleasantly.

"You could." He thought of all the ways the woman could be of service. None included wearing clothing. "I have a meeting tomorrow and I'd like my suit dry-cleaned."

"Consider it done."

Once the suit was tucked away in a back room, he said, "There is something else…"

The blond flashed perfect teeth. "Something wrong with your room, sir?"

"Not at all." He paused for effect. "I'm trying to locate someone. There's been a tragedy in the family."

"Oh my gosh," the woman said, her smile vanishing. "I'm so sorry to hear that."

Winston blinked, as if trying to keep tears at bay. "I need to tell my niece in person. But I don't know where she's staying."

"Where have you checked?"

He gave her the slip of paper with the names of the island hotels he'd called.

The blond frowned. "Are you sure she's at a hotel and not visiting someone here?"

Winston shook his head. "I really don't know. My niece has been a bit elusive lately." He leaned forward conspiratorially. "She had a fight with her father."

"I'm sorry, sir, but the only thing I can suggest is that you check the airports to see if she's flown somewhere."

It wasn't the answer he was hoping for, and he struggled to maintain a friendly smile.

"I've already done that." *Useless bitch.*

He strode toward the front door and had nearly reached it when someone caught his arm.

"Sir, have you tried the marinas?" the blond from the front desk asked. "Maybe she went by boat. Some of the smaller islands have bed and breakfasts."

This time Winston gave her a genuine smile. "Thank you."

"Please let me know if there's anything I can do to make your stay here more pleasurable."

He raised a thick brow. "Anything?"

The woman seemed bewildered at first. Then a small gasp escaped her glossy lips. Clearing her throat, she said, "Have a good day, sir."

He watched her hips sway as she retreated to the safety of the front desk. When she glared back at him, he winked. Any other time he would've taken her up on her offer, but he was saving himself now for someone else. Someone special.

A blistering blast of air hit him as he left the air-conditioned lobby and stepped outside. He immediately began to sweat, though it was a toss-up as to whether he was sweating from the heat or from excitement at being closer to his prey.

"Take me to the nearest marina," he said, climbing into the back of a taxi.

The sullen driver gave a nod, then cranked up the Reggae beat that thudded from the car stereo.

That's okay, Winston thought. *I don't wanna talk to you either.*

He barely noticed the passing scenery, until they reached the parking lot of the Bayshore Marina. At the sight of the nearly two hundred boats tied to the docks, his palms grew clammy and he wiped them on his shorts.

"Damn!" he muttered beneath his breath.

It would take days to question all the boat owners.

He paid the driver and watched the taxi drive away before shuffling down the main ramp. A variety of watercrafts greeted him, from sailboats to speedboats to eighty-foot yachts. He stopped at the first boat that carried passengers—a retired husband and wife.

"I'm looking for my niece." He showed them a photo of Rhianna. "Have you seen her?"

The husband shook his head. "We just got in last night."

Winston moved down the dock, asking everyone he met if they'd seen his niece. But they all gave him the same answer. No one had seen Rhianna.

Frustrated, he waddled toward a speedboat at the end. It had one of those flowery names. *Misty's Dream.*

He approached it with a sense of doomed failure. At the rate he was striking out, it would take him weeks to check every marina. But he didn't have weeks. The longer he searched for Rhianna, the more chances he was taking that he'd be found out. Duke could report his credit card missing. Or his passport.

Only one person was onboard Misty's Dream, a black man in his twenties with tight cornrows in his hair. He was hunched over the outboard, a toolbox at his feet.

"Excuse me," Winston called out. "I'm hoping you can help me."

"What do you need?"

"I'm looking for someone. A young woman."

"What's her name?"

"Rhianna McLeod."

The man glanced up, frowning. "I took her out to Angelina's Isle a few weeks ago."

Winston couldn't believe his luck. He gave the man a huge smile and held out his hand. "Charles Duke."

"Roland Saunders."

"Well, Mr. Saunders, I'd like to acquire your ferry services."

Saunders raised a brow. "Misty's dream isn't a passenger ferry. I told your friend the same thing. It's for supplies only."

"Well, perhaps you can make another exception." Winston slid a wad of bills from his shorts pocket. "Let's say two hundred dollars."

Saunders sighed. "Make it three and you have a deal."

Winston paid the man. "You won't call over there, will you? If Rhianna knows I'm on my way, she'll know something is wrong. I'd prefer to tell her myself. Face to face."

Saunders shrugged. "Can't call anyway. Tyler's radio is broken."

"Tyler?"

"The owner of the island."

Winston hid a frown. He hadn't thought of possible complications. Of course someone else would be on the blasted island. He'd have to be that much more charming. And convincing.

"I can take you over tomorrow morning," Saunders told him. "There's a storm coming in tonight."

Winston looked up at the sky. Fluffy white clouds dotted the horizon and the sun gleamed. "Looks pretty calm to me."

"Trust me," Saunders said with a grin. "You'll want to be inside tonight."

"I'm waiting for a—" Winston caught himself, "a phone call from home anyway. Tomorrow is fine. What time?"

"I'll be fueled and ready to go by nine, Mr. Duke."

That would work perfectly. By morning, Winston would have his Glock.

"See you tomorrow at nine then." He took a few steps, then swiveled on one foot. "I can trust you not to run off with my money and leave me in the lurch, can't I?"

Saunders scowled. "Yeah, you can trust me. I'll be here. Just don't be late."

Delighted with his success at locating Rhianna, Winston trudged up the wooden ramp. At the top, he paused to catch his breath and wipe his brow. A small smirk teased the corners of his mouth.

I'm coming, Rhianna, my love.

Chapter 25

That night, a storm struck the Bahamas, and Rhianna saw nature in all her fury. Though familiar with the hurricanes that besieged Florida on a regular basis, she'd never felt as vulnerable as she did now. Angelina's Isle wasn't that big and there was no way to reach the mainland in the event of an emergency.

Just before the storm let loose, Jonathan had secured all the exterior shutters and placed a number of flashlights on the living room coffee table.

"In case the generator shuts down," he'd explained.

"Does it always shut down in a storm?" Rhianna asked him now, shivering at the thought.

He shook his head. "No, but we can never be too prepared. If the generator shuts down, I won't be able to go outside to fix it. You never know what kind of debris the wind will kick up."

Misty thought the storm was fun. She'd already selected her flashlight and waved it around the living room, even though the lights were still on.

"Don't waste the batteries, Misty," Jonathan signed.

Rhianna smiled.

"What?" he asked.

"You're getting better with ASL. Faster."

"I have a great teacher," he said, grinning.

Me too, she wanted to say.

She sat down on the sofa and watched Misty and Jonathan roast marshmallows in the fireplace. For a fleeting moment, she envisioned living at Lancelot's Landing permanently. She and Misty would play games during the day, and she and Jonathan would play more adult games during the night.

What on earth am I thinking?

Jonathan strode toward her with a well roasted marshmallow on a metal skewer.

"No thanks," she said.

Ignoring her, Jonathan peeled the treat from the skewer. "Just one bite."

She chuckled. "One bite will send me into a sugar high."

He dangled the marshmallow in front of her until she took a timid bite.

"Not bad," she said.

"Not bad?" Jonathan's brow arched. "I'm the king of marshmallows. Just ask Misty."

He gazed into her eyes and popped the remaining piece in his mouth. That small, intimate act made Rhianna's pulse quicken.

"Misty's quite taken with you," he said.

"What about you?" she blurted. "I mean, do you still mind that I'm here?" Her cheeks burned with embarrassment.

Jonathan sat beside her. "What do you think? It hasn't been that bad having you as my castaway. You seem to have a good effect on Misty. She's learned more in a few weeks with you than with her other teachers." He leaned over and kissed her cheek. "Thank you, Rhianna."

"Misty is a bright child."

She couldn't take her eyes from Jonathan's face. She loved him. There was no escaping that.

I've never been so happy in my life.

But listening to the storm churning outside, she had a terrible sinking feeling. Something was coming. She didn't know how she knew it, but she did. Something was going to happen, and when it did, her hopes and dreams were going to come crashing down around her.

Outside, the wind screamed through the trees.

While Jonathan went upstairs to tuck Misty into bed for an afternoon nap, Rhianna stayed behind and cleaned the kitchen. Her mind churned with thoughts of how to approach Jonathan about her feelings, and when he returned to the living room, she was waiting for him.

"Misty passed out three pages into Sleeping Beauty," he said. "Want a drink?"

"Sure."

He poured two glasses of wine. Handing her a glass, his eyes met hers. "Is something wrong?"

She took a deep breath. "I'm just wondering what we're going to do after."

"After what?"

She swallowed hard. "When it's time for me to go back to Miami."

"Maybe you shouldn't go back," he said.

She experienced a brief thrill before reality set in.

"I have a job," she said. "My employer needs me."

Jonathan's expression darkened. "Just what does he need from you? You've never really told me much about what you do, or about your employer."

"I'm a palliative care nurse. My patients trust me not to talk about them."

"So your employer is your patient."

She nodded.

Jonathan sank into the armchair across the floor. "Must be tough dealing with death like that."

She shrugged. "It's all part of life."

"Still, it must get depressing."

"Sometimes," she admitted. "My employer is a very caring, generous man. I'll hate it when he's gone. He's been like a father to me."

She thought of JT waiting for her return. He probably thought she was lounging on the beach, applying sunscreen and drinking margaritas.

If JT only knew.

"You know," she said, "the one thing my employer has taught me is that family is everything. Maybe it's time for you to reconnect with yours."

"The time's not right," Jonathan said quickly.

She sighed. "If you wait too long, it might be too late."

"It's already too late."

She wanted to argue with him, but the scowl on his face made her reconsider. "I'm tired." She gulped down the last bit of wine. "I think I'll have a nap too."

Jonathan said nothing.

In her room, she stripped down to her bra and panties and climbed into bed. But she couldn't get Jonathan's words out of her head.

"It's already too late."

If it was too late for Jonathan and his father, was it too late for her too?

Will I ever have my own family to love?

The dynamics of family were complicated. Blood wasn't always thicker than water. Being born into a family didn't guarantee love. One only had to read a newspaper for proof of that. However, love *could* be found elsewhere, in surrogate parents.

Rhianna had found that with her aunt and uncle before they'd been killed. And then with JT and Higginson.

She glanced at the photo by her bed.

Maybe she could do something to help JT. He had said he was estranged from his son. When she got back to Miami, she would search for this missing son. They'd both need closure before JT passed on. And even if she was unsuccessful at tracking the son down, it would give her something to do to take her mind off Jonathan, Misty and Angelina's Isle.

Jonathan implied that I shouldn't go.

She gave her head a shake. It had been a suggestion. That was all. He hadn't professed undying love to her. Hell, he hadn't mentioned any feelings for her, outside of enjoying her body.

I haven't told him how I feel either.

She couldn't now. It was too much of a risk.

The wind wailed and the shutters rattled as Rhianna slid beneath the soft sheets. She closed her eyes, unable to shake that edgy feeling that something was about to happen. Something that would change everything.

Jonathan checked the back door, then the front. He was restless and he was sure he knew why. Rhianna's comment about contacting his father had bothered him. She made it seem so simple, so easy. Just pick up a phone and call the old man and everything will be forgiven.

But it couldn't possibly be that easy, his mind argued.

It had been too long. His father had probably moved, maybe even remarried.

Now *that* would really burn.

Yet Jonathan couldn't deny a spark of curiosity. Or the need to resolve the past. Perhaps he should go back to Miami.

Maybe I'll go back with Rhianna.

"I don't want her to leave," he muttered to the shadows.

He hadn't spent much time analyzing his feelings, but he knew that the thought of Rhianna leaving bothered him. What about Misty? Where would he find a teacher that his daughter liked?

"You like her too," he whispered.

Rhianna was so different from Sirena. She really cared about others. He could tell she loved Misty.

But how did she feel about him?

He released a huff. "She probably can't wait to get home and tell all her girlfriends about her summer romance."

He glanced at the stairs. Rhianna was sleeping up there, and all he could think of was joining her. But not to sleep.

Jonathan paced the living room floor.

He wanted Rhianna. He needed her. If she left him, he'd feel an emptiness that wouldn't be easily filled. Everything in his body and mind urged him to tell her how he felt. Trust her with his heart. He wanted to wake up every morning with her and go to sleep at night with Rhianna in his arms. He wanted the happily ever after, like in Misty's fairy tales.

Suddenly, he froze. "I'm in love with Rhianna."

As soon as the words were spoken aloud, he knew it was true. He loved her and he never wanted to let her go.

With lightness in his heart, he raced upstairs. Pausing in front of Rhianna's bedroom door, he took a deep breath. Then he quietly pushed open the door and stepped inside.

Rhianna was buried beneath blankets and fast asleep. He moved to her side, then hesitated. Should he wake her? Should he tell her how he felt?

A framed photograph on the nightstand caught his eye.

What in God's name is she doing with this?

Rhianna turned her head, her eyes opening slowly. When she saw him, she gasped in surprise. "What are you doing here?"

Hot anger surged through him. "Is this a joke? Did he send you here to bring me back?"

Rhianna blinked and struggled to sit up. "What are you talking about?"

"This!" He shoved the photo into her hands.

"It's a photo of my employer."

"Your employer? Like hell it is! This is a photo of my father."

Rhianna could barely breathe. "What did you say?"

"You heard me," Jonathan snapped. "This is my father. Jacob Tyler Lance."

"But you said your name was—"

"Jonathan Tyler Lance."

She shook her head, confused. "I thought your last name was Tyler. You never once mentioned Lance."

"Because," he said tightly, "I was doing my best to get far away from it. Being a Lance comes with responsibilities. And apparently I was nothing but a huge disappointment. Or so I was reminded years ago."

"JT is your father?"

He glared at her. "Unfortunately."

She grabbed her robe from the end of the bed, wrapped it around her and sat down on the bed. "I had no idea."

"Sure you didn't."

She caught his gaze and frowned. "What are you insinuating?"

He let out a bitter laugh. "I'm not insinuating anything. I know the truth now. How you came to be *accidentally* stranded on my island. How you happen to know sign language when I needed a teacher for Misty. Jesus! I bought it all."

"Wait a minute," she said, trying to remain calm. "I *was* stranded here accidentally."

Jonathan acted as though he hadn't heard her.

"The bastard sent you here to spy on me. Didn't he? He wants to know if by turning down his millions I'm able to support myself and my daughter. He wants to rub my failed marriage in my face because he predicted it." He shook his head. "I can't believe this. Does he want me back now to take over his *empire*?"

"Your father is dying, Jonathan." She timidly reached out, but he snatched his arm away.

"Don't touch me! You're nothing but a liar, Ms McLeod. I don't know how I could've been so foolish to think I had feelings for you. To think that maybe we had a future together. I thought you were—" His voice cracked. "You're no different than Sirena. You both go where the money is and to hell with anyone else." He spun on one heel and left the room, the door slamming behind him.

Rhianna's eyes burned with unshed tears.

What just happened here?

She thought back to the day JT had given her the plane ticket for her dream holiday. There had been one moment when something had passed between JT and Higginson. Now she knew it had been the glimmer of conspiracy. No matter what Jonathan thought, she couldn't believe that JT wanted anything other than to be reunited with his son. She'd seen the haunted look in JT's eyes when he talked about his estranged son. He wanted resolution and forgiveness—from a son who was incapable of forgiving.

"I finally fall in love and now I've lost him."

"I don't know how I could've been so foolish to think I had feelings for you," Jonathan had told her.

She could almost feel her heart ripping into shreds. Soon there'd be nothing left of it.

"JT?" she cried, clenching the photo. "What have you done?"

Unable to look at JT's smiling face any longer, she opened the nightstand drawer and shoved the photo inside. That's when she caught sight of the Lady in the Mist print. Her tired eyes found the signature and it suddenly became very clear. She knew exactly who had painted it—and the other eight or so paintings JT had purchased over the years.

"Jesus," she hissed. "How can I be so dense?"

JT had been buying up Jonathan's paintings, spending hundreds of thousands of dollars on them. Did he do it because of guilt? Or was he trying to support his son the only way he knew how?

Does Jonathan know?

She doubted it. An art gallery handled all his sales. He probably never gave it a second thought, since the money was funneled through the gallery. She'd hazard a guess that he would never knowingly take money from his father, even if it was payment for a painting. He'd feel like he was being bought off. That it was charity. And Jonathan was far too proud to accept that.

What do I do now?

She slumped on the bed, feeling drained of energy and emotion. JT must have sent her here with hopes that she'd figure it out and bring his absent son back. And his granddaughter.

JT, why didn't you just pick up the damned phone?

The answer was clear. Pride. Both Lance men had too much of it.

She understood why JT wanted closure before he died. It was common with people who knew they were dying to reach out to lost family or friends, to attempt to fix wrongs or mend broken hearts.

But why had he dragged her into this mess?

There were two things she knew without a shadow of doubt. JT had set them up, and Jonathan would never believe she hadn't knowingly deceived him.

As the winds raged outside, she crawled into bed without removing her robe. Maybe she could sleep this nightmare away. Maybe she'd wake up the next morning and discover it had all been a bad dream.

Maybe hell will freeze over and take me with it.

Sleep took her in its tenuous grasp and played with her pained heart in ways that only nightmares can. Between fleeting, troubled visions of loneliness and uncertainty, Rhianna slept.

Chapter 26

When Winston awoke the following morning, he went down to the lobby in search of breakfast. The hotel restaurant was small and empty except for one other table, and the waitress was slower than a sloth, which annoyed him to no end. That and the fact that she'd placed him beside a couple with a screaming baby when there was an entire room filled with empty chairs.

Lazy bitch doesn't want to walk too far, he guessed.

The baby's screams filled the small room.

Winston glared at the parents, but they were oblivious. The mother tried to give her child a bottle, but it was swatted from her hand by a tiny curled fist.

The little bugger was a fighter.

When Winston couldn't stand the crying any longer, he demanded a table in the corner.

Don't make too much of a fuss, Win. Be invisible.

But even the need for invisibility had its limits.

In less than half an hour, he polished off a greasy platter of scrambled eggs, bacon, sausages and pancakes. He also finished a carafe of strong coffee, the kind that flowed thick like syrup from the spout. Food and caffeine would kick his metabolism into overdrive, not to mention keep him vigilant and on his toes. He needed all his faculties to pull off today's venture.

As he was leaving, he noticed the baby had fallen asleep. The parents looked relieved. He paused a foot away and let out a vicious sneeze. He was good at faking them. A well executed sneeze allowed a PI to hover near a target and collect information. It was also great for scaring the be-jesus out of someone—like the baby.

Grinning, he hurried from the restaurant just as the baby's cries were unleashed. He loathed babies. Even more, he detested happy couples.

Returning to his room, he found a newspaper and his freshly laundered suit inside waiting for him. He tucked the remaining Cohiba cigar in the jacket pocket. He couldn't wait to smoke it. Perhaps after he and Rhianna consummated their new relationship.

The red light on the phone was flashing and he called down to the front desk.

"You have a package, Mr. Duke," the attendant said.

"I'll be right down."

With a smile, Winston strode out of his hotel room.

Minutes later, he carried the package containing his beloved Glock into his room and locked the door.

"My little beauty has arrived."

He sat on the unmade bed, stroking the deadly weapon and checking the cartridge. He flicked on the safety. Wouldn't do to have it go off prematurely. Tucking the gun into the inside pocket of his jacket, he arranged the briefcase with the folder on Rhianna on top. He closed the case and locked it.

Stripping off the tourist outfit, he slipped into the suit, selected a silk tie and tucked his fake ID next to the cigar in the jacket pocket. In the bathroom, he looked at his reflection, at the excited gleam in his eyes.

There was nothing stopping him now.

He made a quick phone call to a private airstrip he'd found in the island Yellow Pages. After reserving and pre-paying the pilot of a small plane with Duke's VISA, he hung up, his getaway plan in motion.

He was hungry. But this time, not for food.

Twenty minutes before nine, a taxi arrived to carry him to his destination—the Bayshore Marina. This time, he observed his surroundings on the way. The streets of Nassau were littered with leaves, tree branches and garbage, all victims of the ruthless evening storm. The city already had street cleaners out, unsmiling old men who swept the sidewalks and cleared debris from the roads, which were still slick with rain, the morning sun still struggling to dry them.

It didn't take long before Winston regretted his choice of attire. The suit and high humidity made him sweat profusely. He shifted uncomfortably in the back of the taxi and spread his hefty legs apart, praying he wouldn't find a sweat stain on his crotch. Or on the back seat when he climbed out.

At the marina, he walked almost bowlegged, trying to dry the dampness between his legs. Already a prickly heat rash had formed where his flabby thighs rubbed together.

He spotted Roland Saunders with an older white man. They were loading boxes into the speedboat.

"I hope you haven't forgotten about me, Mr. Saunders," Winston said evenly.

The older man glanced up. "You must be Mr. Duke. I hear you're heading out to Angelina's Isle."

Winston bit his tongue and nodded. Last thing he needed was another nosy parker sticking his big nose in where it wasn't wanted.

"Denny Dorchester," the man said, holding out a hand.

Winston hesitated, then shook it once. "What are those boxes for?"

"Supplies for Tyler," Saunders replied.

"How come you have to drop them off? Doesn't this Tyler guy have his own boat?"

"This *is* his boat," Dorchester cut in.

"Are you coming with us?" Winston hoped the question sounded friendly and not panicked, like he was feeling.

Dorchester's eyes glinted, then he shook his head. "I have to go into town."

Winston could breathe again. "Nice meeting you."

He watched the older man climb the ramp. When Dorchester reached the top, he turned to look back.

Winston scowled. *Keep going, you fuck-wit.*

Saunders started the engine. "Ready to go, Mr. Duke."

"Call me Charles."

Saunders nudged his head toward the back bench of the boat. "You've got lots of room there. Jump in."

Winston climbed aboard and settled his wide girth into the seat. The buttons of his jacket strained against his gut. He sucked in his stomach and covertly patted the side of the jacket. As long as he kept it buttoned, the gun wasn't visible.

Within a few minutes, Misty's Dream slowly chugged away from the marina, and once they were clear of the high traffic area, Saunders opened the throttle.

"Since I'm showing up unannounced," Winston shouted, "tell me a bit about this Tyler guy."

"Tyler likes his privacy."

If Saunders thought that would end the questions, he was wrong. Winston needed to know who he was up against.

"Must be hard living out there," he said.

Saunders shrugged. "Angelina's Isle has everything he needs and wants."

"Except a way to get off it."

"That's what I'm for."

"What's he do for food and other groceries?"

"I usually go out every month or so and take him what he needs."

"Kind of a hermit, is he?"

"Kinda. Once in a while he comes back with me."

Interesting, Winston thought. The island was isolated, and *that* would work in his favor. So would the fact that this Tyler guy didn't seem like he'd offer much of a problem.

"How many people live on that island?" he asked.

"Just Tyler, his daughter and his caretakers—the Atkinsons. Plus your friend Miss McLeod." Saunders hesitated before saying, "Did someone in her family die?"

"Not yet," Winston said, putting on a somber face. "But he's not expected to live past the week."

Saunders gave a nod. "Must suck having to be the bearer of bad news."

"I've delivered worse."

The young man eyed him for a moment and Winston held his gaze. Saunders was curious. Hopefully, he'd stay that way and not become suspicious.

He yawned. He wasn't much of a morning person, especially at this ungodly hour.

"How long does it take to get to the island?" he asked.

"Just under an hour."

Winston's stomach lurched. "Oh shit," he muttered.

Saunders flicked a look over his shoulder. "Something wrong?"

"I shouldn't have eaten such a big breakfast."

"You don't get seasick, do you?"

"I don't know. It's been years since I've been in a boat."

"Try to think of something pleasant," Saunders suggested. "It usually helps."

Winston scowled. He was sick of people giving him advice. "How about you show me how to work this boat," he said. "That'll take my mind off puking."

"Sure."

Saunders slowed the boat and Winston shuffled closer.

"So this thing tells you what direction you're going in?" he asked, putting on his best eager student face. "What do you do when you want to turn around and go back to Nassau?"

Saunders gave him a crash course in watercraft operations, showing him how to use the GPS and how to accelerate, decelerate and navigate the markers in the water.

Boating for Dummies, Winston thought.

Only he wasn't the dummy. Saunders was.

Chapter 27

The morning sun awakened Rhianna early. With a heavy heart, she left the sanctuary of her bedroom and went downstairs, unsure of what she'd say to Jonathan. But she didn't have to worry about that. The house was quiet. Empty.

In the living room, she stared at the photographs of Misty and her father on the fireplace mantle. She'd miss them both when she was gone. With Jonathan out of her life, there'd be a huge hole in her heart. It wasn't so much that she craved the excitement of spending the nights with him. She craved everything about him. He had awakened something in her. A need for human contact. A desire to feel something more. He'd shown her love, even if he'd never said the words.

Tears gathered in her eyes, but she blinked them away. "No more crying."

Taking a deep breath, she squared her shoulders. If she was going to be alone for the day, she might as well make herself useful. Besides, if she kept busy, she wouldn't have as much time to dwell on the fact that Jonathan despised her. He was probably counting the days until she left.

Books were stacked on the floor in the den, so Rhianna started there, shelving them while dusting. When all the shelves were clean, she grabbed a sturdy kitchen chair in order to reach the top of the bookcases. As she was dusting, her rag caught on a pile of loose papers. She pulled them down, planning to replace the papers when she was done.

But luck wasn't with her.

As she strained on her tiptoes, she heard footsteps approaching.

"What the hell are you doing?" Jonathan demanded from the doorway.

She twisted around, about to give him an explanation, but lost her balance. She let out a shriek and toppled sideways, as the papers in her hand fluttered to the floor.

Lucky for Rhianna, Jonathan caught her.

"I'm sorry," she murmured, unable to look at him. "I needed something to do."

"So you thought you'd come poking around in here?" he asked, setting her on her feet.

She could feel the heat in her cheeks. "I wasn't poking around. I was trying to dust up there."

Ignoring her, he leaned down and began gathering the papers on the floor.

A couple of yellow-edged photos caught Rhianna's eye and she plucked them from the carpet. In one picture, she recognized a younger version of her employer. JT stood beside an attractive, dark-haired woman—Jonathan's mother, probably. The next photo showed a happy boy of about six.

Jonathan, she guessed.

She flipped over a third photo. "Oh my God..."

"What's wrong?" Jonathan demanded.

Her hand trembled as she turned the photo toward him.

He shrugged. "What about it?"

Rhianna choked back a sob. "Why do you have a picture of my mother?"

Jonathan was speechless. Had he heard Rhianna correctly?

Clearing his throat, he said, "That can't be your mother."

"Well, it is. I have the same photo at home. At your father's house."

"This," he said, plucking the photo from her hand, "is the picture of the woman my father was having an affair with. I told you about her. I took this from my father's jacket pocket before I left home." His jaw clenched. "I kept it to remind me of how much the mighty JT Lance values family. This woman tore mine apart, with his help."

Rhianna's face went ghostly white.

"I'm sure she just looks like your mother," he said, frowning.

"I'm telling you, that *is* my mother."

"I don't believe this," he muttered. "First, the photo of my father in your room, and now this."

If this woman was Rhianna's mother and his father's mistress, then he and Rhianna were connected in ways they'd never imagined.

"I don't want to talk about this right now," he said, heading for the living room.

"Wait!" Rhianna yelled after him. "You can't just walk away. We need to talk about this, figure things out." She followed him to the bar and poured a drink. "I don't believe my mother would betray my father.

She loved him. I know that."

"How would you know? They died before you were born."

He could tell by the hurt look in her eyes that he'd cut her deeply.

"My aunt told me they loved each other," she said. "They only had eyes for each other."

Jonathan let out a frustrated sigh. "My father kept this picture on him for years. It tore my parents apart."

Rhianna was crying now. "I'm sorry about that, but I still can't believe she—I won't! My parents were happy together." She downed the drink in one gulp and slammed the glass on the counter.

Jonathan's head throbbed. *What a mess!*

"I don't believe JT would sleep with my mother, then years later send me an invitation to care for him," Rhianna said coolly.

"My father has always been a ruthless business man."

"But this isn't business, Jonathan. This is personal. If your father slept with my mother, then they were both adulterers." Her voice grew sad. "And it means JT has been lying to me since day one."

He was unable to offer any words of comfort. What could he say? There was only one person who knew the truth, and he was busy dying nearly two hundred miles away.

"Listen, Rhianna, we don't know for sure—"

She held up a hand. When she finally spoke, her voice was listless, emotionless. "I'm going to lie down."

When Jonathan was alone, he released a pent-up sigh.

"Damn you all to hell, *Dad,*" he said under his breath.

But if his father was going to hell for what he'd done, he wouldn't be alone.

I'm right there with you, Jonathan thought.

He tried to get Rhianna's face out of his mind. Even with these new developments, his feelings for her were strong. That was probably what his father banked on. The old man had sent Rhianna here like the proverbial lamb to a slaughter, and Jonathan took no pleasure in being the executioner.

He recalled the last conversation he'd had with his father. The one where JT had told him he'd made a huge mistake marrying Sirena.

"She'll leave you as soon as someone dangles something better in front of her nose," his father had warned. "It won't matter if it's a role in a major film, more money, or other fringe benefits. Sirena is a classic gold-digger."

"She loves me!" Jonathan had yelled. "And I love her. That's all that matters."

How naïve he'd been back then. Love didn't guarantee a happily ever after. Nothing could.

Just like now.

He loved Rhianna. There was no use denying that now. He loved her with every fiber of his being. If that blasted photo wasn't standing between them he would have asked her to stay. Not that he could guarantee marriage. He couldn't. Not yet. But the thought of Rhianna leaving him, walking out of his life, hit him hard and left him feeling empty.

"How do I fix this?" he said with a groan.

Could he salvage their relationship?

He flipped through the papers Rhianna had found and removed the photo of his parents. They looked so happy. In love? Maybe. But definitely happy. The back of the photo was stamped with a date. Jonathan had been five when the photo was taken.

"Were you happy?" he asked. "Did you really love each other?"

His father smiled back at him.

Jonathan closed his eyes.

There was only one way to get at the truth and it meant facing the man who had betrayed him—*and* his mother. Maybe if he faced his father and asked him point blank about Rhianna's mother, the old man would finally tell the truth.

But would the truth set Jonathan and Rhianna free? Or would it act like a guillotine, severing their relationship and any chance of a future together?

"I have to find out," he said, opening his eyes. "Besides, he owes us that much."

And I owe it to Rhianna to clear up this mess once and for all.

Jonathan glanced toward the stairs. It would be an awkward week or two before Roland returned with the boat. If they could make it until then—without pissing each other off completely—he'd make arrangements to go back with Rhianna.

A knock on the door jolted him from his thoughts.

Frowning, he strode to the door and flung it open.

"I brought Misty back," Marvin Atkinson said, stepping inside. "She wants a popsicle."

Misty grinned and immediately went into the kitchen.

"Thanks," Jonathan told the older man.

"No problem." Marvin's eyes narrowed. "Okay, what's wrong, Tyler?"

"Nothing."

"Yeah, right. You're not a very good liar."

"I guess that's one thing I never inherited from the old man."

Marvin stared at him, then gave a nod. "Woman troubles, huh?"

"You have no idea."

The next thing Jonathan knew, Marvin had confiscated the sofa, along with a glass of brandy, and was nodding and listening while Jonathan unleashed all of his frustration and resentment about his father.

"I've spent so many years distancing myself from him, swearing I'd never be like him," he said tiredly. "Now I don't know what to do. Do I stay out of this mess and go back to life as I know it? Or do I confront him?"

"You say JT's dying?" Marvin asked.

"According to Rhianna, he's got a brain tumor. Cancer of some kind."

"How long?"

"She said he could go any time, although he was given six months. I just don't understand why he thought sending her here would be a good idea. He knows how I feel about him."

Marvin swirled the amber liquid in his glass. "Seems to me that he's reaching out to you. Why else would he send her here?"

"To make my life miserable."

"From what I've seen, you've been anything but miserable these past few weeks."

Jonathan shrugged. "So we had some fun while she was here. It's just a summer fling."

"Really. Nothing more than that?"

"I don't know," Jonathan replied with a groan. "I'd like to think it's just a *thing*, but I think it's more." He picked at a paint splotch on the hem of his shirt before looking at Marvin. "I want it to be more."

Marvin grinned and the wrinkles around his eyes doubled. "Finally. The truth is revealed."

"What truth?"

"You love her, you idiot. The Missus and I have known that for the past week. It's obvious."

Obviously not so obvious to me, Jonathan surmised.

"That's what you two have been doing all day?" he asked Marvin. "Talking about me and Rhianna?"

Marvin snorted. "What else is there to talk about?"

"You probably took bets too," Jonathan grumbled.

The older man gave him an innocent look. "Now, Tyler, don't be so cynical." He paused, taking a long swig of brandy. "You can't deny you have feelings for Rhianna."

Jonathan didn't reply.

"I think she has some pretty strong feelings for you," Marvin said. "And they have nothing to do with JT sending her here."

"But how do I know that? How can I know for sure that she didn't come here to spy on me and report back to the old man?"

"Did you flat out ask her, then actually wait for an answer?"

Jonathan stared at him. "I, uh..."

"Yeah, that's what I thought." Marvin let out a sigh. "Listen, Tyler, you're like a son to me. If you want Rhianna, you have to fight for her."

"I tried that with Sirena and I lost."

"That one wasn't worth fighting for. She had her own agenda."

Jonathan sighed. "Why did everyone see her for what she was except me?"

"Love is blind. And deaf and stupid."

Jonathan clinked his glass against Marvin's. "You said it."

There was a long silence before either of them spoke.

Finally, Jonathan said, "So, are you going to tell me?"

Marvin's mouth curved into a smile. "I lost the bet. I thought it would take you longer to fall for Rhianna. I owe the Missus two weeks of laundry duty and cooking."

"I didn't *fall* for—" Jonathan grinned. "Okay, fine. I've fallen for Rhianna McLeod."

Now he just had to figure out how to get back up.

Rhianna stood on the balcony, a shawl draped over her shoulders. The morning air was chilly, an aftereffect of the previous night's storm.

For a moment, her life flashed before her. Her childhood with her aunt and uncle. The foster homes she'd lived in. The abuse at the hands of Peter Waverley. The lonely years she'd spent in search of a family.

She gripped the railing. "All I want is someone to love. Someone who'll love me back in return. Is that too much to ask for?"

Didn't she deserve to be happy?

Rhianna thought back to the conversation with Jonathan. He was angry at her mother, and rightly so it seemed. She'd realized something when they were discussing the possibility of JT's affair with her mother. The first day she'd met JT Lance, he had slipped in and out of a fog. He'd called her *Anna*. The name hadn't struck a chord with her until today.

When Aunt Madeleine had told her about her parents', the older woman had referred to them as Susanna and Robert, but Aunt Madeleine had also mentioned that Rhianna's father had called his wife by another name—a name he'd called her when they were high school sweethearts. *Anna.*

"Anna!" JT had said to Rhianna that first day. "You came back!"

Rhianna had forgotten about that. Until today.

She slumped against the railing. "Oh my God. Jonathan is right. My mother knew JT."

The question was, how well?

It certainly put everything into perspective. JT's search for her and offer of a job. His confusion over Rhianna's identity. The stunning resemblance she shared with the Lady in the Mist, the painting Jonathan had been inspired to create...

Rhianna gasped. "He painted her as a siren, a temptress, because of my mother."

The Lady in the Mist *was* her mother.

Everyone had told Rhianna how much she resembled the woman in the painting.

"Jonathan sees it too," she whispered.

That's why he now viewed her as a temptress, as someone who had deceived him.

She groaned softly. "I finally have a chance at love and fate rips it away."

There was only one thing she could do now. Leave Angelina's Isle.

But where would she go? She couldn't return to Lance Manor. There was no way she could live there now that she knew the truth about JT and her mother, especially since JT would be a constant reminder of Jonathan.

I don't know if it's the truth though, she thought. *Maybe there's another explanation, one that isn't so...destructive.*

She sighed. "No, running away won't solve anything."

She had to face JT Lance and find out once and for all what kind of relationship he and her mother had shared. If it was as Jonathan says, she would leave and never look back. But if there was even a remote chance at a plausible explanation, she owed it to JT to listen.

She shivered at the thought of an emotional confrontation, but it was time to put everything on the line.

What did she have to lose?

Everything.

Chapter 28

The speedboat skipped along the water and Winston watched the passing scenery like a hawk. There were few watercrafts in the area. That meant fewer witnesses.

He caught Saunders' eye and smiled. "Almost there?"

"Yeah. Another fifteen minutes. The dock is on the western side."

Saunders was steering the boat in the direction of a smaller island with a mildly hilly but lush landscape. The man had been quite accommodating. Winston now knew exactly how to operate the boat. The private airstrip with the waiting plane was a few miles west of Nassau. It would be easy to locate by following the coastline.

"I take it you want me to bring you and Miss McLeod back to Nassau," Saunders said over his shoulder.

"That's the plan," Winston lied. *Bet you had no idea this would be a one-way trip for you.*

Getting rid of Saunders was the only way he could guarantee his plan's success.

"Is the house on the beach?" he asked.

Saunders shook his head. "It's not far in, but you won't be able to see it."

Winston smirked. "Us showing up will be a surprise then."

Saunders gave him a worried look. "Gotta warn you. Tyler doesn't like surprises. He's a very private person."

"Good thing I'm only here for Rhianna then."

Saunders left Winston to his thoughts and focused on steering the boat closer to the shore. As they passed around a spit of land, a wooden dock appeared.

"Five more minutes," Saunders announced. "I'll wait for you here."

"That's fine."

Minutes later, Saunders inched the boat closer to the dock. He agilely jumped out and secured the rope.

"Head into the bushes," he said, pointing to the tree line, "right over there and keep walking. There's no path, but if you head southeast you should be okay."

Winston eyed him suspiciously. "You sure you're not dumping me on some deserted island?"

Saunders laughed. "No worries. This isn't Gilligan's Island. Just keep walking and you'll see the house about forty yards in."

Winston grabbed the man's hand and grunted as he stepped from the boat to the dock. What he didn't figure on was Saunders' keen interest in him, or the fact that the guy would see the Glock when Winston's jacket shifted.

"Are you a cop?" Saunders asked.

"Not exactly."

"You won't need a gun around these parts."

"You're probably right, but one can't be too careful."

The young man gave an uneasy laugh. Then he shrugged and began unloading the boxes.

"Thanks for getting me here in one piece, Saunders."

"No problem, Mr Duke."

"Here's a little bonus."

When Saunders turned, Winston smacked him hard with the gun. The man grunted once, then dropped to the dock, unconscious. With a satisfied smile, Winston grabbed him by the ankles and dragged him down the dock. He had to stop every now and then to catch his breath. Saunders' head plunked down the steps, making a dull thud, then left an indent in the sand as Winston pulled him toward the bushes.

But now Winston had a bit of a dilemma. Saunders could wake up any time and put a pesky dent in his plans. Yet Winston couldn't shoot the guy. The house was too close.

After a moment's hesitation, he leaned down and whacked Saunders in the head again. "If you know what's good for you," he muttered, "you'll stay down."

A small pool of blood gathered near the man's head.

Winston studied the Glock and noticed a smudge of blood on the barrel. He wiped it off with a leaf.

Covering Saunders' body with loose brush, he returned to the beach and headed in the direction his tour guide had pointed out. The dense foliage made him nervous and he took timid steps, checking the ground and trees for snakes. He flicked his hand over his suit, brushing away spider webs he was sure covered him.

Get a grip, Win. Keep calm, cool and collected.

Finally, a two-storey house came into view. There were some

outbuildings on the property in the back. He guessed one of them housed the caretakers. That left Tyler and his daughter.

And Rhianna.

He could barely contain his excitement. His plan was brilliant. Take what he wanted from the lovely woman, then give her back to Lance for a healthy payment. It would be his retirement fund.

He walked around the side of the house. No one was in the backyard.

A movement above him caught his eye.

When Winston glanced up, the very air was sucked from his lungs.

There she is!

Rhianna McLeod stood on an upper floor balcony, the wind fluttering the long strands of brilliant red hair. She gazed up at the sky, unaware that she was being watched. Her expression was filled with sadness.

I can make you happy, Winston promised.

He moved quickly to the door. Taking a deep breath, he painted on a friendly smile. Then he knocked and waited.

A few minutes ticked by and he knocked again.

When the door finally opened, his smile faltered. He'd expected Rhianna, not the tall, well built, angry looking man before him.

"What the hell is this?" the man thundered. "How the hell did you get on my island? And what are you doing here?"

Something about the man's voice and appearance seemed familiar to Winston. He knew this man from somewhere, but he couldn't put his finger on it.

"You must be Tyler," he said, reinforcing his smile. "I need to speak with Ms. McLeod."

Tyler's gaze narrowed. "Really? What business would you have with her?"

"I'm Charles Duke, an attorney for her employer Mr. JT Lance. He sent me to collect her." For effect, he added, "The poor fellow's had a relapse."

Uncertainty flickered over Tyler's face. "Come in."

Winston stepped inside and set his briefcase on the floor. When his host glanced at him, he raised an impatient brow. "Today would be nice."

"Ms. McLeod is lying down," Tyler said. "I'll get her." He took a few steps, then spun on his heel. "How did you get here, Mr. Duke?"

Winston improvised. "I met one of your acquaintances. Roland Saunders."

"Is he waiting at the dock?"

"No, he was unable to join me. He rented me the boat."

Tyler seemed surprised, and for a moment Winston was worried he'd gone too far.

"Guess everyone's scrambling to make a buck these days," Tyler said with a sigh.

Winston was about to answer when he glanced over the man's shoulder and caught sight of beauty in motion. She moved down the stairs as if drifting on fluid or air. He stared at her. His prey. His Goddess.

My bride.

"What's going on?" Rhianna asked.

"This is JT's attorney," Tyler replied.

Rhianna froze. "Did something happen to him?"

Winston shook his head, his smile disappearing. "Ms. McLeod, I'm Charles Duke. Your employer's attorney. I regret to inform you that JT has had a relapse. He's asked me to bring you back."

His bride-to-be responded by promptly passing out.

Chapter 29

Rhianna opened her eyes and found two worried faces watching her. She blinked. "What happened?"

"You fainted," Jonathan replied.

Behind him stood the stranger, Charles Duke. The heavyset man had small, beady eyes, presently trained on Rhianna with the precision of a marine sharpshooter. His bulbous nose was honeycombed with enlarged pores, suggesting a man who imbibed in too much alcohol, and the smile he gave her was thin-lipped and stiff.

Not the friendliest looking man she'd ever seen.

He's a lawyer, she recalled. *For JT.*

She struggled to sit up, but Jonathan gently restrained her. "Just stay there for a minute, Rhianna. You've had a shock." His voice faded. "We both have."

"Do you know Mr. Lance too?" Charles asked. He seemed surprised.

"You could say that, Mr. Duke."

Rhianna took a deep breath. "Let me up. I have to start packing."

The thought that JT had relapsed spurred her into action. No matter what he might have done in the past, she knew now that she had to stay with him. JT had done so much for her. At the very least, she owed him a chance to explain his connection to her mother. Hopefully it was one that everyone could live with.

"Wait a minute," Jonathan said, turning to the older man. "I'm not going to let you whisk her away without some kind of confirmation."

"Let's call Mr. Lance then, shall we? He'll confirm why I'm here."

Rhianna shook her head. "There's no phone here."

Charles wiped his damp forehead. "I can show you the letter he sent me."

"That'll be fine," Jonathan said.

Rhianna let out a huff. "Jesus, Jonathan. He's JT's lawyer, for crying out loud."

"No worries, Ms. McLeod," Charles assured her. "I have the letter with me."

She watched the man as he lumbered to the door and retrieved a leather briefcase. He popped it open on the coffee table in front of them.

"Here we go."

Charles passed a single sheet of paper to Rhianna. She recognized the Lance letterhead immediately. The letter itself was a request for the lawyer to find Rhianna and bring her home. It was typewritten and bore JT's signature.

"I'll pack right away," she said, moving to the stairs.

As she headed up to her room, something made her look over her shoulder. Charles was staring at her, a peculiar expression on his face. One that suggested he knew something she didn't.

She gasped. *Is JT already dead? Is that what he's not telling me?*

With a shake of her head, she forced the thought from her mind and continued upstairs. In her bedroom, she quickly packed and tried not to think about the fact that she was leaving Jonathan, Misty and Angelina's Isle for good.

"Focus on JT," she berated herself. "He needs you."

She thought of Charles Duke. There was something off about the man, but she couldn't put her finger on what. She knew one thing though. She didn't like him. There was a coldness that emanated from him.

Don't be so ungrateful, she thought. *He's taking you home. To JT.*

Would she uncover the truth about her mother before death came to claim him? She sure hoped so.

Lugging her suitcase downstairs, she was surprised to find the lawyer still standing in the living room. Jonathan had even offered the man a martini.

"I'm ready," she said with a nod to Charles.

"Very well then. I've booked a flight back to Miami. It leaves in…" Charles glanced at his watch, spilling his drink on his jacket in the process. "Damn it! I'm so clumsy sometimes." His face puckered and reddened.

"I hope it doesn't ruin your suit," Rhianna said, handing him some paper towel.

Charles snorted. "It's only alcohol."

"How much time until your flight leaves?" Jonathan cut in.

"Just over two hours," Charles replied.

"That doesn't give you much time. Or me."

"Why do *you* need time?" Rhianna asked, surprised.

"I was hoping to go back with you."

"That won't be possible," Charles cut in. "The flight is booked solid. I was lucky to get the last two seats and only because I claimed a medical emergency." He rubbed his two chins. "You could take the next flight, Mr. Tyler. I believe it leaves about four hours after ours."

Jonathan frowned. "I guess that's what I'll have to do then."

"Excuse me for a moment," Rhianna said to Charles. Turning to Jonathan, she said, "Can I speak to you?"

"Sure."

She pulled him into the kitchen. "Why are you being so rude?"

"I'm not. I just don't like some stranger showing up on my island."

"Oh right. Like me." She scowled. "JT asked him to bring me back, so I'm going."

"Then go back with me. On the later flight."

"What's gotten into you? Not that long ago you didn't want anything more to do with me, and now you want to take a trip home together?"

"I wouldn't exactly call it *home*."

"Well, I would," she snapped. "And I do."

Jonathan grabbed her arm. "Listen to me. Something about this Duke guy doesn't feel right."

"What?"

"I don't know. Maybe JT's worse than he's saying. I just don't want to see you get hurt."

"Why would you care if I get hurt? You've hurt me plenty lately."

"Rhianna..." He shook his head. "Look, I'm sorry about going off on you like that. I was in shock. First my father sends you here. Then I find out about him and your mother—"

"Stop right there. We don't know what happened between them."

"You're right." He released her arm and his palm stroked the side of her face. "And now it doesn't even seem to matter. All I can think of is that I don't want you to leave."

She couldn't breathe.

"I care about you," he continued. "A lot."

She glared at him. "You're unbelievable. I guess it's true. Guys always want what they can't have. Now that I'm leaving, you decide you care about me."

Jonathan muttered a curse. "Why does everything have to be so difficult between us?"

"I don't know." She paused, collecting her thoughts and wishing that he'd told her how he felt earlier. "Do me a big favor, Jonathan. In fact, do yourself a favor. Go back to Miami and make things right with your father. For his sake, yours and Misty's." She turned and walked away. "I'll go back with Mr. Duke and tend to JT."

"I'll be on the next plane," Jonathan called after her. "Make sure you send Roland back with the boat. Tell him it's an emergency."

Tears welled in Rhianna's eyes. "Goodbye, Jonathan."

"We need to hurry," Charles called out.

Rhianna glanced upstairs. There wasn't even time to say goodbye to Misty.

"Yes, of course," she said.

As she left the house and followed JT's lawyer through the trees, she peered over her shoulder. Jonathan stood in the doorway, watching her leave.

He almost appeared heartbroken.

Jonathan clenched his jaw and fought the impulse to run after Rhianna. When she turned around, he almost called out to her. *I love you. Don't leave me.*

However, he didn't, and now he was kicking himself for his cowardice. "Way to go," he muttered.

He wondered if he'd ever get the opportunity to tell her how he felt. Maybe it was too late. Maybe their time had come and gone.

Rhianna disappeared into the trees, setting Jonathan into motion. His first stop was the Atkinsons' cottage. He knocked on the door. As soon as Marvin saw his expression, he was ushered inside.

"A lawyer came for Rhianna," Jonathan said breathlessly.

"What would a lawyer want with her?" Marvin asked.

"He works for my father."

Mrs. Atkinson wiped her hands on her apron. "Oh, dear. What does your dad want with Rhianna?"

"It's a long story and I'll explain it all when I have time, but right now I have to pack. Misty and I are going to Miami. To see my father."

"And Rhianna?" Mrs. Atkinson asked.

"Yeah, her too."

"What do you need, son," Marvin asked.

"I just need you to look after the place while we're gone. I'm not sure how long I'll be in Miami."

"Done."

Jonathan took a deep breath. "JT is dying."

It was odd calling his father by name, but that's how Jonathan had grown to know him. As JT Lance. Business mogul and multi-millionaire asshole.

Mrs. Atkinson took his hand. "Don't worry, dear. We'll take care of everything here. You run along and see your dad. It sounds like he needs you."

"How is Ms. McLeod connected to your father?" Marvin asked.

"She's JT's nurse."

Marvin let out a whistle. "I never saw that one coming."

"Me neither," Jonathan said dryly.

"She's a beautiful girl with a great heart," Mrs. Atkinson said. "And she must have her hands full with your dad. I remember you saying he could be very difficult."

"That's an understatement." Jonathan headed for the door. "I'm leaving as soon as Roland gets back with the boat."

Marvin stepped outside with him.

"Thanks, Marvin."

"No problem. Just make sure you bring that girl back with you."

Jonathan shook his head. "It's not that easy."

"Son, if you love someone, you make it that easy. Anything worth having is worth fighting for. Remember that."

Marvin's words rang in the back of his mind the entire time Jonathan packed. The older man was right. It was time to fight.

With a sigh, he took his suitcase downstairs and propped it against the wall by the door. He'd pack Misty's bag later.

There was an eerie silence in the house. Misty was napping, Mrs. Atkinson was with her husband and he was...alone. Had the house always been this quiet before Rhianna had arrived?

He wandered into the den and stared at the bookcase where he'd hidden the photo of his father's mistress. There wasn't any other possible explanation for the old man's obsession with the mysterious Susanna.

Or was there?

Jonathan slumped into the chair and leaned back, folding his arms across his chest. "She's gone," he said to the empty room. "And all you have to do is get on a plane and head home to see her again."

But there was so much bad blood between him and his father. Could their relationship be mended? Rhianna certainly thought so.

Maybe he's changed, Jonathan thought. *Maybe he's not the same hardened man I knew.*

He glanced at a photo of Misty. She'd never met her grandfather. *I'm being unfair to her.*

He let out a hiss of air. "Shit. I have to go home. And I have to bring Misty with me."

When Roland arrived, Jonathan would have everything packed and ready to go. Misty would think it was a vacation. The Atkinsons could look after things at Lancelot's Landing while he was gone. It was all set, everything taken care of. So then why did he feel so antsy, so impatient to get going?

Two words.

Charles Duke.

The man hadn't said anything to warrant suspicion, but the way he'd looked at Rhianna had made Jonathan uneasy. Duke seemed too smooth, like an underhanded car salesman. The man had flown here from Miami at the request of his client. Then he somehow got Roland to rent him the boat and give directions, even though Roland knew very well that Jonathan valued his privacy.

"Now why would Roland do that?"

Chapter 30

Rhianna had only been gone ten minutes and Jonathan was restless. He couldn't ignore the apprehension in the pit of his stomach. It knocked the wind from him, making it hard to breathe.

What was he so afraid of?

Unable to relax, he decided that action was the solution. He'd lug his suitcase out to the dock. Once Roland returned, he'd come back for Misty and her bag.

As he pushed through the bushes, he thought about the situation. His father was dying—Misty's grandfather.

Rhianna's employer.

Where would she go after JT died?

The thought of Rhianna simply disappearing from his life bothered him. He gritted his teeth as he walked. "Get over her! It never would've lasted anyway."

Not with his father in the picture.

Jonathan wondered for the hundredth time why JT had brought Rhianna to Lance Manor to care for him and then sent her to Angelina's Isle. The only reason that made any sense was that JT wanted Rhianna to bring Jonathan back.

"And that's exactly what he's getting," he muttered.

The old man had won. This time.

And if JT's plotting wasn't enough to deal with, now there was another person in the picture to worry about. Charles Duke. Somehow the man had gotten Roland to lend him the boat.

Unless he stole it.

Maybe JT had offered the lawyer too great of a cash incentive for a little thing like transportation to stand in Duke's way. There was only one saving grace. If the man *had* stolen the boat, Roland wouldn't be far behind. Everyone at the marina knew who captained Misty's Dream.

Jonathan stepped from the trees and jogged down the beach, suitcase in hand. When he reached the dock, it was empty. No Duke or Rhianna, and no boat.

He shaded his eyes with a hand and squinted out into the water. Misty's Dream was just disappearing around the western spit.

Disappointment surged through him.

He glanced at his watch. He had about two hours to wait until Roland returned. If Duke didn't give him the message, Jonathan was sure Rhianna would.

Walking to the end of the dock, he stared out over the crystalline water. It was calm, glassy. He breathed in the light, fragrant air and tasted salt in the breeze.

God, he loved this place. Angelina's Isle inspired him like nowhere else on earth. It had helped heal his broken heart after Sirena had left. He supposed it would do the same for the pain he felt now over losing Rhianna.

Distracted, he set down the suitcase. It toppled over and teetered on the edge of the dock. He lunged for it before it ended up in the water.

Stabilizing the suitcase, he paused as a dark substance on a wooden plank caught his eye. He pushed the suitcase aside. A smear of deep red went with it. Crouching down, he examined the substance. Whatever it was, it had seeped into the wood. Had he spilled paint here? No, not possible. He hadn't been to the dock in weeks. Besides, any spilled paint would have dried by now.

Hesitantly, he touched the wet stain. It was sticky, probably from the hot sun. "What the hell—?" He stared at the crimson on his finger, unable to deny what it was.

Blood.

Surveying the plank, he determined there was enough blood to warrant trepidation, but his thoughts were interrupted by a rustling sound behind him.

Jonathan whipped around.

A few yards down the beach, the foliage was moving. Not from a breeze either. Something was alive in the bushes.

He heard a groan. He knew damned well it wasn't the Atkinsons or Misty. So much for a private island.

Who the hell else is on my island?

"Whoever you are," he yelled, "come on out!"

Another groan sounded.

He glanced around the beach. He had no weapon, nothing to use to defend himself. Jumping from the dock to the sand, he moved toward the quivering bushes.

"Don't make me come in there after you."

He took careful steps, constantly eyeing the ground for a weapon. There! A broken branch, compliments of the storm. The end was sharp and thick.

He waved it in front. "I said get out here," he demanded. "Now!"

As Jonathan approached the tree line, he jabbed the makeshift sword into the foliage and moved closer to where there had been movement only seconds earlier.

"This is your last warn—"

A man stumbled from the bushes. Roland!

The young man hit the sand face-first, spurring Jonathan into action. He quickly turned the young man onto his back. Roland's eyes were closed, his breathing shallow and there was a bloody gash on the side of his head.

"Jesus, Roland! What the hell happened?"

There was a moan and fluttering of dark eyes. "Tyler?"

"Yeah, buddy. I'm right here. What happened?"

"Duke..."

Jonathan's heart pounded. "Did he do this to you?"

Roland nodded weakly. Then he said something Jonathan couldn't hear.

"What was that? Say that again, Roland."

"I said...he's got...a gun."

"What would a lawyer need with a gun?"

"Don't think he's a...lawyer," Roland said.

"Me neither. Can you walk?"

"I think so."

Jonathan helped Roland to his feet. "I'll take you back to the house. Marvin will look after your wound."

"Thank you."

"Don't mention it."

They made their way through the woods.

"How's the head?" Jonathan asked.

"Nothing that a few shots of whiskey wouldn't cure," Roland replied. "Did you get the supplies?"

"What supplies?"

"They're on the beach."

Jonathan muttered a curse. He'd never even noticed the boxes.

"The radio—" Roland staggered but Jonathan caught him.

"Did you bring the parts, Roland? Is that what's in the boxes?"

Roland's mouth stretched into a smile. "No parts."

"Then what in God's name are you grinning about? How the hell am I going to get off this blasted island?"

Roland's smile deepened. "With the *new* radio I brought you."

Jonathan grinned. "You're a freaking genius!"

The house came into view, and within minutes, Jonathan had Roland resting on the couch.

"It's just a flesh wound," Marvin assured him. "Might need a couple of stitches, but that's about it."

"There's always a lot of blood with a head wound," Mrs. Atkinson added.

"Roland brought a new radio," Jonathan told them. "It's on the beach."

"Then what are you waiting for?" Marvin asked. "Get going after our girl."

Our girl.

Jonathan had to smile. Yes, Rhianna had become their girl.

He should've realized that sooner.

Jonathan headed back to the beach at breakneck speed. When he emerged from the trees and stepped onto the sand, he scoured the tree line until he found the cardboard boxes. He ripped open the first box and rummaged through it. Painting supplies. No radio. It wasn't until he opened the third box that he found it.

"Roland, my friend, you deserve a raise."

In the bottom of the box were two batteries.

"Mainland Coast Guard, this is Angelina's Isle. I have a 911 emergency."

"Angelina's Isle, what's your emergency?" a male voice asked.

"This is Jonathan Tyler...Lance. My boat's been stolen and the person who took it assaulted Roland Saunders, my captain."

"Does he need medical assistance?"

"He has a head wound, but he seems okay."

"Any sign of concussion?"

"No."

"Do you know who took your boat, Mr. Lance?"

Jonathan took a deep breath to steady his nerves. "The man's name is Charles Duke. He said he was a lawyer from Miami." He gave a brief description and waited for the Coast Guard operator to verify the location of Misty's Dream.

Minutes later, the man said, "Misty's Dream has been sighted about halfway to the mainland, Mr. Lance."

"So you'll get to it before this Duke guy reaches land."

"Unfortunately, we have a bit of a problem."

Jonathan's heart sank. "What kind of problem?"

"All our watercrafts were sent out to a fire on a container ship. The nearest Coast Guard craft is at least an hour away from your boat's position. They'll never get there in time. The helicopter's out there too, along with the police boats."

"Shit."

"Do you have another boat?"

"No. But you could try Denny Dorchester down at the Bayshore Marina. If he's there, he'll come get us."

"Mr. Saunders should go to the hospital. To be safe."

"Will do."

There was a pause. "We're doing everything we can, Mr. Lance. I'll contact the Royal Bahamas Police. They'll have men onshore looking for your boat. And I might be able to get the helicopter. I'm sure your boat will be returned undamaged."

"It's not the boat I care about. Duke's taken a woman with him. A...friend of mine. Rhianna McLeod."

"Are you saying this is a possible hostage situation?"

"I believe so."

"We'll do everything we can, Mr. Lance. Hold tight. We'll get back to you."

The man signed off, leaving Jonathan frustrated and worried. Even if a helicopter was sent out, they couldn't do much. It's not like it could land on the water.

He paced the beach.

A horn blasted and he whipped around. A speedboat was coming in. Fast. Seated at the wheel was an older man with silver hair. The man waved. That's when Jonathan recognized him.

Denny Dorchester.

Jonathan ran to the end of the dock. "How the hell did you get here so fast?"

"I was in the area monitoring radio frequencies," Denny yelled, easing the boat up alongside the dock.

"You heard my emergency call?"

"Yeah."

Jonathan jumped in and Denny turned the boat toward the open water and opened the throttle.

"What were you doing monitoring calls?" Jonathan asked. "That's not something you do every day."

"I met Duke earlier. I didn't like him. Or trust him. I almost left the marina, but then I turned around and followed him out. I was on the southwest side of Angelina's when I saw him heading back to the mainland. Without Roland." He swallowed. "How is he?"

"He's fine, Denny. Marvin's looking after him."

"Then let's catch this bastard."

"When we do, I'm not sure what'll happen."

Denny gave him a worried look. "What do you mean?"

"Duke took something from me."

"Misty's Dream?"

"Rhianna McLeod. The best dream I ever had."

Denny grinned. "About time, Tyler!"

"If you tell anyone I said that, "Jonathan said with a scowl, "I'll fire Roland."

Chapter 31

Rhianna tried to relax as she watched Angelina's Isle disappear from view, but Charles Duke's gaze seemed to rest on her far too often. He was making her nervous.

"Are you sure we'll get through security in time?" she asked him.

"It won't be a problem. Trust me."

She shivered. Trust him? She didn't even know him.

But JT does.

Still, she couldn't picture JT hiring this man as his lawyer.

"So do you handle business cases?" she asked, bored.

Charles glanced at his briefcase. "Business cases?"

"Like lawsuits or mergers."

Charles chuckled. "Oh. Yes, I handle some."

"What about criminal cases?"

"No, I don't touch those."

They drifted into an awkward silence.

"You said JT relapsed," she said finally. "Did he go to the hospital?"

"I believe so."

"But he's still alive, right?"

Charles turned and stared at her. "I can assure you that JT is still alive. But I don't think he's got long."

Rhianna sighed. "I never should've left him."

"You seem to care an awful lot for the old guy."

She stared at him. "Of course I do. He's been very kind to me."

"Has he?"

"Of course he has. Why would you suggest otherwise."

Charles held up a hand. "I'm sorry, Rhianna. I didn't mean to suggest anything. It was just a slip of the tongue. I'm sure he's been very good to you."

It took her a moment to realize he'd used her first name. She didn't like that one bit.

"Mr. Duke, did you handle JT's will?"

This comment seemed to throw the man off.

"I, uh..." Charles cleared his throat. "Yes, I did."

"Do you know if he's leaving anything to his son?"

Charles glanced over his shoulder at her. "Whose son? JT's?"

"Yes," Rhianna said impatiently.

"I didn't know he had a son."

"You just met him."

Charles stared at her. "The guy on the island?"

"Jonathan Lance."

There was a stunned look on Charles face. Then he muttered something and turned his back to her.

What the heck is going on? Rhianna wondered.

Certainly, JT would have left something for Jonathan and Misty. And his lawyer would know that. In fact, it seemed odd that Charles didn't even know about Jonathan. Why would JT hide that fact from his lawyer?

Because Charles Duke isn't who he says he is, came the answer.

Rhianna swallowed hard. "What law firm did you say you work with?"

"I didn't."

There was a drawn out pause, then Duke twisted in the seat. "Ms McLeod, it appears we've come to a crossroads of sorts. You're a very inquisitive young lady, but you're not that smart." He pulled out a gun and pointed it at her. "Don't do anything foolish."

Rhianna gasped. "What are you doing?"

"I'm taking what I want."

The way he said this, combined with the way he looked at her, made her tremble. She'd seen that look before. In Peter Waverley's eyes, right before he raped her.

"Please," she said. "Let me go. I won't say a word. I promise."

Charles smiled. "Don't worry, my love. *I* promise to take very good care of you."

With the gun in hand, Winston twisted in the seat. To keep an eye on his prize. Rhianna McLeod was a beauty. He couldn't wait for their first evening together.

"Who are you really?" she asked.

He smiled. "I'm the man who's going to show you a good time." He saw the fear in her eyes and it excited him.

"Why me?" she said, her voice wavering.

He shrugged. "Blame that on JT Lance."

"So you *do* know him. How?"

"We've done...business together." He checked the GPS. "Right on course."

"Where are you taking me?"

"To paradise." He paused briefly. "Lance will pay a lot of money to get you back. He values you quite highly. I suspect his son does too."

"So you're doing this for money."

"Among other things." He eyed her up and down. "I'm sure we'll have fun together. Before the money comes in."

"I don't think so," Rhianna said tightly.

Winston swung the gun toward her. "My dear, it won't do you well to argue with me."

"So you're a rapist then."

His face burned. "Don't call me that. Ever."

It was clear she got the warning when she turned away.

"You know, good old JT spent a lot of money trying to locate you," he said, changing the subject. "A lot of money and a number of years. I guess I can't blame him."

Rhianna whipped around. "What are you talking about?"

"Lance and I go way back. He hired me years ago to check into some of his employees and to investigate a couple of businesses he wanted to...acquire. He's not as squeaky clean as he likes people to believe." He wiped a trickle of sweat from his brow. "Then a few years ago, he asked me to find you. It took me a long time to find out why he wanted to find you so badly."

"Why?"

He laughed. "I'll let the old guy tell you that himself. I can assure you though, you won't like what he has to say."

"You mean about his affair with my mother?"

Winston stiffened. "Where did you hear that?"

"From a reliable source."

"Who?"

"It doesn't matter, Mr. Duke."

He scowled. "Oh, but I think it does, my dear."

Well, this was a new development. One he'd never expected. If JT had had an affair with Rhianna's mother, it could be a huge problem. Or an advantage.

"None of that really matters," he muttered. "How you feel about JT Lance makes no difference to my plan."

"Which is?"

"To become a very wealthy man and enjoy your company. At least until I return you."

The trembling in Rhianna's hands stopped.

"You're going to let me go then?"

"When this is over," he said, watching her.

There was more to Rhianna than just beauty. The woman was stubborn and defiant. He liked that. If there was one thing he hated it was an easy conquest. He enjoyed the chase too much. Taking down a worthy adversary was immensely satisfying.

He smiled.

The chase was on.

Rhianna stared at her hands, unable to keep her mind from straying to horrific flashbacks from her past. She couldn't go there again. She couldn't be the victim. She wouldn't.

But how could she fight this man?

She peered from beneath her lashes, glancing about the boat for a weapon. Other than a couple of lifejackets and a pair of binoculars hanging from a hook near Charles, there was nothing that could help her. Even if she somehow managed to push him overboard without ending up in the water herself, she didn't know anything about navigating a speedboat. She'd have to wait until they reached the mainland. Certainly, someone there would intervene. Except no one knew she'd been taken hostage.

Her heart sank.

Jonathan thought she was in safe company with his father's lawyer.

Rhianna let out a tearful sigh.

The only thing she could do was wait. Once they were on land, she'd find a way to either escape Charles Duke's grasp, or she'd enlist someone else to help.

She gazed across the water, praying that another watercraft would appear. But it seemed they were alone. The only boat she could see was a tiny white blur, and it was probably heading in the opposite direction.

"Is Charles Duke your real name?" she asked, determined to get as much information out of the man as possible.

"No."

"So what is your name?"

He looked over his shoulder, his beady eyes staring into her soul. "You know what they say in the movies. If I tell you, I'll have to kill you."

She shuddered.

The man grinned, then resumed steering the boat.

"How much money do you think JT will give you?" she asked. "For me, I mean."

"Whatever amount I ask him for."

"You're pretty sure of yourself."

"No, I'm just sure of Lance."

Rhianna absorbed this for a moment.

"Did he really have a relapse?" she asked.

The man shrugged. "Who knows?"

"So he's not in the hospital," she said, relieved. "That's good."

She flicked a look behind them. The white dot of a boat she'd seen earlier was now hugging the shores of the northern islands. It almost looked larger, closer.

Someone please find me.

She batted away a tear and bit her bottom lip to keep it from trembling. She refused to cry. Her captor would take too much pleasure if she did.

She thought about Jonathan. She should've told him how she felt. If another opportunity presented itself, she would. She'd shout it to the world.

Jonathan, I love you.

In her mind, she created a scenario where Charles Duke was captured and she was set free. Jonathan would come running to her, relieved she was okay. He'd hold her and tell her that everything would be all right. Then he'd tell her that he loved her too.

It was a wonderful dream—until reality set in.

Jonathan was miles away on Angelina's Isle, waiting for a boat that would never come. He had no idea the danger she was in. So unlike the gallant heroes and white knights of enchanted fairy tales, Sir Lancelot wasn't going to come to her rescue on his trusty steed.

She'd have to escape on her own.

Charles Duke—or whoever he was—let out a grunt.

"There's the mainland," he said. "It won't be long now."

"Where are we going exactly? Do you have a house here?"

The man pointed the gun at her. "We'll be taking a short trip by plane. I'll have to warn you, if you try anything at all, I'll go back to Angelina's Isle and put a bullet in Lance Junior's head. One in his daughter's head too." He cocked his head to one side. "I never did meet her. How old is the young lady?"

When Charles licked his lips, Rhianna cringed. "She's just a baby."

The disappointment on the man's face was evident.

She gazed into the water. The temptation to jump in was overwhelming, but she knew she'd never make it to shore. She wasn't that strong of a swimmer. Besides, Charles would catch up to her and drag her back onboard anyway. Or worse, he'd run the boat over her and she'd be butchered by the propeller.

As the shoreline came into view, she searched for the marina. If they landed there, she'd look for Roland and Denny. Surely one of them would help her.

The docks came into view and she held her breath.

"Shit," Charles Duke said.

Rhianna's hopes soared. "What's wrong?"

"Nothing."

As the man steered the boat away from the marina, Rhianna caught sight of flashing lights and men in black uniforms. Some of them waved frantically.

Rhianna took a breath and jumped from the seat. "Help! I need help!"

Without warning, something slammed against the back of her head. She collapsed to the deck of the boat. Moaning, she touched the back of her head. "You shot me?"

Charles hovered over her, one hand on the wheel. "I will next time." He hefted the gun in his hand.

A wave of dizziness washed over her and she closed her eyes. When she opened them she saw that Charles was preoccupied by the police on the beach. He kept the boat at a safe distance from shore.

Something made Rhianna glance over her shoulder. When she did, she bit back a gasp.

A boat was speeding toward them.

Please let that be the police.

As the boat approached, she saw two men aboard. One of them was Jonathan.

Her heart raced. *He's coming for me.*

Now all she had to do was make sure Charles kept his focus on the beach.

"What's that up ahead?" she asked, moving closer to the man.

"I don't know," he snapped. "Do I look like a goddamn tour guide?"

"No. Sorry."

The boat veered toward a cove, and she saw a row of small planes parked near a runway and terminal.

"Is that where we're going?" she asked, terrified. "Are we flying somewhere?"

"I told you. We're taking a little trip to a very safe place."

Rhianna flicked a covert look over her shoulder. Jonathan was so close now that she saw him hold up a hand and bring a finger to his lips. She gave a nod and turned back to Charles. She had to keep the man distracted to cover up the sounds of the approaching craft.

"Are we flying somewhere hot and sunny?" She gave Charles a false smile. "With beaches? Because I really love beaches. And hotels. I once went to Mexico and sipped margaritas with those cute little umbrellas in them on the beach. Have you ever been to Mexico? Maybe we could go there."

The Mexico bit was a lie. The only time she'd left the United States was when she flew to the Bahamas.

Was that only weeks ago?

She rambled on about anything she could think of, knowing her prayers had been answered. Her knight in shining armor was on his way.

Chapter 32

Jonathan sucked in a deep breath. "There she is."

When Rhianna glanced at him, he motioned for her to be quiet. The closer they could get to Misty's Dream, the better.

"Roland said Duke has a gun," he said to Denny. "I'll need some kind of weapon."

"I have some small tools."

"I don't think I'd get close enough to use one."

Denny scratched his head, then he smiled. "I don't have a gun with bullets, but I do have something almost as good." He unlatched a small metal door and handed Jonathan a bright orange flare gun. "It's an Orion, breech loaded, 12 gauge. It should do the trick."

Jonathan nodded, then gazed across the water.

Misty's Dream was only twenty yards away.

The thought of Duke laying a finger on Rhianna made Jonathan's blood boil. If the man was lucky, Jonathan would let him live.

Fifteen yards.

He could see the fear in Rhianna's expression, even though she was doing her best to distract Duke.

Ten yards and closing.

As Denny's boat neared Misty's Dream, Jonathan stood ready, the flare gun in his hand.

"Move alongside them," he said to Denny.

Rhianna watched surreptitiously and he waved at her to move to the back of the boat. As she inched away, Duke grabbed her arm.

"Duke!" Jonathan yelled, their boats nearly touching. "Let her go!"

Charles Duke scowled and pushed the lever. As the boat sped up, so did Denny's. They were neck in neck, and Jonathan knew there was only one thing he could do.

When the two boats met within inches, he leapt forward. He hit the side of the boat, the flare gun skittering out of his hand and across the deck of Misty's Dream. He clung to the side of the boat, his feet bouncing hard on the surface of the water.

Rhianna moved toward him.

"No!" he tried to warn her.

Helpless, he watched Duke's gun come down hard between Rhianna's shoulder blades. Down she went, but not before she sent Jonathan a silent plea. *Help me,* her expression said. Then he watched as she crumpled to the deck.

"Rhianna!" Jonathan shouted.

He scrambled over the side and into the boat. When he scrambled to his feet, the boat had slowed and Duke had the gun trained on him. The bastard was grinning.

"So...you're JT's son, huh?"

Jonathan said nothing.

"Tell your buddy to back off," Duke warned. "Or I'll put a bullet in the lovely Rhianna's head." He turned the gun on Rhianna, who wasn't moving.

Jonathan motioned for Denny to move back.

"You bastard," he seethed, turning back to Duke. "If you've hurt her, I'll—"

"You'll what? Kill me? Kind of hard to do when I'm the one holding the gun, don't you think?"

"I don't know what you had planned, but you're not taking Rhianna anywhere. The Coast Guard is on its way and the police have been notified."

Duke scowled. "Yes, I noticed. You're a very meddlesome fellow."

Jonathan tried a different tactic. "Let me take Rhianna and you can go where you want. I can even get you money, if that's what you're after."

"I don't think so. In fact, I think I'll shoot you and dump you overboard." He aimed the gun at Jonathan and smiled. "Say bye-bye."

Before Jonathan had time to move, he heard a loud popping sound. Charles Duke's suit jacket immediately went up in flames. Stunned, the man dropped the gun. With a look of confusion, he staggered backwards. For a split second he was balanced at the very edge of the boat. Then he tumbled backwards into the water.

Rhianna, though dazed, had found the flare gun.

"Oh God," she moaned. "Did I kill him?"

Jonathan flew into action. Reaching her side, he helped her to the seat. "You're safe now."

"What about that man?" she cried.

Jonathan shut down the engine, then peered over the side. Duke was floating face down in the water a few yards behind the boat. He watched as Denny pulled up alongside the man's body and dragged him aboard. A minute later, Denny glanced at Jonathan and shook his head.

"He got what he deserved," Jonathan said.

Rhianna's eyes widened. "He was going to shoot you."

"Yeah, but he didn't."

She let out a sob. "I thought he'd kill us both. You have no idea what he had planned for me. He was going to—"

He pressed a finger against her lips. "Shh...no more talk about him. You're safe, Rhianna. That's all that matters."

The terrified look in her eyes was more than he could bear.

He kissed her. Softly.

While Denny securely tied Misty's Dream to his boat, Jonathan pulled Rhianna closer. Her arms slid up to his neck and she pressed her body against him. She was shaking.

"I would've died if anything happened to you," he murmured against her lips.

She sighed and curled into his arms. "I was praying you'd rescue me, but I thought you'd bought into his lies."

Jonathan shook his head. "I didn't like him the second he showed up on my doorstep."

Her eyes caught his. "But how did you know I was in danger?"

"Roland." When she gave him a puzzled look, he said, "The bastard knocked Roland out on the island and left him in the bushes. When he came to, Roland found me and told me Duke had a gun."

"His name's not Duke."

"Who was he?"

"He didn't say. But he knows your father."

"How?"

"I'm not sure exactly. He said he was going to blackmail your father. He figured JT would pay a lot to get me back."

"If JT hadn't, I would have."

"Really?" She stared up at him, her green eyes pooling with unshed tears. "Why?"

"Why do you think?"

Rhianna shrugged. "I don't know."

"Because I love you, silly," he said, kissing her thoroughly. When he broke for air, he gazed into her eyes. "I was an idiot. I should've told you before you left."

"Say it again," she whispered.

"I love you, Rhianna McLeod. I love you and I want to wake up with you every morning for the rest of my life."

The smile she gave him was almost blinding. "I love you too,

Jonathan Tyler Lance."

He pulled away. "I'm coming back with you."

"To Miami? Charles lied. Your father didn't relapse."

Jonathan breathed a sigh of relief. "That's good. But we're still going back to Miami. I need to see him. I have to try to make things right. Before he..."

She kissed him. "Take whatever time you're given."

Rhianna was right. No matter how much time JT had left, Jonathan wanted to spend some of it with his father. Misty needed to see her grandfather, connect with him. And Rhianna needed to know the truth about her mother.

There's no future together until we know the truth.

Chapter 33

When the taxi drove them away from Miami International Airport, Rhianna glanced at Jonathan and squeezed his hand. "You're doing the right thing."

Sitting between them, Misty giggled. Though still raspy, her laugh sounded joyful.

"Grandpa hasn't seen you since you were a baby," Jonathan signed.

Rhianna watched him converse with his daughter. He'd grown more comfortable with signing, and with Misty's expanding vocabulary.

The little girl tucked a strand of dark curls over her ear, and Rhianna saw the instant Jonathan realized something was different.

"Misty, you're wearing your hearing aid," he said.

Misty nodded. "Rhianna told me I'd miss out on hearing the music."

"What music?" He looked at Rhianna.

"There's music everywhere if you stop to listen for it." She smiled at Misty. "Magic music."

For a long moment, the three of them listened to the sounds of Miami—the buzz of traffic, horns honking, traffic helicopters whirring overhead. The city was alive and breathing.

"Thank you," Jonathan mouthed over the top of Misty's head.

"You're welcome," Rhianna replied.

In this moment, she was happier than she'd ever been.

"Are we going to live here, Daddy?" Misty signed.

"Maybe one day. This is just a holiday."

"Good. Because I miss Lancelot's Landing."

"So do I," Rhianna said, catching Jonathan's eye. "By the way, you never told me where the name Lancelot's Landing came from."

Jonathan shrugged. "It was Misty's idea. When I first bought the island, we just called it Angelina's. When Misty was about five, she wanted me to read the same story over and over again. Sir Lancelot and the Ice Castle. We'd play at sword fighting with broken branches."

Rhianna raised a brow. "You?"

"Yeah," he said with a chuckle. "Misty came up with the name. The funny thing is she didn't know about the Lance legacy. She's always signed her last name as Tyler." His expression grew sad. "I guess I was trying so hard to distance myself from JT that I didn't see what it was doing in my life. And Misty's."

"And you believe me now that I didn't know who you were?"

"Yes, I believe you."

Relieved, Rhianna stared out the window at the passing traffic and buildings. Soon her entire life would change. Part of that change included Jonathan and Misty, a change that thrilled her. But she was still nervous about facing JT.

What would she say to him?

She thought of the day she'd first arrived in Miami. She'd been so overwhelmed by the expansive city and so scared about her future. Meeting JT had changed all that. Now she was getting ready to ask him some very difficult questions. What if the answers made things worse?

She flicked a worried look at Jonathan.

For now she had to leave everything up to destiny. Fate had dropped her on JT's doorstep months ago. Then on Angelina's Isle. Now fate was playing with all their futures.

I'll fight for my future if I have to, she thought, as the taxi pulled into the circular driveway in front of Lance Manor.

They clambered from the taxi, each one taking in the massive home and elaborate grounds.

"Home sweet home," she whispered.

Rhianna stepped inside first, leaving Jonathan and Misty outside on the porch. She figured he'd probably need a few minutes to gather his courage. Dropping her suitcase on the floor, she removed her jacket and hung it in the foyer closet.

The front door opened.

Jonathan poked his head inside. "Is the coast clear?"

"For now. Even if we bump into Higginson, the man won't bite." She gave him a sweet smile. "I promise."

Misty followed her father inside, her eyes two moons as she stared at the rich décor. "Is this a castle, Daddy?"

"Almost."

"Does Sir Lancelot live here?"

Rhianna burst out laughing.

"This is Grandpa's house," Jonathan explained.

As Misty skipped around the foyer, Rhianna watched Jonathan. She could tell he was nervous. He kept wiping his palms on his pants.

Moving close, she took both his hands, then stood on her tiptoes to kiss him.

"What's that for?" he asked.

"You look like you're hurting."

"I am." He touched the corner of his mouth. "I hurt here."

She kissed the spot.

"And here," he said, touching his centre of his lips.

Rhianna was happy to oblige.

"Excuse me," a voice said.

She pulled away quickly, her cheeks reddening. "Higginson. I didn't see you there."

"Apparently," the man said wryly.

Jonathan smiled. "It's been a long time, Higginson."

"That it has, Master Jonathan," the butler said, shaking Jonathan's outstretched hand.

"You don't seem surprised to see us," Rhianna said.

Higginson shrugged. "We thought you might cut your trip short, once you realized whose island you were on."

"So you and JT concocted this whole plan?" Jonathan asked.

"We knew she could convince you to come home."

"But why didn't you just tell me?" Rhianna asked. "I went in blind, thinking I was going to some resort hotel."

Higginson cringed. "I apologize about that. I wanted to tell you, but JT thought…" His voice faded. With a sigh, he said, "It's best if JT tells you himself."

"We've already figured out a few things," Jonathan said. "We have a lot of questions."

"I'm sure JT will answer them. Let me prepare him for your visit. I'll come get you in a few minutes. In the meantime, Master Jonathan—"

"Just Jonathan, please."

"In the meantime, sir, make yourselves at home. Miss McLeod, why don't you take the child and Jonathan upstairs to unpack? I'm sure you'll be staying for a while." Higginson turned cleanly on one heel and disappeared down the hall.

Misty tugged on Jonathan's jacket. "Daddy, is that the king?"

"No, honey. You'll meet the king later."

"Are we going to sleep in this castle?"

"Yes, Misty, we are. This will be our home for a bit."

Rhianna felt a surge of hope and promise in his words. "Come on, you two. Let's go upstairs and pick out your room."

"Does the king have a Sir Lancelot room?" Misty asked her.

"I don't think so, sweetie, but I'm sure we can find you a pretty garden room with lots of flowers."

As she followed Jonathan and Misty upstairs, Rhianna wondered how the meeting between Jonathan and JT would go. Would they finally mend their relationship? Or would the past continue to separate them?

While Jonathan helped Misty unpack, Rhianna took in the familiar surroundings of her bedroom. It seemed like forever since she'd slept in the bed or admired the painting of the Lady in the Mist. She stared at it now, taking in the intricate detail of a master's brush. The foliage was detailed down to tiny veins in the lush plants, and she swore she could almost smell the flowers. She'd never owned anything so beautiful. Or so valuable.

She traced a finger over the artist's indecipherable signature—Jonathan's signature. She recognized part of the floral design from the one he'd painted on her body.

She shivered. It seemed like such a long time ago

A knock sounded.

"Come in," she called.

"Misty's unpacked," Jonathan said in the doorway. "She's having a nap in her room. The trip really tired her—" He stopped dead in his tracks, his eyes widening. "What is the Lady in the Mist doing here?"

"Your father gave it to me for my birthday."

He strode up to the painting and caressed the frame. "He bought it?"

"If you want it back—"

"No," he said. "It's yours now. It's just strange to see it here. The gallery sold it to a collector. But I never knew who."

"You'll probably find there are a few of your paintings here. I've seen at least twelve with your signature on them scattered throughout Lance Manor."

Jonathan shook his head. "I don't get it. He hated that I wanted to be an artist. Said it was a hobby for lazy people, not a respectable career." His voice grew bitter. "He was so pissed when I told him I was going to paint instead of take over Lance Industries. When I married Sirena, I couldn't even talk to him without him judging all my shortcomings."

"So you left."

"What else could I do? He was a tyrant."

"I think you'll find he's changed."

"I'll have to see it to believe it."

She sighed. "Jonathan, if there's one thing I've learned in my line of work it's that people who are dying have a deep need to make amends. JT knows he's made mistakes. I believe he regrets them dearly."

"We'll see, won't we?" He stared at her. "What if he tells you he had an affair with your mother? What if he tells you your parents weren't the happily married couple you've been told they were?"

"I'll deal with that when the time comes."

Higginson appeared in the doorway. "Sorry to interrupt you, Miss McLeod, but JT is bellowing for you. And Jonathan."

Rhianna smiled. "Then we'd better get moving."

"See," Jonathan grumbled. "JT hasn't changed a bit."

She hoped with all her heart that he was wrong.

Sitting in the armchair in his room, JT rubbed his legs. His palms shook slightly.

Nerves.

He had a lot to atone for and he prayed it wasn't too late. The thought of seeing his son after all these years frightened him. Jonathan could be a stubborn one.

Takes after his old man, JT thought.

Dressed casually in tan slacks and a white dress shirt, he waited impatiently for his guests, although it seemed strange to think of his son as a *guest.*

And what about the child? he wondered, scouring his mind for his granddaughter's name. *Mimi? Melanie?*

He scowled. His memory, or lack of it, frustrated the hell out of him.

There was a soft knock on his door.

"Come on in," he called, pasting what he hoped was a smile on his face.

Rhianna entered first and his smile grew genuine.

"I'm so glad to see you," he said.

Rhianna crossed the room and planted a kiss on his cheek. "It's good to be ho—back," she said.

JT pretended not to have noticed the slight slip, though it hurt him deeply that she no longer thought of Lance Manor as home. He hoped to rectify that. Soon.

"How are you feeling?" she asked him.

"Like Death is waiting to throw me a welcome party."

"Ever the optimist," a deep voice said.

Jonathan stepped into the room.

JT studied him. "You look older, Jon."

"I *am* older."

"I'm glad you're here."

Jonathan stared at him. "Are you?"

"Yes."

There was a moment of awkwardness before Rhianna piped up. "We have a lot of questions."

"I am sure you do." JT motioned to the two chairs Higginson had dragged in earlier. "Please have a seat. Both of you." When they were seated, he said, "I'm really happy you're both here. I wasn't sure how long you'd stay away."

"We left right after Rhianna was rescued," Jonathan said dryly.

"W-what?" JT looked at Rhianna, his heart pounding in his chest. "What do you mean, *rescued*?"

"You know a guy named Charles Duke?" his son asked.

JT shook his head. "I don't think so."

"He said he was your lawyer. He told us you had a relapse and that you needed Rhianna back home. But he wasn't planning on taking her home. He had some other destination in mind."

"My God," JT whispered. "What did he look like?"

"Short fat guy with mean eyes."

JT was filled with dread. "Winston Chambers. He's the private investigator I hired to find Rhianna." He gave Rhianna an apologetic look. "I had no idea he'd go after you. He said he'd leave you alone if I paid him. Which I did."

"The bastard was blackmailing you?" Jonathan asked, visibly enraged. "Why didn't you go to the police?"

"I couldn't. He had information..." JT's voice faded as he stared, bleary-eyed, at Rhianna. "He didn't hurt you, did he? I couldn't forgive myself if he did."

"No, he didn't hurt me, JT. I'm perfectly fine."

"Where's the bastard now?"

"He's dead," Jonathan replied.

"I'm so sorry. I never meant for any of this to happen."

JT looked away, hoping no one would see him crying.

Rhianna noticed the slight shaking of JT's shoulders.

"It's not your fault, JT," she said gently. "It all worked out in the end."

"But Chambers—"

"Chambers doesn't matter anymore," Jonathan interrupted. "There are more important things to discuss. Like why you sent Rhianna to Angelina's Isle."

"To bring you back, of course."

"But why didn't you just tell me where I was going?" Rhianna asked.

JT eyed her. "Would you still have gone?"

She knew he had a point. If he'd asked her to go to some island in the Bahamas and bring back his wayward son, she'd have suggested he find someone else.

"I thought if you went and got to know Jon," JT said, "you'd...well, fall in love. That way when I die, my money will take care of all of you."

Jonathan jumped to his feet. "When are you going to learn that it's not your place to mess with other people's lives?"

"I needed to see you, son. I knew you'd never come if I asked."

"Well, I'm here now, aren't I? So what's so bloody important that you had to drag us back here?"

"I don't know where to begin." JT's voice trembled.

Rhianna leaned forward and touched the old man's arm. "Start from the beginning. When you met my mother."

"You know about that?"

"Not the whole story."

"I was in Bangor on business. I met Rhianna's mother and father on my last night there." He glanced down at the floor. "It was all a horrible accident. But I was to blame."

"What are you talking about?" Rhianna asked.

"The night your parents were killed."

JT said this so softly that she thought she'd misunderstood. "But you knew my mother before that day, JT. You had an affair with her. Remember?"

He shook his head. "I *do* remember. But you've got it all wrong. I never had an affair with your mother. The night I met your parents, an important business deal had fallen through. I was pissed about it and scared of the financial ramifications. I was driving back to my hotel room. It was very late." He looked at her then, his eyes filled with torment. "I was on my cell phone, arguing with Jon's mother. I wasn't paying attention to the road. Or the ice."

A tight feeling gripped Rhianna's chest. *Oh God...*

JT swallowed hard. "I had no idea I'd headed into oncoming traffic until I hit them."

Rhianna gasped. "No!"

"Yes. I'm responsible for your parents' death."

This was far worse than she'd imagined.

"But it was a hit and run," she cried out.

"I'm not proud of what I did," JT said hoarsely. "I had a business that was falling apart, nearing bankruptcy. And my family was relying on me. They would've been destitute without me. So, yes, I ran. But not before I checked on your parents and called for an ambulance."

Rhianna's eyes filled with tears. "My father was dead on impact."

"No," JT said. "He was alive when I got to him. He said *'Anna'* and then he died."

"Oh my God," she said with a moan.

"When I realized your mother was pregnant," JT said, "I knew I had to call it in. I called 911 right away, using your father's cell phone. That's when I saw his wallet on the seat. I needed to know their names. For some reason that was vital to me." He took a deep breath. "I found the photo of your mother. Susanna. I don't know why I took it. I don't even recall doing so." He paused. "You look so much like your mother."

Rhianna's mind reeled. She didn't know what to say.

"All these years," Jonathan said, visibly dazed, "you let me believe you'd had an affair."

"I didn't know how else to explain having Anna's photo. The guilt was excruciating, overwhelming." JT gave a weary shrug. "Maybe I wanted someone to blame me for something. So I let you."

"Did my mother say anything before she died?" Rhianna asked.

"She told me about you. She asked me to take care of her baby." A sob escaped him then. "I stayed with her until I could hear the ambulance."

"But you left them," Rhianna cried.

"I know, and there's no excuse for my cowardice. I tried to make things right. I sent money anonymously to your aunt and uncle, but when they died and you went into foster care, I lost track of you. I am so very sorry, Rhianna."

JT's admission filled her with overwhelming sadness. She couldn't even look at him. Or Jonathan. All she wanted to do was to run to her room and lick her wounds.

"Rhianna," JT whispered. "Can you ever forgive me?"

She couldn't speak. She was afraid of what would come out of her mouth.

"I think she needs some time," Jonathan told JT.

Rhianna walked to the window and stared out over the professionally landscaped lawns and perfect flowerbeds. Her parents probably would have given anything to live in a home like this. But they were never given the chance. Because of JT. Because he wasn't paying attention.

Was Jonathan's father really to blame, or was it fate?

Her own words to Jonathan came back to haunt her.

People who are dying have a deep need to make amends.

Could she forgive JT? Was it as easy as just saying the words?

She didn't think so.

Someone touched her shoulder.

"Are you all right?" Jonathan asked.

She crossed her arms protectively. "I don't know. I'm numb."

Flicking a look over her shoulder, she watched JT. He was slumped in the chair, his head in his hands. Quiet sobs came from him—tired, worn out cries of a man who'd suffered, who was still suffering.

Did she want him to suffer more?

No.

Her parents were gone. She'd lived with that knowledge all her life. What was done was done. There was no going back, no way to change things. She'd lost her parents. JT had lost his marriage and his son. Jonathan had lost his father for so many years.

Hadn't they all paid enough?

Exhausted to the bone, she cleared her throat. "I forgive you, JT. Too many people have already suffered because of this secret. I forgive you."

The old man broke down and she hurried to his side, holding him in her arms until his weeping grew quiet. Over his shoulder, she watched Jonathan. He stared at her with a look of amazement. And something else. Hope?

Her heart did a quick pitter-patter.

That evening, after JT had retired to his room, Rhianna sat in front of the living room fireplace, staring into the flames. Her life had taken a series of unexpected turns, the last one leaving her breathless and unsure of the future.

She felt utterly lost.

What now?

Jonathan entered the room, a pensive look on his face.

"Did you have a good talk with your father?" she asked.

"Better than I'd expected. JT was quite taken with Misty."

"I expect the feelings were mutual."

He grinned. "Yeah."

Jonathan sat down on the couch beside her, his thigh brushing against hers. She'd never been more aware of him. Or more terrified of what he might say.

"So what now?"

"Well, I guess that depends, Rhianna."

"On what?"

He took her hand. "On whether you can forgive me like you did JT."

Rhianna tried to ignore the stirrings in her heart. "What do you need forgiveness for?"

"For thinking you were sent to spy on me." His thumb caressed her hand. "For not believing you."

"Water under the bridge."

"Is it?" His gaze intensified. "I've been a complete dolt. A real idiot."

"Go on," she said, smirking.

He entwined her fingers with his and stared at their hands. "I can't imagine going back to Angelina's Isle without you."

Her breath caught in the back of her throat.

"It won't be the same there without you," he added. "And Misty really needs you."

"Misty?"

He pulled her close. "*I* need you, Rhianna."

"For how long?" she asked, gazing into his deep blue eyes. "Summer fling time is over."

"I don't want a fling." He kissed her palm. "I want forever."

Rhianna could feel her pulse beating rapidly.

Is he saying what I think he's saying?

"What's that mean, 'forever'?" she asked.

"Don't you know?" He leaned forward and kissed her. "I love you, Rhianna McLeod."

"Really?"

He chuckled. "Do I have to prove it?"

"Yes, please."

When his lips met hers, Rhianna no longer felt lost. Her knight had found her and rescued her, and soon he would sweep her away to his island castle.

She could think of nothing she wanted more.

Epilogue

Three days later, Rhianna and Jonathan were married in the backyard of Lance Manor. Misty, the flower girl, sprinkled pink hibiscus and rose petals on the grass. Behind her, JT escorted Rhianna down the floral aisle and stood next to his son as the best man. Mrs. Atkinson was Rhianna's Matron of Honor, while Marvin, Higginson, Roland and Denny watched on and exchanged hoots, nudges and proud grins. Rhianna couldn't have asked for a more perfect wedding.

"I have one request," JT told her just minutes before they walked down the aisle.

"Anything, JT."

"I want to see Angelina's Isle. I think I'd like to spend my last days there. With you, Jon and…Sirena."

"Misty," she corrected, kissing the old man's cheek.

"Yes…Misty." He gave her a confused look. "Isn't that what I said?"

She smiled. "Of course it was."

When the music started, JT said, "I think there's a party going on in there."

She took his arm. "Let's go see, shall we?"

They left for Angelina's Isle the next day.

That first night back on the island, Rhianna stood on the dock and watched the setting sun. Seated in a wooden chair beside her, JT stared out at the ocean, a soft smile on his grizzled face. It was wonderful to see him smiling. He'd been experiencing excruciating headaches that day.

"It's beautiful here," JT said, almost to himself. "The air is so fresh and fragrant."

"That was my first impression," she said.

A rustling of leaves made her glance over her shoulder.

Jonathan stood on the beach, waiting for her. In his arms was a large canvas.

"I'll be back in a few minutes," she said, patting JT's shoulder.

"Take your time, dear. I'm not going anywhere tonight."

Rhianna strolled along the dock, her heart filled with love and happiness. "What have you got, Jonathan?"

"A new painting. I couldn't wait to show it to you."

He turned the canvas toward her and she let out an audible gasp. In the painting, a woman reclined on a chaise lounge, with a wisp of silk draped across her naked body and long, auburn hair flowing down over her breasts. Around her neck, she wore a single string of pearls. Her expression was dreamy, as though she were waiting for her lover.

The woman had Rhianna's face.

"You can't sell that," she said, horrified.

Jonathan grinned. "I wasn't planning to."

"Why'd you paint it then?"

"To remind me that you're mine."

Rhianna wound her arms around his neck. "You need reminding, Sir Lancelot?"

"Each and every day, milady," he whispered, his lips capturing hers.

~ * ~

Acknowledgements

There are so many people I'd like to thank, because without all of you, Lancelot's Lady wouldn't exist. So thank you to...

Stan Soper and everyone at Textnovel.com, for giving me a platform to showcase my work on, including Lancelot's Lady.

Dorchester Publishing, for partnering with Textnovel in the "Next Best Celler" contest, and for giving me a reason to go back to an older manuscript and bring it back to life as my debut romantic suspense.

My fans, friends and family who read Lancelot's Lady, especially those who voted, subscribed, commented and kept me consistently in the top 3 "Most Popular" for the contest.

My wonderful beta readers, who pointed out the flaws in the story: Karen Nicholson, Shell Bryce, Kelly Komm.

Author extraordinaire Gail Bowen, whom I so appreciate for the valuable writing advice and for the cover blurb.

Christiana Cameron, my "Next Best Celler" pal, for all your encouragement and support during the longest 5 months of my life—and yours too, I know.

Author Karen Wallace, for allowing me the use of her children's book title, Sir Lancelot and the Ice Castle.

Waheed Rabbani, for participating in one of my contests and supplying me with the name "Winston Chambers", for a character I hope you'll all love to hate.

A special thanks to Michael Iwasaki and Philip Louie at www.24-7PressRelease.com, for being my media sponsor for all things Lancelot's Lady.

My husband Marc and daughter Jessica, for supporting me on this journey and many others. My undying love and gratitude always.

Romantic Suspense by Cherish D'Angelo

Lancelot's Lady

Novels by Cheryl Kaye Tardif

Whale Song
The River
Children of the Fog

Divine series:

Divine Intervention

Novelettes by Cheryl Kaye Tardif

Remote Control

Short Story Collections by Cheryl Kaye Tardif

Skeletons in the Closet

Praise for Cheryl Kaye Tardif's novels

Whale Song

"Tardif's story has that perennially crowd-pleasing combination of sweet and sad that so often propels popular commercial fiction...Tardif, already a big hit in Canada...a name to reckon with south of the border." —*Booklist*

"*Whale Song* is deep and true, a compelling story of love and family and the mysteries of the human heart...a beautiful, haunting novel." —NY Times bestselling novelist Luanne Rice, author of *Beach Girls*

"A wonderfully well-written novel. Wonderful characters [that] shine. The settings are exquisitely described. The writing is lyrical. Whale Song would make a wonderful movie." —*Writer's Digest*

"Tardif again leaves a lasting mark on her readers...Moving and irresistible." —*Midwest Book Review*

The River

"Cheryl Kaye Tardif specializes in mile-a-minute pot-boiler mysteries." —*Edmonton Sun*

"Exciting and vivid. Tardif's latest novel sweeps readers along into uncharted, wild Canadian territory. A thrilling adventure..." —*Midwest Book Review*

"Cheryl Kaye Tardif has once again captivated readers...*The River* combines intrigue, science, love and adventure and is sure to keep readers clamoring for more." —*Edmonton Sun*

"Plunge into *"The River"* for a thrilling adventure! Get carried away by the flow of Tardif's magical prose...Author Cheryl Kaye Tardif hooked me from the first sentence." —Betty Dravis, author of *Dream Reachers*

Divine Intervention

"This chilling page-turner is a genuine Canadian crime novel...Tardif gives her readers plenty of twists and turns before reaching a satisfying ending." —*Midwest Book Review*

"An exciting book from start to finish. The futuristic elements are believable...plenty of surprising twists and turns. Good writing, good book! Sci-fi and mystery fans will love this book." —*Writer's Digest*

"[An] excellent suspenseful thriller...promises to keep readers engrossed...Watch for more from this gem in the literary world..." —*Real Estate Weekly*

"Believable characters, and scorching plot twists. Anyone who is a fan of JD Robb will thoroughly enjoy this one...*Divine Intervention* will undeniably leave you smoldering—and dying for more." —Kelly (Christian) Komm, author of *Sacrifice*

Keep reading for an excerpt of…

*Book **1** in the **Divine** series by Cheryl Kaye Tardif*

Divine Intervention

Prologue

It always began with the dead girl in her closet.

Every night when little Jasmine opened that closet door she expected to see lovely dresses and hangers—not a child her age strung up by a pink skipping rope, her body dangling above the floor…unmoving.

The dead girl had long blond hair. Her blue eyes stared blindly and were surrounded by large black circles. Her mouth hung open in a soundless scream. The pink rope was tied tightly around her neck, a thick pink necklace of death. A purplish-black bruise was visible and ugly.

The most unusual thing about the girl, other than the fact that she was swinging from a rope in Jasmine's closet, was that her skin and clothing were scorched.

Gagging, little Jasmine stepped back in horror.

When the girl's lifeless body swayed gently from a sudden breeze Jasmine let loose a cry of terror and raced down the stairs, searching anxiously for her parents.

"Daddy?"

Her throat was constricted and dry.

"Mommy?"

Then she screamed. "Mommy, I need you! Help me!"

In the lower hallway, the shadows quickly surrounded her.

Then she saw them.

Red eyes flashing angrily at the end of the hall.

Jasmine took a hesitant step backward. She tried to run but her feet would not cooperate. Her small body began to shake while the eyes followed her.

Glancing over her shoulder, she noticed a listless form moving toward her, arms outstretched—pleading.

The girl from the closet wasn't dead anymore.

Blistered hands reached for Jasmine.

The girl's mouth yawned and a horrendous shriek emerged.

Trapped and terrified, Jasmine began to scream…

1

Agent Jasi McLellan awoke from her nightmare screaming and drenched in sweat. Irritated by a piercing sound, she turned her pounding head and glanced at the wall beside her.

A technologically advanced video-screened wall, or *vid-wall*, had recently been added to her daunting security system. The wall was divided into four monitors—each coded for different activities.

The message screen flashed brightly.

Someone was trying to contact her.

"Receive message," she croaked.

She was rewarded with silence.

Jasi eyed the clock. *5:30 in the goddamn morning.* Who the hell would be calling her this early on her day off?

Glaring words flashed across the monitor followed by a voice, deep and urgent. *"Jasi, we need you! Ben."*

She was suddenly wide awake.

"Message for Ben."

When the system connected with Ben's data-communicator, she said, "Give me fifteen minutes. End message."

She glanced at the words on the screen and realized her *holiday* was over. She wondered for a moment what was so important that Ben had to interrupt her downtime. With two days left, she had hoped to catch up on some much-needed rest.

Crawling from beneath the sweat-soaked sheets, she crouched on the edge of the bed and reached for her portable data-com.

She checked the calendar.

A black *X* was scribbled over the date.

"Oh God," she moaned.

Today was her twenty-sixth birthday.

Jasi hated birthdays.

She pushed herself off her bed. In the dark, her toe connected sharply with the corner of the dresser and she let out a startled yelp.

"Ensuite lights on, low!"

Her *Home Security & Environmental Control System* immediately raised the lighting to a soft muted glow. Some days she was very thankful she had allowed Ben to install *H-SECS* in her new apartment. Of course, on the days when she couldn't remember a command or the security code to her weapons safe, Ben would get an earful.

Limping to the bathroom, Jasi shook her head.

Could this day possibly get any worse? Maybe I should go back to bed...wake up tomorrow.

She hugged her arms close to her chest and stepped into the ensuite bathroom. Parking her butt on the toilet, she stared at her throbbing toe. Scowling, she stood up, leaned tiredly against the sink and examined her reflection.

That's when she remembered her recurring nightmare.

"Why can't you leave me alone?" she whispered to a dead girl who wasn't there.

Frowning at her puffy, shadowed green eyes, Jasi splashed cool water on her face and rested her elbows on the edge of the sink. She traced a finger over the small scar that ran down the left side of her chin. It was barely noticeable, except to her.

Spurring herself into action, she cast a self-deprecating glance at her hazy image and then headed for the shower.

"Shower on, massage, 110 degrees," she commanded as she removed her panties and nightshirt. "Radio on, volume 7."

Music from her favorite rock station pounded in through the ceiling speakers as she stumbled into the large shower stall. Stretching hesitantly, she relaxed her tense muscles and breathed a sigh of relief when the steamy water sent thoughts of a dead girl swirling down the drain.

Jasi lathered her long auburn hair and stood under the spray, allowing the water to massage her scalp. Grimacing, she slid a wide-toothed comb through the tangled mess of wavy locks. Her hair had a mind of its own. More than once Jasi had threatened to chop it off but she was afraid she'd end up with a 'fro.

Couldn't have that. No one would take her seriously.

Her central data-com beeped suddenly.

Her fifteen minutes were up.

Cursing under her breath, she spit toothpaste into the sink, barely missing the soap dispenser.

"Data-com on!"

"Hey there, sunshine!" a male voice boomed. "You miss us?" Benjamin Roberts, her friend and partner, didn't wait for a response. "Divine has issued a Command Meet. He says he's sorry to cut your downtime short but we need you."

His voice followed Jasi as she returned to her bedroom and ordered the lights on full.

She sighed loudly. "It's not like I have anything better to do today. Like relax, go to a movie, or hook up with a handsome stranger for a night of passion."

She eyed the closet nervously, then whipped the door open and stepped back, unsure of what or who might emerge.

No one was there.

"Hey, *am* I interrupting something?"

She grabbed some clothes, slamming the door quickly.

"I *wish*! What's up, Ben?"

Stepping into a pair of casual slacks and a light blouse, she waited for her partner's answer.

"You still in the shower, Jasi? Maybe you should put up the vid-wall." She heard him snicker.

"Yeah right!"

"We caught a case near Kelowna—a fire." Ben's voice grew serious. "One victim, Dr. Norman Washburn, ER doc at Kelowna General."

Jasi frowned, and strapped on a shoulder harness.

Kelowna.

She hadn't been there in years. Not since the disastrous Okanagan Mountain forest fires of 2003. Now, nine years later, she would be returning. She'd have to take some precautions, prepare herself.

"Why'd they call us?"

"Sorry, Jasi. I know you're still officially on downtime, but this one is bad. They found a link to another fire. Two victims—a mother and child in Victoria. Unsolved."

There was a long silence.

"Ben?"

She heard a soft chuckle on the other end. "By the way, Jasi, Happy Birthday."

"How'd they link that one to the doctor?" she asked, ignoring the reference to her birthday.

When he told her what the crime scene investigators had found at the scene, Jasi grabbed her 9-millimeter Beretta, checked the safety and jammed it into the holster. Then she dashed from the apartment—a shadow hot on her heels.

A cab dropped her off at an isolated address in the West End. On the roof of a seedy-looking warehouse, a helicopter waited, its engine camouflaged by the busy drone of the streets below. Vancouver was a city in perpetual motion. A city that never slept.

Hiking her handbag over one shoulder, Jasi keyed in her security access code and spoke her name into the VR box. The Voice Recognition program was the latest addition to security.

When the door opened, she stepped inside a small airlock. A man in army greens and a brush-cut greeted her. He was loosely carrying a rifle in one hand.

"Hey, Thomas," she waved.

The weapons tech was tall and muscular, with a face like a pit-bull. Recognizing her, he cracked what was his idea of a smile. "Agent McLellan. Good to see you back."

Jasi removed the Beretta from her pocket and laid it in a clear plastic tray. The tray was carried on a conveyor into a hole in the wall where the gun was scanned and the registration was recorded.

Thomas buzzed her through.

She followed a short hallway that opened to a large room filled with computers and electronic equipment. Another guard escorted her through a body scan, metal and powder detector and a fingerprint analyzer.

The last stage was the Retinal Scanner Device.

"I spy with my little eye," the RSD tech, Vanda, greeted her cheerfully.

"Eyes that are puffy and bagged…and belong to a sixty-year-old," Jasi muttered when the RSD clicked off and Vanda waved her on.

"For a sixty-year-old, you're lookin' pretty damned good, girl," the woman teased.

"Yeah? Well, next time Divine calls me out on my downtime, I'll roll over and play dead!"

Jasi neared the final scanning gate.

It examined the small tracking device that had been surgically implanted in her navel. The tracker was used when an agent went missing—and for identification purposes. Especially if an agent's body was recovered in an unrecognizable state.

Benjamin Roberts greeted her from the other side of the gate. "Pass on through, oh Queen of Darkness." He made a sweeping motion with his black-gloved hand.

Thomas slid the tray with her gun toward Ben.

Examining it, Ben said, "You know, Jasi, we do have better weapons than this old thing."

She shrugged. "I know. But it has sentimental value."

He handed her the gun.

"Happy Birthday, Agent McLellan," Thomas called out.

Jasi glared at Ben, her eyes shooting daggers. "What'd you do? Take out an ad in the newspaper?"

"Naw, just a vid-wall ad on Hastings," he said, laughing. "Ouch! Watch that elbow!"

Jasi examined her co-worker, taking in his broad shoulders and gray eyes. Benjamin Roberts was in his mid-thirties. He was a tall striking man who wore Armani suits like a second skin fitted to every contour of his muscular body.

"New ones?" she asked, indicating his gloved hands.

"I needed a better lining."

She thought of how challenging it must be for him.

Ben was a Psychometric Empath.

If he touched someone, he often sensed flashes of thought or emotion. He wore specially designed gloves when he was out in public. Inside the black leather gloves, a protective coating blocked his empathic abilities. It was essential that he keep his mind fresh, so that he could focus on each case without unnecessary interruptions.

Ben was also an expert in various martial arts and the best profiler the CFBI had. He had been with the Canadian Federal Bureau of Investigators for over fifteen years, before it was ever known as the CFBI.

Back in the late 1990's, the Canadian government requested a more 'open-door' policy with the United States—-and the sharing of information. It started with computer programs designed to be accessed from either country so that information on every criminal perpetrator, rapist, pedophile, kidnapper, or serial killer was available at the touch of a keyboard. CSIS was still dedicated to protecting Canada's national security and focussed primarily on international terrorist activities.

Then in 2003, the CFBI was formally introduced as a Canadian counterpart to the previously established FBI organization in the US. Eventually the CFBI took over CSIS and integrated a variety of divisions. Agents were employed and deployed from either side of the border, anywhere they were needed.

Some agents were Psychic Skills Investigators—*PSIs*.

Of course, the public was naively unaware that both governments were implementing the use of psychics. Even now, in 2012, it was a closely guarded secret.

"Hey, Jasi! Ben! Over here!" a woman called.

Jasi's other partner, Natassia Prushenko, was tall and leggy—and had breasts Jasi would kill for. Her black hair was razor-cut in a short wispy style. Her sapphire eyes twinkled mysteriously. It had been almost two weeks since they had seen each other but Jasi immediately sensed that something was different about Natassia. Something other than the copper streaks in her jet-black hair.

Natassia passed her a sealed manila envelope.

Then she gave a similar envelope to Ben, saluting him cockily. "Agent Prushenko, reporting for duty, sir."

"Aw, cut it out, Natassia," Ben growled, rolling his gray eyes before pulling himself into the helicopter.

The woman smirked, then climbed in beside him. "Aye, aye, *mon capitaine.*"

Jasi curiously eyed Natassia.

Why, she wondered, was her friend grinning like a Cheshire cat?

When Ben leaned forward to talk to the pilot, Jasi nudged Natassia's leg.

"You'd better tell me what's going on."

"Later."

Jasi shrugged, then stared out the window. They were flying low under the canopy of clouds. As always, the beautiful British Columbia scenery with its lush forests and majestic snowcapped mountains entranced her.

When the flight ended, they landed safely on the heliport in the center of a gated complex. Perched high on the electric wall, numerous cameras zoomed in on their arrival. A sterile concrete field surrounded two large buildings in the center of the complex. Both held a reception area and countless offices.

Most were empty—a front.

To civilians, the complex was known as Enviro-Safe Research Facility. To Jasi and the rest of the CFBI, it was Divine Operations. Or *Divine Ops*, as most agents referred to it. But the real Divine Ops was not visible. It was actually a maze of underground tunnels and offices more than fifty feet below the surface.

"Well, now I *know* this is a big one," Natassia mouthed, her eyes glittering darkly while she followed Jasi from the heliport.

On the tarmac ahead of them, a man paced restlessly.

"Yeah," Jasi agreed. "A power-figure must be involved. I think this fire has someone hot under the collar."

She nudged Natassia and they hurried toward the creator of Divine Ops.

Matthew Divine's investigation of psychic phenomenon had initiated the construction of the first PSI training facility in Canada. The Federal government had listed the building as nothing more than a laboratory—one that researched the environment and its effect on people, animals, plant life and weather patterns.

The locals knew nothing of the CFBI's presence. They were unaware that a web of offices existed underground, stocked with high tech computer equipment. They had no idea that the people they saw flying in and out of Enviro-Safe were highly trained government agents with specialized psychic skills.

They *did* know that Matthew Divine and Enviro-Safe had brought prosperity to the area. When Enviro-Safe was first built, there was one existing town nearby. Originally called Mont Blanc, the town's name was changed in 2005.

Through a unanimous town council vote, it was renamed *Divine*.

Jasi straightened to her full five feet, eight inches as she reached Matthew Divine. He was a man of average height, average looks but above average intelligence. His long gray hair was tied back with a strip of leather. Intense brown eyes were framed with outdated tortoise-shell glasses. No one dared ask him why he hadn't gone for the ever-popular SEE—sectional eye enhancement—to restore his vision.

Divine's arms were crossed.

The grim expression on his clean-shaven face made Jasi gasp.

A serial killer was on the prowl.

2

Jasi followed Divine while he led the PSI team into the primary operations station—Ops One. An assortment of security scanners recorded each agent's various stats before admitting them to a small corridor. The same programmers that designed *H-SECS* created the Divine Ops security system. Ever since the kidnapping and murder of the Prime Minister in 2008, security programmers had been rallying to design a system that was impenetrable and virtually flawless.

Jasi allowed a technician to scan her with the paranormal electroencephalograph unit, an apparatus that recorded brain waves and psychic residue. This security precaution safeguarded PSI agents against overuse of their skills.

Heaving a sigh of relief, she smiled when the PEU flashed green. She was clear.

"Welcome back, Agent McLellan," Divine finally said with a curt nod. "I hope you enjoyed your well-deserved holiday. Sorry I had to cut it short. Have you been given details of the case?"

Jasi held up the envelope. "Ben told me that the killer left something behind...a lighter?"

Divine pulled her aside. "A *Gemini* lighter. Same as the one you received in the mail two months ago, Agent McLellan. The same brand found at a fire in Victoria last month."

They waited for Ben and Natassia to clear security, and then the four of them crowded into an elevator. When the elevator doors opened, an electronic voice informed them that they had reached the PSI floor where an expansive maze of halls and pale mauve cubicles lay before them.

"Happy Birthday, Agent McLellan," a co-worker greeted her.

Jasi whacked Ben in the arm, hard.

They wove through the maze of hallways, passing agents and technicians engrossed in their work. Artificial light hovered over occupied cubicles while the empty ones remained in darkness.

Abstract paintings lined the wall—someone's attempt at personalizing the underground lair. One painting showed a window opening onto a garden. Beside it, a photograph of a wooden maze tempted two rats to find their way out.

We're all just a bunch of lab rats, Jasi mused. *We live underground, running through this insane maze every day.*

Part of her wished that her downtime hadn't ended. On the other hand, two weeks of pretending to be normal, living in her empty apartment in North Van, had been about as much as she could take of herself. Even her plants couldn't live with her. The last ivy had died a slow, torturous death, its neglected soil shrinking from lack of water.

"Why didn't we hear about the Victoria fire a month ago?" she asked Divine.

"Victoria PD thought they had an isolated case last month so it didn't show up on our radar. Until this morning's case, just outside of Kelowna. The current victim is Dr. Norman Washburn. He was the head of Surgery at Kelowna General Hospital. He's also the father of Premier Allan Baker."

There's the higher influence.

Divine escorted them to the Command Office.

As they sat down around the conference table, Jasi opened the manila envelope and slid one picture from the stack of photographs.

A blond-haired man smiled confidently into the camera.

Premier Allan Baker.

Allan Baker was the youngest Premier ever voted in by any Province in Canada. Now, at thirty-two years old, he had set the precedent for bringing in young blood. Baker was now a front runner for Prime Minister of Canada.

She passed the photo to Ben, then carefully examined a surveillance photograph taken the year before, in which the Premier of British Columbia and Dr. Washburn were engaged in an intense argument.

Jasi recalled that the newspapers had created a frenzy when it was discovered that Baker's mother had given birth to the son of a prominent, *married* doctor. The scandal had almost cost Baker the position. It had cost Washburn his marriage.

Divine flipped a switch on the box embedded into the table in front of him. Two oak panels in the wall parted slowly, revealing a large vid-wall. He pressed the remote and a photograph of a lake appeared.

"Dr. Washburn's remains were found at Loon Lake early this morning. Loon Lake is less than an hour's drive from Kelowna."

The photo zoomed in to reveal a smoldering mass that was once someone's holiday home.

"Who reported it?" Jasi asked.

Without missing a beat, Divine answered, "Shortly after four o'clock this morning an anonymous caller reported a cabin fire near the lake. Fire fighters were sent to the area, and ten minutes later, the Kelowna PD arrived and secured the scene."

Jasi's eyes locked on Divine's. "How secure?"

Divine flipped to an aerial photo, revealing neon orange perimeter beacons that surrounded the crime scene.

"Kelowna PD has guaranteed that there has been no contamination of evidence—other than water, of course. The fire was almost out by the time the trucks got there."

Ben cleared his throat loudly. "We've heard *that* before. How'd they know there was a body?"

"Kelowna PD used an X-Disc," Divine explained. "As you are all aware, very few departments outside of Vancouver and the major cities have access to X-Discs. And our PSI division is the only unit to have the Pro version. Kelowna PD has one of the original prototypes."

"What's the estimated time of death?" Ben asked.

"TOD is between one and two this morning."

The wall photo switched to a black and white of the esteemed Dr. Washburn. The man had posed for the hospital staff photo as if it were a painful experience, his brow pinched in a wrinkled scowl. His receding white hair looked wiry and stubborn.

Like the man himself, Jasi thought.

She had met Dr. Washburn a couple of years ago during a symposium on children's health. The man had not impressed her. There was something about him she didn't like, something she couldn't quite put her finger on.

Divine turned to Natassia. "Forensics came back as a positive on Washburn. His dental scans matched. I'll need you to dig deep on this one, Agent Prushenko."

Jasi saw Natassia's head dip in agreement.

"We need any information pertaining to the victim. His life, his career—everything," Divine said.

Jasi rubbed her chin. "If this is his second fire, then what's the connection between the victims? What can you tell us about the Victoria fire?"

Divine's data-com beeped suddenly.

He examined it, then shook his head. "I'm sorry, Agent McLellan. I have a meeting with the Premier in half an hour. You'll have to upload that info into your data-communicators." He walked to the door, then paused. "The sooner you pick up your supplies, the sooner you can get your team moving. I need you at the Kelowna crime scene A-SAP. Allan Baker's going to want some answers—fast."

Divine held her gaze. "Get me some."

Then he left.

Jasi plugged her data-com into the Ops mainframe and began reading aloud while the computer uploaded to her portable. "Case H081A. Two victim's. Charlotte Foreman, sixty-three, and Samantha Davis...four years old."

Poor baby.

Her voice faltered slightly. "TOD is 9:05 p.m. on Charlotte Foreman. She was pronounced in the hospital. The child died shortly before. Smoke inhalation."

"Who called it in?" Ben asked.

"A neighbor. When the fire department got there the rain had already extinguished the fire. Victoria PD exhausted their leads. The case was cold. Until now."

Her eyes gleamed with determination.

"So we have jurisdiction over *both* fires, now that it's a serial arson case."

For the next half-hour, Jasi examined the evidence, including the fire investigator's statements and forensic reports on the two bodies found at the scene in Victoria. There wasn't much to go on. A cable truck would warrant investigating but other than that, no one in the neighborhood remembered seeing anything remotely suspicious.

"Let's start with Washburn and work backward," Ben suggested. "I'll call ahead, Jasi, and make sure that everything's ready for you in Kelowna."

He disappeared down the hall.

Meanwhile, Natassia continued flicking through the wall photos of the Washburn murder.

"See anything?" Jasi asked her, moving beside the dark-haired woman for a closer look.

Natassia pointed to the close-up of a strange melted mass of plastic. "There's a few possibilities. The X-Disc found IV tubing. Washburn was secured to his recliner with it. Funny thing, though. The recliner was fully extended."

Jasi chewed on her bottom lip, wondering why someone would bother to recline the chair...or use plastic IV tubing.

Wouldn't a rope have been better? And how did the arsonist get possession of the tubing?

"Back in a sec, Natassia. I have to get my pack."

She walked down a narrow corridor to a door marked *PSI Prep Room*. Swiping her ID card, she was buzzed inside. The room held a row of lockers lined against one wall.

She inserted her card into the slot on locker *J12*.

It beeped, then opened.

Removing a hefty black backpack, she silently cursed its necessary weight. She placed the bag on a metal table in the middle of the room and kicked the door to her locker shut. The zipper to the main compartment of the bag jammed. Frustrated, she tugged at it until it finally opened, revealing two thin flashlights, evidence markers, a piece of florescent chalk and other field supplies.

From a shelf above the lockers, she grabbed the last can of *OxyBlast* and shoved it inside the bag. Satisfied, she closed the backpack, heaving it over her shoulder.

Then she returned to Command.

"Okay, ladies, we better get moving," Ben suggested, poking his head through the doorway.

"Ladies?" Natassia asked with a laugh. "Jasi, did Agent Roberts just call us *'ladies'*?"

"Well, one of you certainly doesn't fit that description," Ben grumbled under his breath.

"Come on, Natassia," Jasi said with a snort. "Focus."

"I *am* focussing."

Watching her, Jasi chuckled. She couldn't help but admire Natassia Prushenko. Not only was the woman gorgeous, she had self-confidence up the ying-yang.

Natassia was a Russian immigrant. In some ways, she was a trade from the Russian government in return for favors from the PSI division. She spoke five languages and was the best VE Jasi had ever worked with.

And Jasi had worked with a number of Victim Empaths over the years.

Natassia had joined her team just over two months ago, during the Parliament Murders. Jasi had seen firsthand what her partner's skills could take out of her. A VE sometimes assimilated the emotions of the victim, to the point that it was almost impossible to separate—to come back to reality.

"Happy Birthday, Jasi. Great way to be spending it, huh?" Natassia's grinning mouth snapped firmly shut when Jasi whipped her head around.

"Okay, the chopper is ready," Ben announced.

Covering their ears, they dashed across the tarmac. The four-blade rotor of an Ops helicopter sliced through the air, droning and choppy. The sound was deafening until the pilot handed each of them a headset.

A few minutes later, they were onboard and gliding across the treetops.

"We'll do the scene first," Jasi said, plugging her data-com into the outlet in front of her.

Natassia nodded. "Okay. After that, I'll see if I can get a read off Washburn's remains. Maybe I'll get a hit. There's a good chance Washburn knew the perp."

"I'll get the reports for both fires and make some calls to set up interviews," Ben said, removing his gloves. "Then I'll start my profile. So far, what do we have?"

"A sick bastard who likes to set fires," Jasi murmured.

"Yeah, we have that. Hey, are you going to be okay in Kelowna? Do you need anything special?"

She handed him a short list. "Just this. I have everything else."

Ben read the list quickly, then keyed in the request on his data-com.

A few minutes later, his unit beeped a response.

"Everything will be waiting for you, Jasi. Just see the Chief of Arson Investigation on-scene."

She knew that her day would be long and grueling. She recalled the disaster that occurred years ago. A raging forest fire had swept over Okanagan Mountain, burning almost three hundred homes to the ground and destroying over twenty-five thousand hectares of natural forest.

As the private helicopter soared closer to the dreary crime scene, Jasi settled into the seat, pulled her long auburn hair up into a quick ponytail and closed her eyes. She would need to be alert and rested.

Agent Jasi McLellan could already taste the bitter smoke in the air.

And something more—death.

3

~ *Loon Lake near Kelowna, BC*

The helicopter deployed Jasi and her PSI team one mile from the fire. A fog of gray smoke greeted them. It hung in the air over the crime scene like a smothering electric blanket set on *high*. The scorching sun smiled down upon them, adding to the heat.

Fire trucks were parked on the side of a grassy field surrounded by thick trees and weedy underbrush. An oversized khaki-colored army tent had been pitched in the center of the field while an exhausted group of firefighters slept nearby in the shade. A variety of police vehicles slanted across the gravel road, blocking off public access.

A tired, sooty police officer strolled toward them. "Hey, Ben."

Ben grinned and introduced the man. "This is Sgt. Eric Jefferson, Kelowna PD."

"How's it hangin', Ben?" Jefferson asked, after introductions were complete. "Are you supervising this case?"

"Actually, *I* am," Jasi said, only slightly offended.

Ben grimaced apologetically. "Eric and I trained at the VPA range together."

The Vancouver Police Academy was highly regarded worldwide for its superior training of police officers. The academy owned acres of land outside the city limits. The rough terrain had been converted to a firearm training facility used by CFBI agents and police officers.

There was also a separate area for the bomb squad.

"A van's coming to get you," Jefferson said. "And someone'll be here any minute with the supplies you requested."

"Where's the Chief of AI?" Jasi asked him.

"Over by the tents, I think."

Jefferson glanced over his shoulder at an approaching truck. "Your supplies are here."

A police officer in his mid-forties, dressed in a fresh uniform, jumped from the truck. When he spotted them standing by the edge of the road his eyes narrowed. A firefighter wearing fire gear, minus the hat and mask, climbed from the passenger side carrying a bright red equipment bag. He had a stocky build and blond hair that was cut in a surfer style, long on the sides.

The man reminded Jasi of an advertisement for steroids.

She caught his eye and he aimed a withering look in her direction. Uh oh, she thought. *Steroid-man* wasn't happy to see them.

"Detective Randall," Jefferson murmured, indicating the officer. "He's the lead on the Victoria case."

"He *was* the lead," Jasi corrected him.

She watched while Randall and the stocky firefighter lumbered closer. When the two men reached her, she held out a hand.

"Agent McLellan, CFBI."

The detective winced at her words. Then his hand crushed her fingers, challenging her to back down.

Jasi squeezed harder until Randall let go.

After introducing her team, she caught Randall fighting with Ben for *alpha male* status. Detective Randall lost. Tension sliced through the air, thick with male testosterone. She saw Ben wave Eric Jefferson aside.

Jasi stole a glance at the firefighter.

The man's head was turned slightly away. On the shoulder of his jacket, a blue firefighter's patch flapped loosely in the breeze. *R. J. Scott, KFD*, the patch read.

"Have you got the supplies?" she asked him, feeling a shudder of pain behind her eyes.

Scott dropped the red bag on the ground, crouched down and jerked the zipper open. "Right here."

Her head began to pound. The smoke was invading her pores. She reached into her black backpack and extracted the can of *OxyBlast*. For half a minute, she sucked on the mouthpiece, inhaling pure oxygen and clearing her lungs.

"The oxy-mask is in the bag," Scott muttered in a voice that was hoarse from breathing in too much smoke.

When he brushed the hair from his eyes, she sucked in a puff of air. The left side of the man's face was scarred—a motley web of spidery burns.

"Hazard of the job," he shrugged when he noticed her shocked expression.

Detective Randall joined them. "You done here, Scott?"

"Yeah," the firefighter grunted.

Randall stared at Jasi and laughed rudely. "I don't know why she needs the mask."

Scott scowled at her. "Yeah, it's as useless as tits on a bull—unless she's gonna go into a live fire."

The men grinned at each other, then caught her eye.

"Detective Randall," she said coldly. "There are *many* things that are useless on a bull."

She allowed her eyes to slowly drift down past Randall's waist, locking in on his groin area. The man's face grew pinched, and then he muttered something indistinctly.

She turned her back and reached into the bag, removing the familiar navy-blue mask. It had a built-in filtration system that eliminated air contamination, giving the wearer a clean source of oxygenated air. Small and lightweight, the oxy-mask fit securely over the nose and mouth.

She drew it snugly over her head and adjusted her ponytail. Fighting back a feeling of claustrophobia, she took a deep breath.

"I'm fine," she assured Natassia who was watching her intently. "The residue is bad out here."

The oxy-mask muffled her voice.

"It wasn't *that* big a fire," Scott huffed.

"Not *this* fire. The Kelowna fire."

The firefighter eyed her suspiciously.

"What? That fire was years ago." The scarred side of his face stretched tautly and barely moved when he spoke.

"Agent McLellan?" Ben called out, hurrying to her side with Sgt. Jefferson in tow. "Everything all right here?"

"Everything's fine," she assured him.

Her head swiveled and her eyes latched onto Detective Randall's. "Right?"

The man flashed her a dangerous smile. "We don't need your help. Victoria PD is more than capable of handling—"

Jasi threw the man a frigid glare.

"This isn't a pissing contest, detective. The CFBI was called in and it's our case now. Both of them. And if you have a problem with that, then take it up with *your* supervisor."

Outraged, Randall tipped his head toward Scott, then stomped back to the truck and sped away in an angry cloud of dust. Scott watched him go. A second later, he rasped a quick goodbye and headed for the field. Joining a small group of firefighters, he pointed in Jasi's direction and circled one finger beside his head.

Crazy.

Cursing under her breath, she spun around and looked Eric Jefferson directly in the eye.

"What about you, Sgt. Jefferson? You have a problem with us being here?"

The police officer smiled. "Whatever gets the job done, Agent McLellan. That's my motto. With a serial arsonist on the loose we can use all the help we can get."

"Too bad those two don't feel the same way," Jasi growled, casting a shadowed look in Scott's direction.

Jefferson glanced toward the field. "Scott's just a rookie with a big mouth. Randall, on the other hand, he's a hotshot. He needs the collar." He nudged his head in Detective Randall's direction. "It's guys like *him* you need to worry about…and maybe Chief Walsh."

"I'll take care of the chief," she muttered. "As soon as I find the man."

Jefferson elbowed Ben. "If Scott or Randall get in your way, you let me know. I'm the CS Supervisor."

Jasi caught a brief nod then the man headed for a patrol car.

"Good luck with the chief," Jefferson called over his shoulder.

When the officer was gone, Ben removed two mini-cans of OxyBlast from the equipment bag and passed them to Natassia. Natassia tucked the cans into Jasi's backpack and pulled out a small protective nosepiece. She handed it to Jasi who carefully tucked it away in the top pocket of her black PSI jacket.

"Thanks," Jasi smiled beneath the oxy-mask.

She shoved her arms through the straps of her pack, shifting it slightly so the weight was balanced on her back.

Natassia nudged her. "Let's find the AI Chief. He's supposed to be here somewhere. Then we can get a ride to the scene. Man, I'm starved! I could go for lunch right about now—maybe a nice marinated steak."

Jasi grinned. "Yeah, with sautéed mushrooms."

"Excuse me for interrupting your culinary exchange," Ben nudged dryly. "I'm going to talk to the police. You gonna move or stand there swapping recipes all day?"

Laughing, Jasi adjusted her backpack while Natassia picked up the red bag. Then they headed toward a group of firefighters.

Jasi noted their smoke-covered faces and sooty yellow fire jackets. The men were in the middle of a serious discussion and no one noticed their approach.

"Excuse me, gentlemen," Natassia called out.

The men stopped talking.

Oh Jesus! They're gonna start drooling any minute.

Jasi rolled her eyes when she saw the firefighters focus in on Natassia like a swarm of bees. One of the firefighters stepped forward, grinning unabashedly. The man's eyes slowly perused Natassia's body, then his ice blue eyes turned and rested on hers. One eyebrow lifted when he registered the mask she wore.

She stiffened slightly, registering his obvious contempt.

"Well, well. What have we here?" the man drawled sarcastically. "Uh, ma'am? The fire is out now. There's no need for that mask."

The firefighter was over six feet tall—a lumbering, magnificent personification of man. He had eyelashes that most women would die for, and eyes that were such an unusual pale shade of blue that she wondered if he had visited a SEE office. A jagged scar intercepted his right brow, narrowly missing his eye. A slight cleft in his chin gave him an air of stubbornness. Dark wavy hair clung to his head and she couldn't help but wonder what it would feel like to run her fingers through those curls.

Jasi held his gaze while she examined him like a lab specimen in a jar. Built like a tank, she thought.

"I think maybe you're a bit lost, ma'am," he said, his lip curling disdainfully.

He turned toward the men, brushing her off like an annoying wasp at a barbecue.

She stared at the back of his head and then flipped her badge. "That's Agent McLellan, not *ma'am*. Where's the chief?" Her voice was cool, her eyes unwavering.

"Whoo-eee!" the man whistled when he caught sight of her ID. "An agent with an attitude. How rare!"

He shifted so that he was standing in front of her. Behind him, some of the men snickered loudly.

Jasi's smile was deadly sweet. "Listen, you arrogant asshole. When I find the chief and report you I'll have you on desk duty for a month. Now where is he?"

The man's eyes snared hers, turning her knees to mush.

Suddenly he reached for her arm, gripped it firmly and led her away from the laughing eyes of the firefighters. She felt the heat of his fingers through her jacket, branding her as his possession.

Natassia nudged her sharply. *"Jas—"*

"Shh!" Jasi interrupted her, glaring up at the man whose tanned fingers still curled around her upper arm. "I could have you up on charg—"

"Check out his shoulder patch!" Natassia hissed.

Jasi glanced down. Then her eyes found the patch.

Walsh, Chief of Arson Investigations.

Her eyes traveled back to the man's face. His expression was dark and smug. For a second her composure flickered. There was something annoyingly attractive about the man.

But damned if she would let *that* cloud her judgement.

"Brandon Walsh, at your service," he said blandly, interrupting her thoughts. "AI *Chief* Walsh, that is."

Jasi ignored his outstretched hand and felt her temper rising when his eyes scoped Natassia's hip-hugging jeans and tight blouse. *Men!*

When he turned to issue a command to the firefighters, Jasi couldn't restrain the snicker that erupted from her throat. The back of the man's fire jacket was well worn. The lettering in some places was covered with black scorch marks.

Walsh, Chief of Ars In stig tions.

"Arse, all right," she muttered under her breath.

Abruptly, Walsh turned, piercing her with a frigid stare. Then he frowned and jerked his head.

"This way, *Agent* McLellan."

"Now isn't he a fabulous piece of work?" Natassia mumbled in her ear. "Check out the size of those hands."

"Natassia!"

Although Jasi had to admit, his hands were well shaped—like the rest of him.

Beside her, Natassia giggled beneath her breath. "You know what they say about large hands—"

"Shhh! Wouldn't want him to hear you. It might go to his head."

And that's big enough already!

She followed Walsh to a table standing beneath the shade of a tent.

He pulled out a chair beside his, offering it to her.

"You gonna tell me why you're wearing that mask?"

Jasi's eyes fastened on his and she took the chair across from him instead. "Allergies."

Walsh watched her for a long moment. "As the AI Chief, I've been informed of your…uh, special team. I wasn't given much info though."

"What have you got so far on the victim?"

"We've only received a few of the reports. Dr. Norman Washburn, age fifty-eight. He's the only victim. The fire originated in his livingroom where Washburn was tied to his recliner with IV tubing."

"Time of death?"

"Estimated TOD, one to two a.m.," Walsh replied. "We believe he died from smoke inhalation. We'll know for sure when the autopsy's in."

"What about neighbors? Anyone see anything?"

Walsh shook his head. "The cabins are separated by trees and bushes. He had no immediate neighbors."

"Did you ask around?" she asked impatiently.

"Listen," he said glibly. "I'm well aware that we've been ordered by the CFBI to cooperate with your team, but personally, I think AI is capable of handling this ourselves. And I don't really buy into the whole psychic thing."

She detected a trace of bitterness in his voice.

Jasi bit back her reply, frustrated.

She was sick and tired of having to defend herself—and her team. This wasn't the first time that someone had questioned the PSI's value.

"Chief Walsh, we've got two fires, three murder victims and few leads to go on. We're here to aid this investigation, not hamper it. You're not too macho to take help wherever you can get it, are you?"

Walsh laughed. "Macho? Now there's an outdated term."

Jasi refitted her oxy-mask.

She desperately wished she could tear it off her face and rip into the man before her. His attitude grated on her and left her feeling uneasy.

Walsh pointed to a Qwazi laptop and touched the screen with a stylus.

"Here's the data from the X-Disc. Have a seat and read through it. And yes, we asked around. No one saw anything. I'll go check on the other agent. Where'd he go, anyway?"

"Agent Roberts is busy drafting up a rough profile and arranging for transport to the scene," Natassia spoke up for the first time.

"Upload the data, Natassia," Jasi ordered. "*I'll* go check on Ben."

She cast a warning look in the AI Chief's direction. "I'm counting on your support. Don't get in my way, Walsh."

The man raised a well-shaped eyebrow. "I have no intention of getting in *your* way. Just stay out of mine."

She clenched her teeth. "Trust me, I'd be happy to stay away from you."

"Jesus, thanks. I think. And here I thought I was irresistible."

Jasi huffed in exasperation.

The man was insufferable. The sooner she finished her job here, the sooner she could put Brandon Walsh out of her mind.

Walsh accompanied her outside, and slipped on a pair of dark sunglasses.

"Need anything else?" she asked tightly.

"Yeah. What's Agent Prushenko's role?"

"She's a Victim Empath."

The man stared blankly, his lip curling in disbelief.

"She picks up vibrations—pictures from the victims," she explained. "Usually she sees their final moments."

"Yeah, right," he scoffed.

Jasi gripped Walsh's arm, her eyes flashing angrily.

"Agent Prushenko has empathic abilities, whether you believe in them or not. She's been a PSI for eight years, traveled worldwide and is recognized as one of the best VE's in the CFBI."

She wanted to slug the man.

Walsh grinned. "What about you?"

"I've been with PSI for almost six years. That's all you need to know."

"What do *you* do?"

"She reads fires," Natassia interjected, poking her head from the tent.

Wordlessly, Jasi glared at her partner.

"He needs to know, Jasi. Otherwise he's useless."

Brandon Walsh—useless?

Jasi hid a sly grin. "I can usually tell you where and how a fire started. Sometimes I pick up the perp's last thoughts or the last thing he saw."

"She's a Pyro-Psychic," Natassia bragged. "Jasi is the best there is."

"Jasi?" Walsh smirked.

"That's *Agent* McLellan to you!" Jasi snapped.

She'd make Natassia pay for that slip-up.

Oops, Natassia mouthed silently, raising her open hands in the air.

"Time for you to leave, Walsh," Jasi said rudely. "I'm sure there's something out there for the Chief of AI to do. Just remember we're running the show here."

Walsh's breath blew warm against her ear. "We'll see about that."

Then he hurried from the tent. "See ya later…*Jasi*."

With her eyes glued to his back, Jasi cursed aloud.

"Not if I can help it!"

Brandon Walsh walked away from the tent, unsure about the PSI's role. He had heard of the Psychic Skills Investigators in his dealings with various police departments, but his cases rarely required CFBI intervention. Or interference, as he thought of it.

As the AI Chief, he was compelled to assist the CFBI in any investigation involving serial arsonists. And that didn't sit too well with him—not one bit.

He'd show Agent Jasi McLellan who was boss.

After all, wasn't he the one responsible for capturing the arsonist involved in the Okanagan Mountain forest fires of 2003? He had led the AI team that had tracked down the arsonist and the accelerant used to set the blaze.

The press had blamed an unattended campfire for the raging fires that consumed a massive portion of the BC forest. Then a week later, it was rumored that a single cigarette had ignited the blaze. That was before the public ban on smoking became official—before people were restricted to smoking in the privacy of their homes, in well-ventilated smoking rooms.

Brandon had never believed the fire had started from a cigarette. He personally sifted through acres of destroyed forest, searching for a clue. He had explored the land until he discovered an abandoned cabin deep in the mountains.

There, he found remnants of liquid methylyte and zymene, highly flammable chemicals used in the underground production of Z-Lyte. Z-Lyte, with its sweet musky scent, had become the hallucinogenic drug of the new generation.

Public homeowner records listed Edwin Bruchmann as the owner of the cabin. An hour later, Bruchmann was in custody. When the old man was escorted into an interview room by his caregiver, Brandon was disappointed to discover that Bruchmann suffered from Alzheimer's.

Brandon's leads were slowly disintegrating—until his suspicions turned to the caregiver. Gregory Lawrence, thirty-nine, had been employed by Bruchmann for the past two years and had access to all of the old man's documents. But Lawrence denied knowing anything about a cabin.

"When was the last time Mr. Bruchmann visited his lakeside cabin?" Brandon had asked the caregiver.

Lawrence's face had registered confusion.

Then, without thinking, he had blurted, "You idiots! Edwin Bruchmann's cabin is not by any lake. See? I told you, you have the wrong person. Mr. Bruchmann's cabin overlooks the *valley*."

Brandon had smiled then. "I thought you knew nothing about the cabin?"

"I, uh..." the man stuttered. "Well, I m-might have heard about it once. But that doesn't prove anything!"

A knock on the door halted the interrogation and a detective passed Brandon a toxicology report.

"Maybe not," Brandon had agreed. "But this sure does."

Earlier he had recognized the sweet-smelling body odor common with Z-Lyte users. Suspicious, he offered Lawrence a can of pop. When the man had finished it, Brandon dropped it into a plastic bag and handed it over to the lab for analysis.

It came back positive for Z-Lyte.

The case was immediately closed, Gregory Lawrence locked away, Bruchmann established in a care facility and Brandon promoted to AI Chief.

All accomplished without any outside help.

And Brandon certainly hadn't needed a PSI!

This new case was no different, he reasoned. What could Agent Jasi McLellan possibly offer?

Psychic mumbo-jumbo?

He laughed suddenly, adjusting his shades.

How could the woman expect him to believe she had the power to see into a killer's mind?

I'd have to see it to believe it.

4

Jasi fumed indignantly while she waited for Natassia.

"I've uploaded all pertinent info from Walsh's laptop," her partner grinned. "And a few extra files to boot."

"I don't want to hear it, Agent Prushenko," Jasi scolded, covering her ears with both hands. "You know better than to illegally hack into another investigator's computer."

Even if he is an ass!

"Hacking?" Natassia said with a grin. "Hey! Chief Walsh gave me permission to upload. Not my fault if some extra files found their way onto my data-com. It's not as if he'll know."

Jasi sighed. One day, her friend was going to hack into the wrong person's files. And then there'd be hell to pay.

A dark green van rolled up alongside them.

Ben sat in the driver's seat.

"The ME's already taken the remains to the coroner's office," he said as they climbed inside. "Natassia will have to get her reading later."

Jasi sat in front and cautiously peeked out the window toward the tent.

Brandon Walsh was insolently leaning against a wooden support post, his legs crossed at the ankles. His candid gaze caught her off guard.

If I'm lucky, the posts will come crashing down and knock him unconscious.

As they neared the crime scene, Jasi readied herself.

The unpaved road was a mess of mud and water. The van lurched forward into potholes, stopping suddenly every once in awhile to navigate carefully over the boggy ground. It ventured down a narrow lane and into the thick brush. Spruce and cedar trees surrounded the vehicle, long branches scraping restlessly against metal.

Ben drove cautiously down the road, cursing loudly when the tires spun rebelliously.

"This is the worst part of it. There's grass up ahead."

Sure enough, the marshy ground opened to a grassy field. The ground hardened and they parked a few yards from what was once a rustic summer cabin.

Stepping out of the van, Jasi surveyed the scene.

The emptiness hit her, assaulting her senses. The area was devoid of life—except for her PSI team.

Off to one side, charred wood and clumps of black mud covered a cement pad. Washburn's cabin. Perimeter beacons were spaced every twenty feet. The beacons emitted a six-foot-high screen of orange light that quarantined the area. Anyone stepping through the beam would automatically trigger an alarm that would then activate a GPS, pinpointing the intruder's location and identity.

Jasi stepped closer to the scene and surveyed the damage.

"Okay, *shake 'n bake* time."

This was her ritual—something she said before entering every crime scene.

"Natassia, you're on data. Remember, don't tell me anything that you've gotten from the X-Disc. The less I know the better."

Jasi turned to Ben. "While we're inside you can send in the X-Disc Pro. Maybe we'll get lucky—fingerprints, trace fibers. Hell, anything would be good right about now. We need a break, something."

Natassia brought out her data-com and programmed it for automatic voice recording. With a simple voice command, the data-com would pick up every word.

Jasi opened her backpack and pulled out the *OxyBlast*.

"Give me a sec."

She peeled back her mask and took a few quick puffs of oxygen. Then she grabbed the nosepiece from her pocket and slipped it over her nose. Once the mask was attached to a cord on the side of her jacket, she pocketed the *OxyBlast*.

Ben tugged on Natassia's arm. "She can't use a mask when she's reading so—"

"I know," Natassia said, cutting him off. "Keep an eye on her."

"Stop talking like I'm not here," Jasi groaned. "I'm not deaf, you know. And I don't need babysitters. Come on, Natassia."

When they reached the edge of the crime scene, Jasi entered the code on the main beacon to deactivate the perimeter alarm. The blackened ruin of the cabin beckoned her closer. Ashes fluttered in the breeze and she walked slowly, so as not to disturb them. Smoke from the extinguished fire teased a trail toward her. She could taste its acrid bitterness.

A man died here, she thought. Burned beyond recognition.

"Voice record on!" Natassia ordered.

Jasi closed her eyes, anxious to clear her thoughts. She stood at the edge of the crime scene, her hands stretched above her. Trying to relax, she brought her arms slowly to her sides.

Focus. Deep breaths…in, out.

The wind began to stir. She could hear birds in the distance. *Breathe.* The smoke clung to her skin and swirled around her body. It entered her mouth, assaulting her senses.

In her mind, she saw Washburn's cabin. She could visualize it as it once was. Smoke rising from a chimney, the curtains ruffling in the breeze.

A body strapped into a recliner, unmoving.

Jasi took a step forward, one step closer.

The darkness sucked her in, deeper…

The man muttered a curse. His fishing rod had disappeared again. Maybe he was just getting too old.

Maybe 'old timer's' had kicked in.

"Son-of-a-bitch! Where did I put it?"

I observed him from the bushes, and laughed scornfully at the old doctor's complete lack of attention. He was easy prey. I wrapped the IV tubing around my hands, testing its strength. I saw the moment the old man noticed the fishing pole I had leaned up against the railing. I crept forward and slipped behind a large screen that separated part of the deck.

Then I held my breath.

Dr. Washburn, with his snow-white hair and paunch belly, teetered through the doorway onto the deck.

Fate had delivered him to me.

I pulled a black ski mask over my face. Then I crept up behind him, reaching above his bent head and brought the tubing around his neck. I could feel him buckling and straining beneath my hands.

"Don't fight it, Doctor," I whispered in the man's ear.

His body slumped forward and I dragged him inside the cabin. Hoisting the unconscious man into an old leather recliner, I tugged his inert body until his head rested at the top. Leaning over, I gripped the lever and reclined the chair. I quickly wrapped the rope around his body, looping it around his neck.

And then I sat on the threadbare sofa.

And waited.

I heard the doctor groan a few minutes later. I laughed when he cried out in terror at finding himself tightly tied to the chair. A rope of tubing bound his legs, waist, shoulders and neck.

"I wouldn't try to move your legs too much. The more you move, the tighter the tubing will get around your neck. It's a neat trick I learned."

I reached for the gas can at my feet. The diesel was Super Clean. Only the best for the best. I poured it around the chair, savoring the horrified expression in the doctor's face. The fumes were strong and my eyes teared slightly.

"Why me?" he cried.

I stared at him for a moment, daring him to remember me.

"Because you burned me once."

I reached into the pocket of my jeans, pulled out a Gemini lighter. The gas can leaked diesel behind me as I carried it toward the door.

I peered deeply into the old man's eyes. He sobbed like a child and I watched a tear roll down his wrinkled cheek.

"Who are you?" he croaked, his eyes bulging with terror.

Without answering, I flicked the lighter in my hand. I lit a piece of newspaper, then heard the old doctor scream as I tossed it toward him.

"I don't know who you are!" the old man shrieked. "I don't know you!"

The fire licked the floorboards, searing the old cedar planks. It crawled voraciously up the chair, over his writhing body, and a low keening moan was the last sound Dr. Norman Washburn made.

Satisfied, I glared at the man engulfed in flames.

Strolling outside, I stood a safe distance away. I smiled when the cabin went up in a blazing inferno and a small explosion ripped through the wall. Tossing the lighter on the ground, I glanced back at the wreckage. Thick black puffs of smoke billowed from the roof.

I rolled up the ski mask so I could breathe.

Reaching into my pocket, I brought out my list and meticulously crossed off Dr. Washburn's name.

"You might not remember me, but I sure as hell remember you."

Then I began the long hike past the moonlit beach, listening to the wind and the occasional crackle of fire behind me.

A hollow darkness surrounded Jasi, blinding her.

"Ben! She's barely conscious," a woman's voice said apprehensively.

I sure as hell remember you!

Jasi fought to open her eyes.

"She's coming around," she heard Ben say. "She'll be okay."

"Here. Let me have a look at her." The voice was deep and arrogant.

Jasi opened her eyes slightly, squinting at the sudden sharp pain in her head. She hazily examined her surroundings. She was safe, inside the van.

Then Brandon Walsh leaned over her.

He grinned when he caught her gaze. Turning her head gently, he examined a small scrape on her forehead.

"You fainted," he said scornfully. "And landed on your head."

She knocked his hand away, ticked off by the man's attitude. "It's just a bump."

"Well, Agent McLellan, I guess it didn't knock any manners into you."

Walsh leaned forward, then dabbed the cut with peroxide.

"Ouch! Damn it, Walsh!" she hissed.

His expression was smug, insolent. "Oh, sorry. I forgot to warn you. This might sting a bit."

"Walsh," Ben growled softly. He leaned down and settled the oxy-mask over her face.

When Jasi noticed his bare hands, she said, "Shouldn't you be wearing your gloves?"

Ben threw her a warning look. "I'll put them on when I get out of the van."

Walsh glanced at them—puzzled, suspicious. Then he opened a bandage wrapper and gently covered the wound on her forehead.

Jasi endured Walsh's touch, mostly because of the raging headache that threatened to rip her eyeballs from their sockets. Her head felt like someone was shooting a nail gun into her skull.

She cautiously eased herself into a sitting position, watching the man suspiciously. "What are you doing here? Thought we left you back at the tent."

"Gee, thanks for the warm welcome," Walsh remarked sarcastically.

"Who said you're welcome?" she snapped.

Natassia grinned widely, her head bouncing back and forth as if watching a tennis match. By the expression on her face, it was a thoroughly enjoyable game.

"Agent Prushenko, haven't you got work to do?" Jasi growled. To Ben she said, "I'll be fine. Just give me a few minutes to recuperate."

Then she glared at Walsh.

"Alone!"

5

Benjamin Roberts gripped Walsh's arm firmly with a bare hand. Steering the man away from the van, he swore under his breath. The AI Chief wore too many layers. Ben couldn't get an accurate read but Walsh's intense frustration and skepticism wasn't difficult to pick up.

"Man, she's a feisty one," Walsh grinned, jerking his head toward the van.

Ben lifted his hand from the man's arm. "Agent McLellan is one of the best PSI's in Canada. Don't underestimate her, Walsh. She's very good at her job."

"So am I, Roberts."

Walsh strode across the field, making a beeline for Natassia. He cast a smirk over one shoulder, then steered Natassia under a tree.

Ben clenched his teeth in exasperation.

Walsh was becoming a pain in the ass. There was something about the man that Ben didn't like. Maybe it was Walsh's grating insolence. Or the way he deliberately flirted with both Jasi and Natassia.

Ben ventured a look at Natassia who was persuasively drilling Walsh for information. He almost laughed aloud at the man's clumsy attempts at withholding facts. Yeah, Chief Walsh wouldn't know what hit him—once Natassia was through with him.

Ben knocked hesitantly on the side of the van. He slid the door open and Jasi beckoned him inside. She was huddled on the bench seat, wrapped in a blanket. Her face was pale and it worried him.

"Are you ready?" he asked her.

"Let's do it."

"Agent Prushenko!" Ben hollered.

A minute later, Natassia's head appeared, a smirk lingering on her face. "You bellowed?"

Ben released a sigh. "Just get in."

"Let's play back the data recorder first," Natassia suggested.

"What about me?" Brandon Walsh inquired innocently, poking his head inside the van.

"Sorry," Ben said smugly. "CFBI only."

He closed the van door with a slight slam, barely hiding his satisfied grin.

Walsh was definitely a nuisance, he thought.

"Thanks, Ben," Jasi smiled.

His eyes flicked toward the closed door. "Any time."

Forcing Walsh from his mind, Ben listened while the data-com replayed Jasi's voice.

Her words were low and hoarse. *"Don't fight it, Doctor."*

When Jasi went under, she took on the perpetrator's emotions, thoughts and actions. She literally saw through the eyes of the arsonist. Jasi relived moments in time, as if she were there in body.

Ben, on the other hand, was a highly skilled profiler with the ability to touch someone and feel his or her thoughts. But his psychic abilities were unreliable and infrequent.

The data recorder played back Jasi's voice. *"You might not remember me but I sure as hell remember you!"*

Ben watched her carefully. He noticed the small shiver as she heard herself laughing insanely. Even after all these years, it was something that Jasi still had difficulty with.

Who could blame her?

"Previous knowledge of the victim is a positive," Natassia said, consulting her data-com. "I'd say we're looking for a male, based on the lower vocal tone in your voice."

"Anything on the accelerant?" Ben asked.

"It's Super Clean diesel fuel."

"What about our X-Disc?" Jasi interrupted suddenly.

Ben scrolled through his data-com and downloaded from the X-Disc Pro's data site. "We've got a partial boot print. About six yards from the house, behind the apple tree. Could be our perp. The Disc also took a soil sample from the tread. We'll have it analyzed back at Ops."

"You want a list of known contacts now, Jasi?" Natassia asked.

"Yeah," Jasi said. "Search all data regarding previous contacts of Dr. Washburn. All complaints issued against him, either personal or professional. Lawsuits, wrongful death, misdiagnoses. Someone had a hate-on for the doctor."

"Give me thirty minutes. Maybe an hour. I have a feeling it could be a very long list."

Jasi stood and reached for the door. "I'm going back to the crime scene."

Ben grabbed her arm. "Twice in a short time-frame might be too much. You've given us plenty to go on. Why don't you—"

"I'm fine, Ben. I won't go under again. I just want to see everything."

She adjusted her oxy-mask and climbed out of the van before he could say another word.

"Jesus Christ!" he heard her say.

Ben leaned out the door and followed her gaze.

Brandon Walsh was leaning against the bumper of the van. "Well, not quite."

Jasi ignored the man and doggedly headed toward Washburn's cabin.

Ben was furious. "Walsh!"

He led the fire chief away from the van, fuming under his breath. "Listen, don't mess with any of us. This town might be your territory, but Agent McLellan is *my* territory. She's gone through too much to be messed with by an egotistical redneck who—"

"Hey! I surrender!" Walsh managed, throwing his hands into the air. "Look, I just want to help. Trust me, your Agent McLellan has nothing to worry about with me."

Ben clenched his teeth. "Just keep your hands off her—and Agent Prushenko too, for that matter."

The tension between them mounted.

Then Walsh turned on his heel and walked back to a nearby police car. Walsh said something to the driver who immediately handed him the radio.

Ben watched, suspicious.

What are you up to, Walsh?

Glancing away, Ben held up a hand to shield his eyes from the sizzling sun. Jasi was moving closer to the crime scene. He saw her muscles tighten in response to the chaos. He prayed that the mask would keep out the toxic fumes that triggered her psychic abilities.

Jasmine McLellan was like a sister to him. A stubborn, self-reliant, younger sister who sometimes needed rescuing. There was an air of innocence about her, yet she exposed herself to evil every day. Ben guarded her, protected her and even loved her…as a brother would.

But most of all, he owed her.

Ever since the Parliament Murders…

He hopped inside the van and leaned over Natassia's shoulder to check the data-com screen.

"The good old doctor had enough enemies to fund his own political campaign," she smiled grimly.

"Anyone we know?"

"A few wrongful deaths. Remember the actress, Stacey Beranski? Her son filed a WD because she died on the operating table after what was supposed to be a routine appendectomy. Rumor is, Dr. Washburn was intoxicated while he performed the surgery and he botched the job."

Ben leaned closer to see the monitor. "What happened to Washburn? Did he get charged with wrongful death?"

Natassia wrinkled her nose. "He was reprimanded internally. It appears the alcohol was covered up, made to look like he had suffered from a mild stroke during the operation. He got off. Case closed."

"What's the son's name?"

"Jason Beranski, age twenty-nine. He's a pharmacist, works at Pharmacity Drugs in Kelowna." Natassia glanced up from her data-com. "Now, *he* would have access to medical supplies."

"You and Jasi want to check him out?"

Natassia gave him a smirk that said *Hell yeah!*

He was positive that somewhere in the list of names was a clue—the identity of a serial arsonist. It was only a matter of time before they found him. But time was running out.

Ben sensed that the arsonist would strike again…soon.

Divine Intervention is available in paperback and ebook from your favorite retailers, including Chapters, Amazon, Kobo and Smashwords.

Book 1 in the Divine series by Cheryl Kaye Tardif...

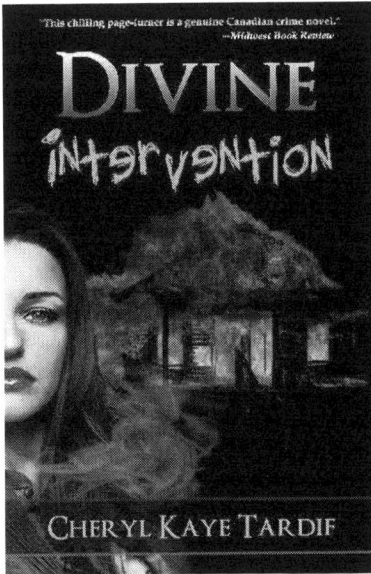

Divine Intervention

CFBI agent Jasmine McLellan is assigned a hot case—one that requires the psychic abilities of the PSI Division, a secret government agency located in the secluded town of Divine, BC.

Jasi leads a psychically gifted team in the hunt for a serial arsonist—a murderer who has already taken the lives of three innocent people. Unleashing her gift as a *Pyro-Psychic*, Jasi is compelled toward smoldering ashes and enters the killer's mind. A mind bent on destruction and revenge.

Jasi's team, consisting of *Psychometric Empath* and profiler, Ben Roberts, and *Victim Empath*, Natassia Prushenko, is led down a twisting path of dark, painful secrets. Brandon Walsh, the handsome, smooth-talking *Chief of Arson Investigations,* joins them in a manhunt that takes them across British Columbia—from Vancouver to Kelowna, Penticton and Victoria.

While impatiently sifting through the clues that were left behind, Jasi and her team realize that there is more to the third victim than meets the eye. Perhaps not all of the victims were *that* innocent. The hunt intensifies when they learn that someone they know is next on the arsonist's list.

The case heats to the boiling point as Jasi steps out of the flames…and into the fire. And in the heat of early summer, Agent Jasi McLellan discovers that a murderer lies in wait…*much closer than she imagined.*

ISBN: 9781412035910 (trade paperback)
ISBN: 978-0-9865382-2-3 (ebook)

Available at various retailers, including Amazon, Chapters and KoboBooks

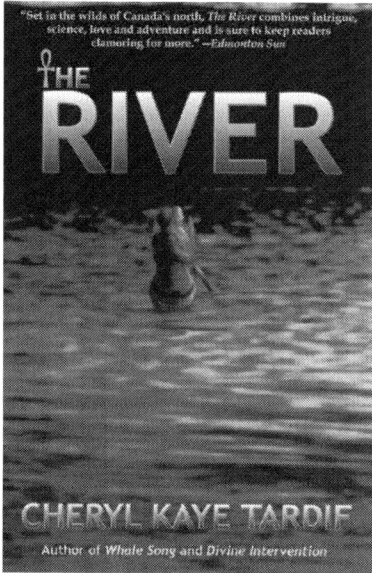

The River

How far do we go until we've gone too far?

The South Nahanni River has a history of mysterious deaths, disappearances and headless corpses, but it may also hold the key to humanity's survival—or its destruction.

Seven years ago, Del Hawthorne's father and three of his friends disappeared near the Nahanni River and were presumed dead. When one of the missing men stumbles onto the University grounds, alive but barely recognizable and aging before her eyes, Del is shocked. Especially when the man tells her something inconceivable. Her father is still alive!

Gathering a group of volunteers, Del travels to the Nahanni River to rescue her father. There, she finds a secret underground river that plunges her into a technologically advanced world of nanobots and painful serums. Del uncovers a conspiracy of unimaginable horror, a plot that threatens to destroy us all. Will humanity be sacrificed for the taste of eternal life?

And at what point have we become...God?

"Tardif specializes in mile-a-minute potboiler mysteries." *—Edmonton Sun*

ISBN: 9781412062299 (trade paperback)
ISBN: 978-0-9865382-3-0 (ebook)

Available at various retailers, including Amazon, Chapters and KoboBooks

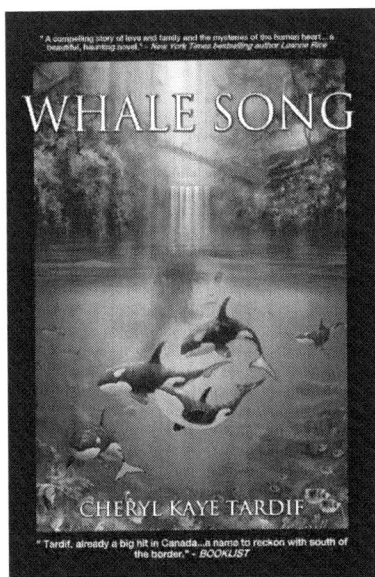

Whale Song

A haunting story that will change how you view life...and death.

Thirteen years ago, Sarah Richardson's life was shattered after the tragic death of her mother. The shocking event left a grief-stricken teen-aged Sarah with partial amnesia.

Some things are easier to forget.

But now a familiar voice from her childhood sends Sarah, a talented mid-twenties ad exec, back to her past. A past that she had thought was long buried.

Some things are meant to be buried.

Torn by nightmares and visions of a yellow-eyed wolf and aided by creatures of the Earth and killer whales that call to her in the night, Sarah must face her fears and recover her memories—even if it destroys her.

Some things are meant to be remembered—at all cost.

"Moving...[a] perennially crowd-pleasing combination of sweet and sad."
—*Booklist*

"Whale Song is deep and true, a compelling story of love and family and the mysteries of the human heart...a beautiful, haunting novel." —New York Times Bestselling novelist Luanne Rice, author of *What Matters Most*

"I read Whale Song and loved it." —Jodelle Ferland, actress in *Eclipse*

ISBN: 978-0-9866310-5-4 (trade paperback)
ISBN: 978-0-9865382-7-8 (ebook)

Available at various retailers, including Amazon, Chapters and KoboBooks

In the tradition of Stephen King, The Twilight Zone and The Hitchhiker, comes a terrifying collection of short stories in…

Skeletons in the Closet & Other Creepy Stories

Thirteen stories take you from one hold-your-breath chapter to the next.

Enter the closet…

A Grave Error
The Death of an Old Cow
Maid of Dishonor
Atrophy
Picture Perfect
Sweet Dreams
Separation Anxiety
The Car
Deadly Reunion
Remote Control
Ouija
Caller Unknown
Skeletons in the Closet

ISBN: 978-0-9866310-2-3 (ebook)
ISBN: 978-1-926997-05-6 (trade paperback)

Available at various retailers, including Amazon, Chapters and KoboBooks

YOU HAVE 10 SECONDS TO MAKE A DECISION:

**Let A Kidnapper Take Your Child, Or Watch Your Son Die.
Choose!**

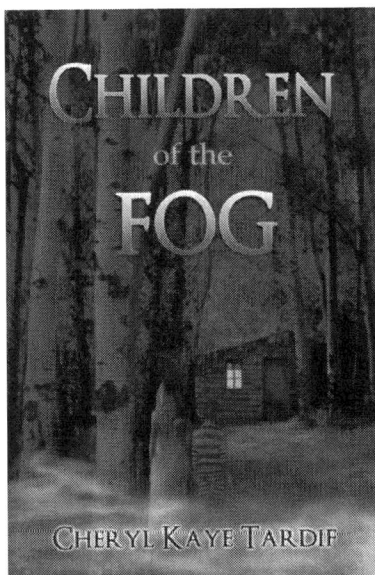

Children of the Fog

Sadie O'Connell is a bestselling author and a proud mother. But her life is about to spiral out of control. After her six-year-old son Sam is kidnapped by a serial abductor, she nearly goes insane. But it isn't just the fear and grief that is ripping her apart. It's the guilt. Sadie is the only person who knows what the kidnapper looks like. And she can't tell a soul. For if she does, her son will be sent back to her in "little bloody pieces".

When Sadie's unfaithful husband stumbles across her drawing of the kidnapper, he sets into play a series of horrific events that sends her hurtling over the edge. Sadie's descent into alcoholism leads to strange apparitions and a face-to-face encounter with the monster who abducted her son--a man known only as...The Fog.

"Reminiscent of *The Lovely Bones*, Cheryl Kaye Tardif weaves a tale of terror that will have you rushing to check on your children as they sleep. With exquisite prose, *Children of the Fog* captures you the moment you begin and doesn't let go until the very end." —bestselling author Danielle Q. Lee, author of *Inhuman*

"Ripe with engaging twists and turns reminiscent of the work of James Patterson, Tardif once again tugs at the most inflexible of heartstrings...*Children of the Fog* possesses you from the touching beginning through to the riveting climax." —Kelly Komm, award-winning author of *Sacrifice*

ISBN: 978-0-9866310-6-1 (trade paperback)
ISBN: 978-0-9866310-7-8 (ebook)

Available at various retailers, including Amazon, Chapters and KoboBooks

About Cherish D'Angelo

When romance author Cherish D'Angelo is not busy relaxing in her hot tub, sipping champagne, eating chocolate-covered strawberries or plotting romantic suspense with scintillating sensuality, she is ruthlessly killing people off in her thrillers as bestselling Canadian suspense author, Cheryl Kaye Tardif.

Cherish's debut romance, Lancelot's Lady placed in the semi-finals of Dorchester Publishing's "Next Best Celler" contest and went on to win an Editor's Choice Award from Textnovel. Currently living in Edmonton, Alberta, she enjoys long walks on the beach, except there aren't any around so she has to make do with trips around the hot tub or a vacation to a tropical paradise. And margaritas.

Cheryl Kaye Tardif is an award-winning, bestselling Canadian suspense author. Her novels include Children of the Fog, The River, Divine Intervention, and Whale Song, which New York Times bestselling author Luanne Rice calls "a compelling story of love and family and the mysteries of the human heart...a beautiful, haunting novel."

Her next thriller, Divine Justice (book 2 in the Divine series), will be published in spring 2011, in ebook and trade paperback editions.

Cheryl also enjoys writing short stories inspired mainly by her author idol Stephen King, and this has resulted in Skeletons in the Closet & Other Creepy Stories (ebook) and Remote Control (novelette ebook).

Booklist raves, "Tardif, already a big hit in Canada...a name to reckon with south of the border."

Cherish's website: http://www.cherishdangelo.com
Official blog: http://www.cherylktardif.blogspot.com
Twitter: http://www.twitter.com/cherylktardif

You can also find Cheryl Kaye Tardif on MySpace, Facebook, Goodreads, Shelfari and LibraryThing, plus other social networks.

7515372R0

Made in the USA
Charleston, SC
13 March 2011